The Bethune Murals

To Peggy

Tom Hill

By the same author

Fiction

The Strange Malady of Alessandro's Uncle (Short story)

Axton Landing (Book One of Adirondack Trilogy)

The Railroad (Book Two of Adirondack Trilogy)

Forever Wild (Book Three of Adirondack Trilogy)

Blame a novel

Non-fiction

Proceed with Caution: Predicting Genetic Risks in the Re-combinant DNA Era

Promoting Safe and Effective Genetic Testing in the United States (with Michael S. Watson)

Assessing Genetic Risks: Implictions for Health and Social Policy (with Arno Motulsky, Jane Fullarton, Lori Andrews)

The Bethune Murals

A Novel

Tony Holtzman

CLOUD
SPLITTER
PRESS

Cover: The Angel of Death mural (#9) by Norman Bethune, courtesy Historic Saranac Lake
Cover design by Eva Cohen

For individual orders, go to thebookstoreplus.com or amazon.com.

Bookstores can order from www.northcountrybooks.com

For more information visit www.cloudsplitterpress.com

ISBN 978-0-9984893-3-9

Library of Congress Control Number 2018938520

PROLOGUE

The sun momentarily blinded Arnold Springer as he emerged from the City Hall subway station. After the dank rush-hour train, the crisp air stung Springer's face and he lifted the collar of his overcoat. Of average height and build, he blended in with other men, similarly attired, heading to their jobs along the cavernous streets of lower Manhattan. Getting his bearings from the street signs at the nearest intersection, he walked briskly to his destination, the Federal Bureau of Investigation. Once there, he scanned the directory in the lobby for the agent who had been assigned to his case, knocking on his door punctually at ten o'clock, January 12, 1953.

Larry Crane opened the door himself, shook hands with Springer, hung up his coat, and waved him to a straight-backed wooden chair. Seating himself behind his desk, he picked up Springer's folder, the only paper on its surface. "You have remarkable credentials, Dr. Springer: director of the Trudeau Foundation's Saranac Laboratory, and before that, during your stint in the Navy, medical attaché to Secretary of the Navy James Forrestal."

"He was a great American whose end was untimely. But he was right about the communist menace," Springer replied.

Crane looked up and stared directly at Springer when he uttered those last two words. Some attributed James Forrestal's fatal jump from his sixteenth-floor room at the Bethesda Naval Hospital in 1949 to an irrational fear of Communists.

When he joined the FBI after his honorable discharge from the Army at the end of World War II, Crane thought he would be investigating bank robberies, murder suspects, and known criminals. He did his job well and before long was promoted to J. Edgar Hoover's pet project—weeding out Communists. Some of his leads came from reputable sources, like government agencies, and were based on credible suspicions, like an employee's refusal to sign a loyalty oath. His job then was to establish whether the employee was or had once been a member of the Communist Party. Other leads came from private citizens like Dr. Springer. Crane's first task was to distinguish accusers who had legitimate concerns from those who were carrying out personal vendettas, or who had fallen prey to the anti-communist hysteria sweeping the country, seeing a red under every bed. Crane wondered which most accurately described Arnold Springer.

He would have preferred investigating bank robberies, murder suspects, and criminals, but weeding out Communists was the path to advancement. Already with wife and young child, he was eager to get ahead. Getting down to Springer's complaint, Crane asked, "What makes you think the Trudeau Foundation is harboring Communists?"

"They're out to destroy capitalism," Springer blurted.

"Who is 'they'?"

"The Foundation's Board of Trustees."

"Have you done anything to stop them?"

"I've refused to arrange publication of studies conducted at the Saranac Laboratory and papers from last year's Saranac Symposium, which they keep asking me to do."

"And how will publication 'destroy capitalism'?"

"It will bring some of America's leading mining and manufacturing companies to financial ruin. What more could Communists want?" Crane noticed Springer's voice getting unnecessarily loud. He picked up Springer's letter and leaned back in his chair. "You wrote to the FBI under the letterhead of the Saranac Laboratory. Your complaint is against the Trudeau Foundation. What's the relation?"

Pleased that the agent had read his letter, Springer took a deep breath. More subdued, he continued, explaining to Crane that after the death in 1915 of the Sanatorium's founder, Dr. Edward Trudeau, the Saranac Laboratory and the Sanatorium were amalgamated under the Trudeau Foundation, "although the Saranac Lab is geographically separate, built adjacent to Trudeau's home in the village of Saranac Lake, while the Sanatorium is outside the village.

"I joined the staff of the Saranac Laboratory after my discharge from the Navy in 1946 and was appointed lab director in 1948, succeeding Dr. Leroy Gardner after his death in 1946; the position I've held for the past five years. Last year, the trustees rejected my proposal to make the Saranac Laboratory independent of the Foundation."

"Why did they reject it?"

"I need to give you some more background." Crane nodded for him to continue. "Since the 1920s, the focus of the Trudeau Laboratory has been on tuberculosis while the Saranac Laboratory's research has been on diseases thought to be caused by inhaling various types of industrial dusts: coal, cotton, silicon, asbestos, and more recently beryllium. The Saranac Laboratory established safe levels of exposure and helped companies monitor dust concentrations and reduce exposures to harmful dusts. Workmen's Compensation funds, to which the companies contributed, were used to pay workers who could show that their lung disease was work-related and prevented them from continuing to work."

Crane's father had been a steelworker, and when he was injured and could no longer work, the compensation had been a pittance.

"Mining and manufacturing companies supported much of the lab's work," Springer continued. "With industry support, the Saranac Lab studied low-dose and short-term exposures to asbestos in animals and found that much lower levels, previously assumed to be harmless, could cause lung disease. My predecessor, Dr. Gardner, also discovered that animals exposed to asbestos developed lung and other cancers at a much higher rate than unexposed animals. The papers that I am holding back report these findings."

Astonished, Crane searched for a rational explanation. "Holding back because the results are different in humans?"

"Quite the contrary. It wasn't long before asbestos workers began to turn up with the same type of lung cancer. And more workers who had only worked with asbestos for a short time when they were much younger were diagnosed with asbestosis."

"What's that?"

"The textbook case occurs in workers who have had a long history of exposure to asbestos—you know, that miracle fiber that will not burn. In the early stages, it's like T.B., with coughing and shortness of breath. As the lungs get progressively scarred, patients can't get enough oxygen to their tissues. Eventually, this kills them. These new findings suggest it doesn't always require prolonged, heavy exposure for asbestosis to develop. Based on the animal studies, wives and children of asbestos workers could contract asbestosis and asbestos-related cancers through second-hand exposure."

"What will happen if these findings are published?"

"The courts could allow workers and others to sue on the basis of liability. The companies could go bankrupt."

"Liability?"

"If asbestos is shown to be harmful to most people who come in contact with it, the companies that mine or manufacture it could be liable for the harm that it causes, no matter how long ago the exposure occurred, and even if the exposure was not work-related. So if the wife of an asbestos worker, or his children, or a consumer using a product that contained asbestos, developed signs of asbestosis, they could sue the company."

"Which they can't do under Workmen's Compensation?"

"That's right, suits based on liability, not on job exposure, do not fall under Workmen's Compensation. But people can bring liability suits only if their disease occurred after the date when the dangers of exposure become public."

"Now I see what you're saying," said Crane. "Once the dangers of asbestos are published, the companies will have a hard time denying that asbestos causes widespread harms. They could be sued out of business. In fact, we'd have to find a substitute for asbestos."

"Exactly," confirmed Springer.

"What's at stake for you if the findings are published?"

"Not for me as much as for the future of the laboratory and for the village of Saranac Lake." Crane looked at Springer quizzically. "The companies who fund our research will withdraw their support, the lab will close, and more people in the village will lose their jobs. Coming on the heels of the Sanatorium closing—"

"Is that imminent?"

"Any day. Since anti-tuberculosis drugs have become available, the number of T.B. patients coming to Saranac has dwindled."

"And if the lab closes, you lose your job?"

"I have several job offers. My family and I will miss Saranac Lake, but I'll be earning more elsewhere and I'll still be able to conduct my research."

"I take it, then, that the Trudeau Board believes the papers should be published in the interests of science"—he paused—"and workers."

"Yes. They refuse to see the implications for the Saranac Laboratory, for the industries that support it, and for the village of Saranac Lake."

Crane was sympathetic to the Board's point of view but did not say so. "Do you have any other evidence of what you see as communist sympathies at Trudeau?"

"My wife told me that Dr. Warner's wife—"

"Who's Dr. Warner?" Crane interrupted.

"He's the executive director of the Foundation. Dr. Warner's wife asked my wife to sign a petition asking for clemency for the Rosenbergs."

"Did your wife sign it?"

"Are you kidding? Save the life of those commie traitors? I'd give her a good piece of my mind if she did."

Agent Crane stood. "Well, thank you for coming down to the city, Dr. Springer. You've provided some interesting information."

After Springer left, Agent Crane sat at his desk, reflecting on everything he'd been told. *Dad might have worked with asbestos. He was a member of the United Steelworkers. Yeah, companies go broke, but keeping secrets that can hurt workers—is that the American way? What if I report that Springer is a fanatic and there's no need to investigate? But then the papers he's hiding are published and the companies go bust. J. Edgar will want to know why I didn't follow up, why I didn't intimidate the Trudeau Foundation to the point maybe of putting it out of business.* "No," Crane said aloud, "I don't have enough evidence to do that."

———————

A week after Springer's visit, Larry Crane was sent on special assignment to the FBI headquarters in Washington, D.C. to help reduce the backlog of subversive activities cases. One of his first cases concerned a high-ranking official at the National Institutes of Health who had failed to sign the loyalty oath required of all federal employees. Crane drove out to Bethesda, a Maryland suburb, enjoying the gently rolling countryside in clear, crisp winter weather. Past the town, the scenery changed abruptly, gouged out by NIH's growing campus. Most of the construction was taking place around the enormous Clinical Center, Building 10, still a skeleton of steel girders. His FBI badge did not get Crane a parking space, so he circled around the visitor parking areas until someone left. After finding a space, he walked along dirt roads, muddy from recent rains and rutted by heavy construction vehicles, several of which passed him, spattering his briefcase, trouser cuffs, and highly polished wingtip shoes. He finally reached the National Microbiological Institute just in time for his appointment with Dr. Harold Hungerford, its deputy director.

Just under six feet and husky, Hungerford was a few inches taller than Crane. He was working in his shirtsleeves, his rumpled pants held up by broad red suspenders. He took Crane's coat and hung it on the back of the door. "Ahh trust you didn't have too much traffic comin' out from the District," he greeted his guest in a deep southern drawl. Throughout their conversation, Hungerford spoke slowly, in a resonant, soothing baritone.

"Not much at all, and the drive was very pleasant until I reached NIH." Hungerford followed Crane's glance as he looked down at his soiled trousers and shoes.

"Pretty messy, but when it's finished, NIH will be the biggest medical research center in the world." Hungerford offered Crane a seat and took one opposite him. "Ahh hope the matter for which you've braved the wild west of Bethesda is an important one. How can I help you?"

Crane snapped open his briefcase and pulled out a single sheet of paper that he flashed in front of Hungerford. "The Subversive Activities Control Office at NIH informed the FBI that you have failed to sign this loyalty oath. I know that when you first came to NIH in 1946 no loyalty oath was required, but since then it's gone into effect retroactively." Laying the single sheet down in front of Hungerford, he continued. "This is a copy of the one you were asked to sign."

Hungerford nodded.

"Perhaps you overlooked it or were too busy. If you'll sign it now, we can cut this visit short and you can go on to more important things."

"This is an important matter. May I see the oath?"

Assuming that Hungerford's remark meant he would sign the document, Crane handed it over, agreeing obsequiously. "Yes, it is important."

When the oath was first sent to him in the privacy of his office, Hungerford had stared at it for several minutes. He could honestly sign it, knowing that if he did, the government had no grounds for investigating him. Still, he hesitated. A good friend of his, also a prominent physician, had signed the oath and shortly afterward had signed a petition urging clemency for Ethel and Julius Rosenberg, sentenced to death for spying for the Soviet Union. Within weeks of signing the petition, he was investigated by the FBI and accused of perjuring himself when he signed the oath. Several leading physicians, including Hungerford, wrote to the Department of Justice insisting on their colleague's integrity and the case was dropped. However, the atmosphere of the country was laced with fear, with senators like Joseph McCarthy and Karl Mundt and congressmen like Richard Nixon rooting out the "red menace" at full throttle. Ten Hollywood writers and directors were fired and went to jail for refusing to say whether they had ever been Communists. Having to say he wasn't a Communist in order to prove he was a loyal citizen wasn't Hungerford's idea of what America was all about. He tossed the unsigned oath in the waste paper basket.

The document Crane handed him was the same as the one he had trashed. "This oath says," he spoke slowly and calmly, "Ahh am not now nor ever have been a member of the Communist Party or any other organization that advocates the overthrow of the Government by force or violence."

"Is that not true?"

"Between you and me, it is true; I never have been. But I'm not going to sign this." He paused. "For a couple of reasons. First, Ahh don't see what my political beliefs, or affiliations, have to do with my ability to serve loyally as deputy director of the National Microbiological Institute. Second, 'advocating' is a form of speech, not action. I believe the oath violates the First Amendment of the Constitution, 'Congress shall make no law—'"

Crane cut him short. "I know what the First Amendment says. The courts don't agree with your interpretation. Let me ask you one question, Dr. Hungerford. Give me a straightforward answer, and I'll be on my way." Hungerford had anticipated the question. It was another reason he would not sign. "Have you ever known any Communists?"

Hal had friends who were Communists, people who had fought to free the Scottsboro Boys, a cause célèbre of the Communist Party, and who feared Hitler's rise until the Nazi–Soviet non-aggression pact in 1939, when they became pacifists until Hitler invaded Russia in 1941. They were upright citizens who cherished their constitutional right to speak freely and did not advocate violent revolution. One friend who declared himself a Communist in 1937 had died. Hungerford saw no harm in mentioning his name.

He stared up at the ceiling and after a minute said, "Yes sir, Ahh've known one."

"What's his name?"

"Norman Bethune."

Crane whipped out his notebook and unscrewed his fountain pen. "That name doesn't ring a bell," he said as he jotted it down.

"Well, maybe because he was Canadian."

Crane looked disappointed. "Is he currently in the United States?"

"No, he's in China."

"Conspiring against the United States, no doubt."

"No doubt?" Again, Hungerford paused. "Mr. Crane, let me tell you a little about Norman Bethune." Crane's pen was poised to add details.

"Norman Bethune became a friend of mine in 1927 when we met as tuberculosis patients at the Trudeau Sanatorium in New York State."

Instantly, Crane recalled this was the sanatorium Arnold

Springer had mentioned. He wrote "Trudeau 1927" in his notebook.

Hungerford continued. "He was a physician like me. In 1937, Bethune declared he was a Communist. I was surprised, but when I thought about it, it wasn't so shocking; when Bethune felt strongly about something, he went whole hog at it. And when Generalissimo Franco attempted to overthrow the democratically elected"—he paused and repeated the last three words, staring straight at Agent Crane—"the democratically elected government of Spain, Bethune and a lot of others offered to serve the Spanish Republic. Bethune wasn't interested in overthrowing our democratically elected government but in *preservin'* a democratic government elsewhere."

Hungerford noticed Crane look at his watch and looked at his own. "Mr. Crane, you asked for half an hour of mah time. Ahh see we have ten minutes left, so let me tell you something else about Norman Bethune." Realizing he was trapped, Crane sat back and listened. "In 1938, Bethune went to China to help set up medical and surgical units for Mao Tse-Tung's army. At that time, Mao and Chiang Kai-shek were both repelling the Japanese invasion of China—the same Japanese who bombed Pearl Harbor a few short years later. Neither in Spain nor in China did Norman Bethune go to fight; he went to use his medical skills. And when wounded Japanese prisoners were brought to him he operated to save their lives, just as he did wounded Chinese. Yes, Agent Crane, Bethune said he was a Communist, but really he was a humanitarian."

"So, this Bethune is still in China helping the reds?" Crane asked.

"He's still in China, but he's buried in a tomb there." Crane looked up sternly, realizing that Hungerford, knowing Bethune was dead, had intentionally deceived him.

A dead Communist is of no use to the United States government, Crane said to himself.

"Bethune cut his finger while operating on a soldier. The wound got infected, he developed septicemia and died in ten days." Hungerford got up. "No, I'm not going to sign your loyalty oath."

"Did you keep in touch with Dr. Bethune after 1927?"

Again there was silence before Hungerford answered. "I'm not going to answer that."

"Do you think Bethune was a Communist when you first met?"

"I'm not going to answer that question either."

"You realize you are putting your job in jeopardy."

"So be it," Hungerford sighed. He went to his bookshelf, picked out a book, and showed it to Crane. "*The Scalpel, the Sword*," he said, reading the title out loud. "This is a biography of Norman Bethune written by avowed Communists, published last year. Having known Bethune, I wouldn't say it's completely accurate, but it gives you an idea of the man."

"I'll have to get it," Crane replied, as Hungerford helped him on with his coat. They shook hands and Crane left, stopping briefly to see the director.

With his hands hooked in his suspenders, Hungerford gazed out the tall window of his office that looked over the front entrance of the National Microbiological Institute. Ten minutes later, Agent Crane emerged and walked down the muddy path toward a distant parking lot. *Wallowing in mud*, Hungerford thought, *with inordinate power to destroy people, including me.*

A few minutes later, the director of the institute knocked, entered, and pulled up a chair alongside Hungerford's desk without being asked. "I wanted to make sure you survived the visit from the FBI."

"For the time being, yes. You knew about it?"

"The agent stopped in my office after he saw you, said you weren't cooperative."

Hungerford gave a hearty laugh. "You know me well enough not to be surprised," he drawled.

"Why do you make life difficult for yourself, Hal?"

"I've asked myself that a lot since this loyalty oath matter arose." He paused, debating whether to tell his story. "You know, I grew up in a small town near Selma, Alabama. Mah daddy was a doctor. He came down south with Union troops just after the Civil War and decided to stay. When the Army withdrew in 1876, he didn't have the good sense to leave. In 1880, he married a nurse, the daughter of a Congregationalist minister. Together, they cared for colored folks as well as whites. I was their third child, born in 1890.

"When I was fourteen and daddy was close to death, he called his children to his bedside and told us about a ten-year-old girl brought into his office by her parents—I guess it was in the 1880s. They said she had been molested by a colored boy and wanted his corroboration. Daddy took her into his examining room, without the parents, and called my mama in to assist him. He asked the girl what happened. 'Papa said some of his friends saw the boy touch me,' the girl said. 'Did he?' daddy asked. 'He brushed against my arm coming out of the general store.' 'Is that all?' daddy asked. She nodded and started to cry. 'What's the matter?' mama asked. 'Papa said the boy gave me a baby.' My parents looked at each other. 'No, he didn't,' they said in unison."

"What happened to the boy?" the director asked.

Hal looked at him as if it was a foolish question. "He was in jail by that time. Daddy told the parents that their daughter hadn't been raped. A mob had already gathered in front of the jail and was yelling at the sheriff to release the boy into their custody. 'You go out there,' daddy told the couple, 'and tell them your daughter hasn't been raped.' For the rest of his life, he regretted not going to the jailhouse and telling the mob himself."

"Lynched?" the director asked.

Hal's look made it clear that if not foolish, the question was superfluous. "After daddy told us the story, he said to us, 'Promise me, children, when you see injustice, don't look the other way.' Does that answer your question?" he asked the director.

"Look, Hal, all you have to do is sign the loyalty oath. I guarantee you'll be better off and nobody will be worse off. That's different than the story you just related."

"I don't see it that way. I'm not going to become another sheep. That's not the way democracy should work."

"You may not want to join the flock, Hal, but if you don't sign the oath, you'll become the sacrificial lamb." Hal looked at him strangely. "I know where you're coming from now," the director continued, "but I won't be able to come to your defense."

"You mean that bastard Crane is blackmailing you?"

"He told me that the House Un-American Activities Committee is thinking of launching an investigation into subversive activities at NIH. They will certainly subpoena you for your refusal to sign the loyalty oath. With appropriations coming up in Congress, the institute has too much at stake for me to go out on a limb."

"What do you want me to do?"

"Sign the oath."

"And if I don't?"

He looked Hungerford straight in the eye. "I'll have to ask for your resignation."

"You mean fire me."

"However you want to put it." The director got up and left without another word.

———

Driving back to the Capital after seeing Harold Hungerford in Bethesda, Agent Crane tried to tie Dr. Springer's information to what Hungerford had told him. *If Springer is to be believed, the Trudeau is a hotbed of Communists, and here is the deputy director of the National Microbiological Institute spouting the Communist Party line and saying he and Bethune were patients at Trudeau together—in what year was it?* He pulled his notebook from his pocket, flicked it open, and taking his eye off the road for moment, read the year: 1927. *Were there Communists on the staff of the Sanatorium or the Saranac Laboratory then, and are there still now? Maybe Springer is not such a fanatic.* Crane stopped at a bookstore in D.C. to purchase *The Scalpel, The Sword.* In his temporary office, he wrote up his visit with Hungerford, mentioning the Trudeau Sanatorium and Dr. Springer's allegations. His report reached the top echelons of the Bureau and he received permission to return to the New York office to investigate whether communists had infiltrated the Trdeau Foundation in 1927.

PART ONE

1927

Chapter 1

When Great Britain declared war on Germany in 1914, twenty-four-year-old Norman Bethune promptly interrupted his third year of medical school to join the Canadian Army. Enemy shrapnel pierced his left leg in the second battle of Ypres, ending his active duty and allowing him to finish medical school in 1916. He joined the Royal Navy in 1917, serving as a medical officer on HMS Pegasus, on which over half the crew came down with influenza in October 1918. Even after he contracted the flu, Bethune continued to care for the debilitated sailors until he collapsed and was relieved from duty. The Russian Revolution of 1917, and the Soviet Union's condemnation of World War I as internecine capitalist conflict, did not seem to affect his loyalty to the Allied cause.

Returning to civilian life, Bethune did internships in several London hospitals, living lavishly on his meager paychecks and throwing splendid parties, but going broke as a result. Handsome, well-dressed, and well-spoken, with a Canadian-American accent, he charmed English women, who found him attractive, entertaining, and seductive. Immediately taken with a woman who was brought to one of his parties by a friend, Bethune took her arm and whispered, "It's too noisy to talk in here, let's go for a walk." As they walked to the Thames a few blocks to the south, he asked, "Are you an artist? Most of my friends are, you know."

"I have a keen interest in the arts, but no, I'm a medical

student," she replied.

Walking alongside her, he stopped in his tracks and turned to face her. "That's marvelous. I wish more women would use their brains."

"It's not easy you know. Trying to fit in classes when I have children who need my love."

"And a husband?" he asked disappointedly.

"My husband has disappeared. Fortunately, the wealth at my disposal enables me to undertake a career and have nannies to help with my children."

They reached the Victoria Embankment. Pleased not to be scolded about entering the male world of medicine, Isabelle Humphreys-Owen took Bethune's arm and they strolled for several blocks before returning to Bethune's apartment long after midnight, the party in full swing despite the host's absence.

In the ensuing months, Beth (as his friends called him) and Isabelle spent their holidays visiting Madrid, Rome, and Vienna, ostensibly for business. Traveling largely on her money, Beth had devised a scheme that he was sure would make him rich. "We can't lose," he told her. "We'll hunt antique art dealers and book stores for paintings by the old masters that have been overlooked and then buy them for a song. Then we'll bring them to London, get them appraised, and sell at a huge profit." He never found them and remained heavily in debt to his lover, all the while continuing his lavish lifestyle and his devotion to the visual arts, even showing promise as an artist.

Eager to become credentialed as a surgeon, Bethune traveled to Scotland in 1921 where he studied to become a Fellow of the Royal College of Surgery in Edinburgh. He fell in love with Frances Campbell Penney, a twenty-nine-year-old, intelligent, shy beauty from a wealthy Scottish family. Based on his dress and debonair manner, Frances thought Beth was wealthy but was disabused of this notion when he confessed that he had to return to Hammersmith Hospital in London as a house surgeon for £50 a year. Wanting to break away from her domineering, recently widowed mother, Frances went to London as a volunteer social worker and quickly took up with Bethune.

While vacationing at Dover during Frances's first summer, they got into a terrible row—later neither could remember what it was about— in the midst of a ferocious storm. Beth emerged from the bathroom of their rented bungalow in his bathing trunks. "I'm going for a swim," he shouted at her.

"It's frightful out—" He slammed the door in her face. From the window of the bungalow, she looked at him as he disappeared into a wave. Fully dressed, Frances ran to the beach searching frantically for him. No one was about. The storm abated, and far out she spotted a man swimming desperately to escape the undertow. Beth eventually dragged himself on to the beach and lay gasping at her feet. The gasps turned to laughter and they quickly made up.

Back in London, Frances was notified that she had received a legacy of £1,250 pounds from her uncle's estate. Despite the flaws in their relationship, she decided to accept Beth's marriage proposal, and they spent their six-month honeymoon traveling in Europe, living on the legacy until it ran out and Frances had to wire her bank in Edinburgh for more money.

The honeymoon did not begin or end auspiciously. On the coast of France, on the first day, she put on a new dress that particularly pleased her. Beth expressed his distaste unequivocally. "If you insist on keeping it on, go and walk into the North Sea." To his amazement, she promptly did. He ran after her and pulled her out before the waves had reached above her waist. "I still love you," he said tenderly. She burst out laughing, as did he, and they hugged.

Six months later, in Vienna, they ran into Isabelle Humphreys-Owen, who was stunned to learn that Beth was married. He insisted on paying off his debt—although he did not know how he could manage it—but she refused, and they never saw each other again. He had told Frances about their relationship (which was, he said, strictly for business), but to placate her jealousy he bought her an expensive vase with part of the money her bank had wired. She unwrapped it and, realizing what he had done, threw it at him. He ducked and the vase broke into several pieces. Frances tried to paste them together.

Having completed his fellowship in surgery, Bethune persuaded Frances to come with him to his native Canada, but he was unable to find a medical-surgical practice there that would support them, so they moved across the border in 1924, to Detroit, a city booming because of the expanding automobile industry. He started a medical practice in the apartment that he and Frances rented in a working-class neighborhood flooded with poor whites, Negroes from the south, and immigrants looking for jobs in the nascent industry. They and the city's prostitutes formed the mainstay of Beth's practice. Charging only what his patients could afford, he barely made enough to pay the rent and put food on the table. His patients loved Bethune and he became popular in the neighborhood. On top of Beth's irregular hours and erratic behavior, Frances did not appreciate his patients tramping through her living room. Raised in a sedate, upper-middle-class neighborhood in Edinburgh, she shuddered every time she went out.

Beth came down with a severe cold and fever in September 1926, undoubtedly contracted from his patients. His cough grew worse and he developed night sweats. Afraid she would catch whatever he had, Frances refused even to kiss him. In October he saw a doctor, who collected a sputum sample. The day he received the report, Beth announced to Frances as they sat down to dinner, "I've got T.B."

Horrified, Frances gasped. Silently, she put down her fork and collected her thoughts. Finally, she announced, "Until you're cured, I'll sleep on the sofa, and I'm going to boil all your dishes and utensils."

Infuriated, Beth picked up his dinner plate and threw it across the room. As he stalked out, he screamed, "Sorry I'm such a burden; that's one less dish you'll have to boil." His physician advised Bethune to enter the Trudeau Sanatorium.

———

The sanatorium for the treatment of tuberculosis stood on a flank of Mt. Pisgah, northeast of the village of Saranac Lake in the Adirondack Mountains of northern New York State. Overcrowding and malnutrition contributed to the spread of tuberculosis, and to the pallor—hence the "white plague"— that accompanied it. Though striking them disproportionately, tuberculosis was not limited to the poor. Near death from the disease, Edward L. Trudeau, a prosperous physician on Long Island, came to the Adirondacks in 1874, where with rest and the bracing air he went into a long-lasting remission that enabled him to study tuberculosis and open the sanatorium in 1884, only dying of the disease in 1914.

"What a terrible New Year's Eve. I can't stand this enforced bed rest," Beth wrote to Frances from the Sanatorium's Ludington Infirmary two weeks after he had been admitted in December 1926. "How I long to be cured and back in your arms."

But Frances's love for Beth was fraying. She visited him at Trudeau early in 1927, arriving by taxi from the train station in the village. The temperature had warmed to the low twenties, but a darkening midday sky hinted that snow might be on the way. Frances emerged from the cab as beautiful as ever, wrapped in a black wool coat with a fur collar. "That coat doesn't suit you," were Beth's first words. "And why on earth did you bob your hair?" He had loved to bury his face in her luxuriant chestnut hair. "Your hair was one of your best features." He put his arms around her and started to kiss her.

She turned away and his kiss landed on her cheek. "You know I'm not going to kiss you while your T.B. is active," Frances said in the husky voice that Beth loved.

He took her gloved hand. "You're right, of course. I've caused you enough trouble. You don't need this wretched disease as well."

They sat on one of the two alabaster seats that curved out from each side of the statue of Edward Trudeau at the front entrance of the sanatorium." The ground was covered with snow that had fallen a few days earlier, but the seats had been cleared and were dry. Neither of them spoke for a while and a few flakes of snow fell, glistening white on Frances's coat before melting. "I'm going to file for divorce, Beth." Frances looked at him with her large brown eyes. "I love you, Beth, probably always will, but I can't live with you. You should know that by now." A single tear trickled down her smooth, white cheek.

His reply surprised her. "You're right, dearest. I would be lying if I said a divorce would kill me. It will be the white plague. You should leave me; I can offer you nothing and I'll probably die soon anyway." She stayed in the village that night and returned to Detroit the following day.

Beth's condition had not improved at Trudeau. He had not been a model patient; unable to tolerate complete bed rest, he had broken the rules several times. Despite an outward countenance that entertained his fellow patients and most of the nurses, particularly the young ones, he increasingly felt that he would not survive his disease. Anticipating the terms of the divorce, he signed himself out of the Sanatorium in March 1927 to make as much money as he could from his practice.

Back in Detroit but separated from Frances, his condition rapidly deteriorated; he tired easily, became short of breath, and coughed up blood. In July 1927, he readmitted himself to Trudeau. When he arrived for his second admission that summer, he got an ovation from the patients who were there in 1926. Delighted at the welcome, he produced a top hat, and twirling a patient's cane as he strolled down the aisles between beds, he sang *It's a Long Way to Tipperary*, slightly off key, to boisterous applause.

Chapter 2

Residing in the black belt of cotton-picking Alabama, the Hungerford family remained close to sharecroppers and tenant farmers and continued to be sympathetic to their plight. Harold's older brother studied law at the University of Alabama and set up practice in Montgomery, where many of his clients were poor blacks. His older sister became a nurse like their mother, married, and lived close to their mother outside of Selma. After their father died in 1904, their mother, an amateur botanist, became the president of the local horticultural society. As a child, Hal loved trekking through woods and fields with her to look for wild flowers and identify them. His interest spread to fauna, and to the well-being of all living creatures. For a few years, he helped support his mother by getting logging jobs in federally owned forest reserves obtained from Indian tribes through treaties and seizure. They were extensively logged around the turn of the twentieth century. In hiking and camping in the reserves, his favorite pastime, Hungerford was horrified to see the dangers of uncontrolled logging—the devastation caused by forest fires and, alternately, flooding.

Harold won a scholarship to the Johns Hopkins University in Baltimore, Maryland, and then to the Johns Hopkins School of Medicine, which he entered the same year Norman Bethune graduated medical school in Toronto. One of his three assigned partners in his first-year anatomy course was

Betty Granger, a slender, quiet young woman from Montana. Ahead of its time in many ways, Hopkins was one of the few medical schools that accepted women; one of its benefactors made their admission a condition of her bequest. Hal took an immediate liking to Betty when he learned that she loved the outdoors, having hiked in the Rockies and fly-fished in Montana's streams. Their two male dissecting partners were disdainful of Betty, insisting that she read the manual aloud while they did the dissecting. Hal said nothing when they made their opinion known, but he stayed behind after they left to walk with Betty to their anatomy lecture. "Do you think that's a fair arrangement?" he asked.

"What do you think?" she replied.

"No, Ahh don't."

She broke into a broad grin—the first time he had seen her smile.

"Got any suggestions?" she asked him.

"Why not refuse?"

She looked at him sideways. "Will you back me up?"

"Ahh wouldn't have made the suggestion otherwise." From then on, the four partners took turns reading from the manual.

Soon Betty and Hal were dating. Tired of the formalin stench of the dissecting room, they often went in search of fresh air. Some weekends, they'd walk down to Baltimore's inner harbor and stroll along the shore, past the freight train sidings, warehouses, and factories, shut down for the weekend, to look over the water to Federal Hill and watch sailboats heading out to the Chesapeake. One of their friends had a car, and they'd sometimes drive out of the city and hike for miles around Lake Roland or on trails in the Patapsco Valley. In their second year, the friend lent them his car and they drove out to Harpers Ferry, where John Brown had seized a federal arsenal in 1859, hoping to start a slave insurrection. They hiked into a primitive campsite nearby and spent their first night together wrapped in blanket rolls. Around the campfire, Hal told Betty about his family's roots in Alabama, and she described how her great grandfather had led his family out of Kansas, "bleeding Kansas" she called it, in 1856 as the territory violently seesawed between pro- and anti-slavery forces, the latter including John Brown and his sons.

They both contracted tuberculosis during clinical rotations in their last two years of medical school. Hal, who showed symptoms first, was horrified by the possibility that he might have infected her. Betty's disease was more fulminant. Too ill to complete her internship, Betty became a patient on the Osler wards, reversing roles with good humor. They were married at her bedside. As she lost weight but not her good humor, it became clear that she was not going to rally sufficiently to qualify for admission to a sanatorium. She died in 1925 in the Johns Hopkins Hospital. The following year, Hal applied for admission to Trudeau, weak from the disease and severely depressed following the loss of Betty.

Hal was at the Sanatorium when Bethune first arrived in December 1926. He was amused by Beth's supreme self-confidence, flirtatious behavior, and high jinks in front of the other patients and nurses, not realizing it was a façade until August 1927, when Beth was assigned to Lea Cottage, where Hal was staying with three other men. Hal had returned from a short hike up Mount Baker and immediately recognized Bethune standing just inside the threshold. "Hello, I'm Dr. Norman Bethune, your new cottage mate. You look familiar but I haven't had the pleasure."

"Harold Hungerford." He shook Beth's hand, then added with a sarcastic smile, "Ahh'm just a poor white boy from Alabama—that's in the deep south in case you're a foreigner. Or you might just be tryin' to impress me with your doctorate and accent."

Beth laughed. "Well, I do have an M.D. degree, but it was pompous to mention it. So far as the accent, I was born and raised in Ontario and lately lived in the British Isles, where I may have acquired a flourish or two."

"Well, if you're going to join us in Lea Cottage, let me advise that although three of its tenants are physicians, includin' me, we don't go around callin' each other 'doctor.' Here we are just lowly patients." Hal removed his battered felt hat, soaked with sweat around the rim.

"Looks like you've been hiking." Hal was wearing hiking boots, suspendered dungarees, a plaid shirt, and a bandanna around his neck. "And you have T.B.?"

"In remission," Hal replied. "Been here over a year and Ahh seem to be on the mend. Ahh couldn't have climbed Mt. Baker when I was in your condition." Though by no means short, Bethune was thin and pale next to Hungerford, muscular and tanned. "It helps that I've been hiking all my life. Worked as a lumberjack, too."

"So did I," Bethune said. They spent a few minutes comparing notes before Bethune told Hal, "Next time you go out for a hike, I'd like to come along." Hal looked at him skeptically.

"Let's wait until the weather cools off a bit. In the meantime, you can rest up and put some more meat on your bones."

Two of the other Lea patients, Al Blalock and Lou Davidson, entered shortly and Hal made the introductions, omitting any mention of professional status. That soon became evident as they often discussed their disease in medical terms.

Ideal hiking weather prevailed in early September, and Hal and Beth set out together to climb nearby Scarface Mountain. Hiking on fairly flat terrain, they became better acquainted with each other's woes, Beth confessing that his erratic behavior had precipitated Frances filing for divorce. "I still love her and she says she still loves me, but she couldn't go on putting up with my antics."

The trail passed through a clearing with a small boulder in the center. Hal stopped a moment until Beth caught up and then described his short-lived relationship with Betty, which had culminated in death rather than divorce. "We had it all planned out: As soon as we got well, we'd walk across the moors in England on our delayed honeymoon, then settle in Montana near Betty's folks and raise our kids to relish the great outdoors." Out of breath, Beth perched on the boulder and drank from his canteen. Hal was unsure Beth had heard his story. "Are you okay?"

Beth did not answer right away. "I'm not going to make it to the top, Hal. I'll certainly slow you down. Why don't you go on and I'll rest here awhile and walk back slowly. You'll probably reach me before I get to the trailhead."

Hal became concerned. He had had some trepidation about taking Beth along, but he had put on a little weight since coming to Lea Cottage and had color in his cheeks. "No, Ahh'm not feeling up to it myself. Let's stay here a while longer and go back together." They sat quietly for a few minutes before starting back down the trail until Beth had a paroxysm of coughing that caused them to stop. When it was over and he withdrew his handkerchief from his lips, Hal noticed blood on it.

They finally got back and Beth fell exhausted across his bed. The next day he confessed to Hal, "I thought climbing a mountain would cure me; I can't just lie around in this 'pure' air waiting to get better."

"Ahh never should have brought you along, Beth. You've got to be patient, man. It worked for me."

Despite his outward appearance, Beth was deeply depressed. He was not sleeping or eating well, and neither he nor Trudeau's doctors could see improvement. After he got permission to use the Trudeau staff library to study tuberculosis, he was drawn to studies on the collapse of the lung when disease was limited to one side of the chest, as his was. In the 1890s, a doctor in Italy reported that after pumping air into the pleural space around a tuberculous lung in order to collapse it, the patient's disease often showed improvement when the lung was re-expanded. In the following decades, other reports appeared of artificial pneumothorax, as the procedure was known. A book published in 1925, recently acquired by the staff library, summarized much of the data. In moderately severe cases, improvement occurred in about half of the patients. Improvement was much less likely in advanced cases. The procedure was relatively simple and did not require general anesthesia, but there were complications and collapse of the lung was not always accomplished. To keep the lung at rest, the procedure had to be repeated periodically.

As he walked slowly back from the library to Lea Cottage, Bethune saw a glimmer of hope. True, he coughed and spit blood, but he did not consider himself to have advanced tuberculosis. *Is a 50–50 chance of improvement after pneumothorax better than this abominable bed rest?* "And if pneumothorax worked," he exclaimed out loud, "I'd know right away; none of this infernal waiting around feeling like a prisoner." Nobody heard him.

In early October, after two senior physicians had turned down his request for pneumothorax, Bethune was given the opportunity to present his case to the entire medical staff. Dressed in his bathrobe and slippers, Bethune felt at a disadvantage standing in front of the professionally attired doctors. The staff could not fail to be impressed by his presentation, explaining as he did the rationale for pneumothorax and summarizing the benefits and risks. "In conclusion, gentleman, bed rest has not worked in my case. My right lung is healthy, I am relatively young, and I am an ideal candidate for artificial pneumothorax of my left pleural space. Please allow me to undergo it before my disease advances and I am less likely to survive."

Dr. Lawrason Brown, the highest medical authority, spoke first. "How long have you been at Trudeau, Dr. Bethune?" he asked.

"This time, almost three months. Before that, four months."

"Do you know the average length of stay of patients at Trudeau?" Before Bethune could answer, Brown went on. "And let me remind you that many of these patients were healthier than you were when we first admitted you."

"I don't know," replied Bethune.

"It's about two years, and then most go home on limited activity, not back to a busy practice and teaching." Again before Bethune could reply, Brown asked another question. "Have you been a model patient, Dr. Bethune?" Some of the staff tittered and Brown answered his own question. "Your fellow patients and even some of our nurses—particularly the students—may find your antics amusing, but I dare say you have not set a good example, and you have not done your own health any good."

Bethune suppressed a cough by sipping some water from a glass he had by his side. "No, I have not been a model patient and I have not given bed rest the chance that many others have. But, my colleagues, you would have to tie me down like Prometheus if you expect me to give up the best years of my life rotting in bed when I am confident that artificial pneumothorax can restore my health quickly."

"Are you willing to take a chance you might die? What if we punctured your lung, or you went into shock, or had a hydrothorax?"

Bethune paused to take another sip of water. "It has been called to my attention—I might embarrass the person if I reveal my source—that when Dr. Trudeau's condition worsened, he requested and received pneumothorax here a few years before he died." The room stirred; several physicians were not aware that their guiding spirit had had the procedure.

"But he died," Dr. Brown retorted.

"We all die in the end, sir. Dr. Trudeau, sicker and older than I, survived the procedure. Would he have survived as long afterwards had he not had artificial pneumothorax? We'll never know. But if you pump air into my chest and I improve, and you give pneumothorax to others whose condition is like mine, and they improve, and you soon discover that their stay at Trudeau has been shortened, you will have made a major contribution to the field."

"Are you not being grandiose, perhaps delusional, Dr. Bethune, to compare yourself to Dr. Trudeau, and to believe that you can have such an effect?"

"I have tuberculosis. Dr. Trudeau had tuberculosis. In that

sense we are equal. He understood the risks as well as the possible benefits, just as I do. Your predecessors did not refuse him the procedure. Whether I will save as many lives as Dr. Trudeau and you and his other disciples, I don't know. But I would like to live and have the chance to try."

Dr. Fred Heise, head of the medical staff, stood. "Thank you, Dr. Bethune. You've given us a lot to think about and we may want to consult with others. If you will return to Lea Cottage, we will deliberate and let you know our decision. It should be but a few days." Bethune started to protest but thought better of it. He turned and walked out.

"My life is finished," Beth told his cottage mates. "They've turned down my request for pneumothorax. Dr. Heise mumbled something about consulting with others, but these gentlemen are so hidebound, they'll never agree."

"We're all in the same boat," Al Blalock replied. "We're young. We see the future of medicine as dependent on experimentation—on animals first, on humans if necessary." He paused. "Let's go into the village and drown our sorrows."

This was Beth's initiation into the occasional night sojourn of his cottage mates to one of the village's speakeasies. Their favorite was in the rear room of an art gallery on Broadway. Surreptitiously, they left the Sanatorium soon after the evening meal, took the short walk to the village in the fading light, and entered the gallery. Casually, they examined the art, slowly making their way to a door to the back room. They stood back as Hal knocked and gained their admission. The room was used for framing pictures during daylight hours but equipment had been moved up against the walls to make room for a few tables. The doctors ordered, and while Hal and Lou waited for their drinks, Beth and Al went back to the gallery to look at the paintings. Beth was attracted to a series of prints in one poorly lit corner. "I saw the originals in the Soane's Museum in London," he whispered to Al. "Hogarth's *A Rake's Progress*." He guided Al through the pictures. "In the first panel, a young Tom Rakewell, having come into a fortune, is being fitted for a new set of clothes. In the subsequent seven, he squanders his fortune on whores and gambling and marries a wealthy woman, despite being married to a poor woman who is pregnant with his child and is desperately trying to save Tom. He quickly runs through the fortune from his second marriage, continuing his wanton ways, ending up in London's notorious insane asylum."

After their drinks had been served, Beth told his friends that Hogarth lived to sixty-six, painting these incredible scenes, then engraving them. "Let me live until sixty-six and I'll show the world what I can do," Beth announced as he gulped his whiskey and ordered another.

They left the gallery at nine and arrived back at the Sanatorium a few minutes before the ten o'clock curfew, brazenly walking past the main entrance, where Beth's flashlight revealed an entwined couple on the alabaster bench to the left of Trudeau's statue. Beth, a little more intoxicated than the other two, turned his light on the boy. "Are you a patient here?" he asked.

"No sir," the lad answered. "I'm an assistant in the research laboratory."

"Ah, a budding scientist," Beth observed. He turned to the young woman. "Watch out for these scientists. They can do devilish things." The four patients laughed, but the young couple was not amused.

The next day, Beth paced around the rooms at Lea Cottage,

jotting figures with pencil and pad. "I need something to keep me busy," he told his inquiring roommates. I may not be as good as Hogarth but I can give it a try. I'm calculating how many murals I can fit on our walls, leaving space for windows and doors." In the few months he'd been at Lea he had sketched the faces of all his cottage mates. They were impressed by their likenesses.

Beth borrowed ten dollars from Hungerford and got a ride in the Sanatorium's station wagon, which shuttled patients to the village for shopping and the like and then picked them up for the return trip at an appointed time and place. The station wagon dropped Beth off at the art gallery he had visited earlier. A slim woman of indeterminate age, who was not there on his previous visit, greeted him. "Can I help you find something?" she asked, coming up close and peering at him from behind horn-rimmed glasses.

"Yes, you can, but I'm afraid it's not a painting I want." Beth's smile disarmed her look of disappointment. "I am planning to paint something but I need the proper supplies."

"Will you be painting outside, with need for an easel as well as paints and brushes?"

"No, nothing as grand as that. Only a mural."

"Only a mural?" she replied. "That's really grand."

"Not really. You see, I'm a patient at Trudeau"—with a look of concern, she took a half-step back, then came forward again when Beth lied that he was not contagious— "and I want to cover the walls of Lea Cottage with a pictorial story." He pointed to *A Rake's Progress*. "Something like Hogarth's."

"Will they let you paint on the walls?"

"No, no, I can't do that. I'll have to cover the walls with a material I can paint on. Paper is all I can afford."

"Then you'll either have to use watercolors, which might get messy, or chalk crayon, like pastel. There's an art supply store where Main turns off Broadway. We have lots of artists—or would-be artists—in this town, as well as, umm, visitors like yourself who like to draw."

Beth procured the art supplies, deciding that chalk crayon would be easier than watercolors. Other than sketch pads, which were far too small and expensive, the store had no paper to cover the walls. As he walked back to meet the station wagon, he saw a customer emerging from a Chinese laundry holding a package, presumably his clean laundry, wrapped in brown paper and secured with twine. Beth walked into the store.

"You have laundry?" the proprietor asked.

Beth did not answer right away, his eye roaming around the store until he spotted a spool of five-foot-wide brown paper mounted on a cast iron frame with a horizontal cutting edge. "No," he replied, putting his hand on the spool. "Want to buy the paper."

"Not for sale," said the owner. A boy of about ten came through a curtain from a back room. He exchanged remarks in Chinese with his father.

The boy put his hand on the frame. "This is not for sale; my father would not be able to cut paper to wrap clean laundry."

Beth was puzzled for a moment until he realized the misunderstanding. "No, I just want a roll of paper. No frame."

Again, father and son exchanged remarks. The father laughed and ordered his son to go to the back room, from which he emerged a few minutes later with a full roll of paper. He laid it on the counter.

"How much?" Beth asked.

"One dollar."

Beth paid him and made his way back to the Trudeau station wagon, the roll of paper cumbersomely lodged under one arm, his art supplies in the other.

When he returned to Lea, Lou Davidson told him that Dr. Heise wanted to see him in his office the next day.

"You caused quite a stir," Heise told him. "The staff could not come to an agreement on your request and so we invited Dr. Edward Archibald, the leading authority on the surgical treatment of tuberculosis, to come down from Montreal, examine you, and give his opinion."

"Yes, I've heard of Dr. Archibald. He's at the Royal Victoria and on the faculty at McGill."

"Dr. Archibald has agreed to be here on Monday."

Bethune laughed. "That's Halloween. Will he give me a trick or a treat, I wonder?"

He came to his appointment dressed as a lumberjack in a plaid woolen shirt, britches held up by red suspenders, a bandana around his neck, an axe slung over his shoulders. Dr. Archibald invited Dr. Edgar Wren, who had just joined the Trudeau staff after a fellowship with Dr. Archibald, to sit in on the consultation.

Deadpan, Dr. Archibald shook Bethune's hand. "Have you done much jacking?"

"Started at Martin's Camp of the Victoria Harbor Lumber Company on Lake Panache when I was twenty-one."

"And since then?" Archibald asked.

"Naw, I had to give it up when the white plague got me."

"Well, why don't you set your axe by the door, take down your suspenders, remove your shirt, and let me examine you." He took his stethoscope from his medical bag.

Wondering whether Archibald had not been informed of

his professional status, Bethune obliquely brought it to Dr. Archibald's attention. "Stethoscope's not much good." Instead of unbuttoning his shirt, he flicked the light switch on the view box on which his X-ray hung. "You can see that my right lung is clear but there's cavitation and some inflammation in my left."

Archibald looked at the X-ray then returned the stethoscope to his bag. "Which, I suppose, makes you an ideal candidate for artificial pneumothorax."

"Don't you agree, Dr. Archibald?"

Sternly, Archibald told Bethune to pull his suspenders back up. "I came all this way to have a lumberjack tell me what should have been obvious to the esteemed physicians of Trudeau. If I had the right equipment, I would perform the procedure myself. I'm sure someone here is qualified to do it, young Edgar Wren here, for instance." He turned to Wren. "With what you've learned at McGill, Wren, it will be quick and easy. I'll arrange to send the apparatus from Montreal." Turning back to his patient, he said, "Happy Halloween, Dr. Bethune. If the procedure works, and there are no complications, look me up when you get out of here. Maybe I can find a place for you at McGill."

Bethune's elation was amplified as he walked up the hill to Lea Cottage by the maples and birch on the mountainsides, aglow in reds and yellows that would have set anyone's heart on fire. He burst in on his roommates at Lea and announced, "I've won. Ed Archibald thinks I'm a good candidate for pneumothorax."

Hal Hungerford asked, "Are you on first-name terms with Professor Archibald?"

"Not exactly," Bethune admitted, "but we are kindred spirits."

"Did Dr. Archibald say anything about risks?" Hal asked drily in his southern drawl.

"He did say, 'If the procedure works, and there are no complications—,' so yes, he did."

"Ahh don't know, Beth. The risks you surgeons take go further than what an internal medicine man like me would tolerate."

Beth liked Hal immensely and admired his reasoning on medical matters. After lunch, he walked back to Lea alone, thinking about risks and complications. *Have I been fooling myself, grasping at straws? My chances are no better than 50–50—that is, if I survive the procedure.* Gloom replaced elation. *Down I go with nothing to show for it. My wife's divorcing me. I have no future. I was cut out to do better.*

The next day, Dr. Heise informed Bethune that the apparatus for artificial pneumothorax was expected to arrive from Montreal on Tuesday, and that Edgar Wren would perform the procedure on Thursday morning. While he waited, Beth tacked up the brown wrapping paper he had obtained at the Chinese laundry and began sketching out his ideas for the murals.

Chapter 3

Dr. Wren was busy for several hours Thursday morning. Bethune had taken it on himself not to drink or eat, even though he was not undergoing general anesthesia. He prolonged his fast, foregoing lunch. Not until three o'clock did he get a call that Wren was ready.

The treatment room in which the pneumothorax would be performed smelled faintly of disinfectant. All its light came from a 150-watt bulb screwed into the base of an inverted, shiny, metallic dish suspended over the examining table in the center of the room. Bethune, stripped to the waist, ribs visible through his gaunt chest, sat on the edge of the table, his slippered feet dangling over the side. "If you count down to my sixth rib and insert the needle so it rests on top of it," Bethune reminded Wren, "you'll avoid the blood vessels and nerves that run along the bottom of the ribs."

Emily Jenkins, a willowy student nurse, finished prepping the injection site. Waiting for the alcohol to evaporate, Wren attached the newly arrived air pump and manometer to the hub of a long, hollow needle, which he held with one gloved hand while he located the top of Bethune's sixth rib with the other. Locating the point of entry, he placed the tip of the needle on Bethune's skin. As he did so, Bethune reached for Emily's hand and pulled her closer, wincing as the needle penetrated his skin.

"Push harder, doctor," he said to Wren, who slid the needle

over the rib, puncturing the pleural space. "Yeow!" Beth screamed, erupting into a brief spasm of coughing. "I didn't think it would hurt that much; I think the needle has pierced my lung." Both doctors looked at the column of fluid in the manometer, which was rising and falling irregularly. "Pull the needle back slightly," Bethune ordered, gritting his teeth in pain. The fluid stopped fluctuating. "Have adhesions obliterated my pleural space?" he asked, more to himself than to Wren. Emily gently mopped the beads of sweat that had formed on his brow with the dry sponge in her free hand. "Pull the needle out very slowly," Bethune commanded. As Wren did so, the fluid in the manometer began to rise as Beth let out his breath. It fell when he inhaled, rising and falling rhythmically as he breathed. Still in pain, he announced, "That's more like it. Now start pumping air in."

Wren pumped the air in a jar hooked to the manometer into Bethune's pleural space. Markings etched into the jar indicated how much air had gone in. As more air was pumped in, the pressure in the pleural space began to rise. When Wren had pumped in 500 cc's, the magnitude of the manometer's excursions diminished; the increased pressure was preventing the lung from expanding when Bethune inhaled. By 700 cc's, the excursions had stopped completely. Keeping his eye on the manometer, Bethune said, "Congratulations, doctor, you've collapsed my lung. I hope the compression will seal off the puncture wound so it doesn't reinflate my lung." Dr. Wren withdrew the needle.

Emily released her hand from Bethune's grip, helped him put on his pajama top and robe, and then walked away from the operating table. "Where are you going?" he asked weakly.

"To get a wheelchair for your return to Lea Cottage."

He put one foot on the floor. "No. I can walk there. I'll soon be cured, you know." He put the other foot down and stood momentarily without support. Taking a step, he would have toppled over had Dr. Wren and Emily not grabbed him. Leaning against the table, he seemed to be studying Emily's face.

"What's your name?" he asked.

"Emily."

"If you accompany me, Emily," he grimaced but forced a winsome smile, "I'm sure I can make it on my feet." He put his arm around her waist. To brace him, she reciprocated. They made it into the corridor, down the steps of Ludington, and into the crisp November sunset, walking like tightly linked lovers.

The other nursing students envied Emily her assignment to assist at Bethune's artificial pneumothorax. He was the legendary older man with whom anything could happen. Handsome, with light brown hair swept back over his bullet-shaped head, beautifully chiseled features, penetrating blue-green eyes, straight nose, full lips, and a slim moustache, he was known to give his favorite nurses a pleasant pat here and there and had even invited two of them to join him on a clandestine after-hours visit to the village. Emily was aware of all this as she tended to Bethune. She, too, found him attractive and began to imagine a life with him. That they both had T.B. removed an obstacle to an intimate relationship.

Neither of them spoke as they started up the small hill to Lea, Emily's heart thumping wildly. As they approached Lea, Beth looked sideways at her. "You look familiar. Have I seen you before?"

"Uh, yes," she blushed. "Last week, I was sitting next to Dr. Trudeau's statue—"

"Oh yes, necking with the young scientist."

They walked on silently, Emily debating whether to tell him that she wasn't really serious about the young scientist, when Beth turned, put his free arm around her, and drew her close and put his lips on hers. Instantly, she forgot professional propriety. Slowly, his tongue parted her lips and pressed against her teeth insistently until they parted and his tongue met hers. She clung to him, savoring the new sensations. When he started to pull away, she hung to him more tightly. Gently, he released her. "I bet your boyfriend doesn't kiss like that."

"Oh no," she sighed as they continued to the cottage, arms around each other's waist.

"Now I'll be able to continue work on my murals," he said at the entrance to Lea.

"Are you an artist, too?" she asked.

"Not really, but I have this urge to leave something tangible behind if I should—"

Emily held him tighter, "Oh no, you're not going to die."

After Emily helped him inside, she noticed the laundry paper covering the walls. In the foreground of the wall to her left, a small church and a churchyard had been penciled in on the paper. Seven tombstones stood engraved with names of the deceased and the years of their deaths. Norman Bethune was one of the names, and his year of death was 1932. "That's so sad," she said.

"I 've drawn the last panel first in case I die before I get to the early ones."

Grasping his hand tightly, she reassured him, "You'll finish."

He pointed to a large blank space higher up on the right side of the panel. "There's a problem, Emily. I need a model for the Angel of Death. A beautiful woman." He turned to face her and moved back, holding her at arm's length, scanning her from top to bottom. "Like you," he said.

"I've never modeled before."

"You're not bashful, are you?"

Naïvely she asked, "Why?"

"You'll have to pose in the nude."

She blushed for being so stupid. "Will there be other people around?"

"I hope not," he smiled. "It shouldn't take long, maybe an hour. If there's some deserted cottage, I can do the sketches there and then transfer them to the mural."

That night, barely able to stand, Bethune began work on the first mural, continuing well past the ten o'clock curfew. His coughing grew worse, troubling the sleep of his cottage mates. Around two in the morning he came into the bedroom and started to roll his bed out to the porch. Hungerford was still awake. "What are you doing, Beth?" he asked.

"I'm keeping you awake," he gasped.

Hal helped Beth roll his bed out and then rolled his own, closing the French door so the others could sleep. When Beth stopped coughing, Hal checked to make sure he was still breathing. His coughing started again shortly after dawn, waking Hungerford and Blalock, who went to get a wheelchair. He and Hal wheeled him to Ludington Infirmary. Dr. Wren was awakened and he fluoroscoped Beth's lungs. Not only did the left lung have a total pneumothorax, but the air pressure in it had pushed his heart and aorta to the right. Inhaled air had continued to enter the pleural space through the lung puncture, impairing his good right lung and causing considerable pain. The only solution was to withdraw air to reduce the pressure.

Once again, Wren put a needle into Bethune's chest, this

time to withdraw air, leaving the lung partially collapsed. Bethune tolerated the procedure well but his cottage mates insisted he return to Lea by wheelchair, which they pushed, and then made him go to bed. His coughing diminished, he was in less pain, and he completely finished the contents of a lunch tray they had brought him. He slept the entire afternoon and awoke at dinner time, ravenously hungry. With his friends' help, he walked to dinner and again cleaned his plate.

He resumed work on the murals, making steady progress, his cottage mates making various comments about their meaning. Beth decided he'd have to write a few lines of verse at the bottom of each panel to make clear what the drawing meant.

Dr. Wren scheduled a follow-up a week after the first pneumothorax. Emily Jenkins was again assisting. As she prepared to prep him, she handed Bethune a tightly folded piece of paper. As she swabbed his chest, he unfolded it, read the message, then crumpled the paper and tossed it into the trash can in which Emily had discarded the used sponges. Just as Dr. Wren entered, Bethune whispered to her, "I'll be there."

Quickly, she whispered back, "If I get caught, it will be the end of my nursing career."

The note instructed Beth to come to the deserted Brown cottage, which was awaiting demolition, at noon the following day, when patients and staff would be at lunch. She arrived a few minutes early, not wanting Beth to show up first and then leave if the cottage was empty. He came on schedule, carrying a large sketch pad and a folded, clean bed sheet. Without a kiss, and in a very business-like manner, he instructed Emily to drape the sheet over her shoulders after she undressed. Then he wandered around the cottage, seeking the proper light.

"This will do," he called, beckoning her to a sunlit room.

He had her kneel on her left knee and cradle her hands on her right thigh. Then he loosened the sheet from her left shoulder, lowering the edge so her breast was exposed. He sat in a chair with his sketch pad on his lap and began to work. They didn't talk. After a few minutes, he put his pad and pencil down and walked over to her. She looked up at him, expecting a kiss. Grasping her head between his hands, he turned it to the right and bent it down. "I know this will be difficult," he said, "but I'd like you to hold this pose and smile beatifically."

Holding the pose was difficult, let alone smiling, and Emily realized that modeling was difficult work.

After about an hour, they heard the voices of patients as they returned from lunch to the nearby cottages. "Why don't you leave first, uhh, Emily," Beth said. "I'll leave when the coast is clear."

In the weeks following the modeling session, Beth neither spoke nor signaled recognition when he passed Emily on the Sanatorium grounds. When he left Trudeau on December 10, 1927, in a remission that proved permanent, he didn't say goodbye. A week later, as she was helping decorate the Sanatorium for Christmas, Emily overheard one of the older nurses tell another, "I'll miss Dr. Bethune. He would liven up the holiday."

"He livened me up, all right," replied the second. "Thought I'd snared a husband, then he dropped me like a hot potato." Emily felt sick to her stomach and went outside. She realized that she, too, had been jilted.

—◆—

The choices were limited for a poor girl like Emily, graduating from high school in 1925. Women had to be extremely smart to get a college scholarship, and that was the only way Emily, who was smart, could afford to go to college. But being smart, or showing it off, was not fashionable—not the way to get a husband. Besides, few opportunities were open to women with a college diploma. Although she was voted prettiest in her class and had lots of boyfriends, Emily Jenkins had not found anyone she wanted to spend the rest of her life with. That left her with few options: finding an ordinary job, or becoming a teacher, secretary, or nurse, each of which required some additional training. Emily opted for nursing and applied to the Trudeau School of Nursing. Students entering the program had to have had tuberculosis or test positive for it. Emily tested positive but her sputum was negative for the tubercle bacillus. Her disease was quiescent, the doctors told her, and would probably remain so for the rest of her life, even if she were to be intimately exposed to the tubercle bacillus.

Emily was well liked by the nurses, doctors, and patients, especially the male ones. By the end of her second year she was assigned difficult cases, including some that would ordinarily be assigned to a registered nurse but that her instructors felt she could handle, like assisting Dr. Wren. One of her easier duties was to help a staff physician in the examination of new employees, and that was how she met Thomas Steele at the beginning of her second year in the summer of 1927.

After his senior year in college, Tommy's plan to go to graduate school was sidetracked when his father was diagnosed with tuberculosis. Whatever savings the family had went to renting a cottage in Saranac Lake so his father could take the cure. When Thomas tested positive for T.B. and his chest X-ray suggested minimal involvement, his doctors thought the fresh Adirondack air would help his lungs heal completely. In

September 1927, he moved to Saranac Lake with his parents and applied for a job at the Trudeau Research and Clinical Laboratory adjacent to the Sanatorium, a twenty-minute up-hill walk from the Steeles' cottage in the village. On his first climb there, Tommy admired the turning leaves and the distant views of high peaks. *I really could like living here*, he thought, not considering the snow and bitter cold of winter. He was steered to the administrative offices, where a clerk told him his letter of application had been received but that he would need to pass a physical examination before it could be acted upon.

"Sounds like the Army," Tommy declared with some anxiety. He lowered his voice and bent toward the clerk, a man about Tommy's age. "Tell me, sir, does having tuberculosis disqualify one for a job?"

The clerk laughed. "It's almost a qualification—as long as it's quiescent." He directed Tommy to the Ludington Infirmary, where he was shown into an examining room and told to strip to his waist. A few minutes later, a tall, attractive young woman in a student nurse uniform, her black hair spilling out from under her cap, entered.

"Hi," she said, "my name is Emily and I'm here to take your blood pressure and temperature."

"Temperature?" Tommy asked, a bit embarrassed.

Emily laughed, "Orally." She proceeded to perform her tasks, then felt his pulse, timing it with the watch pinned to her apron. "Now please just breathe quietly so I can count your respirations." Tommy wondered if her proximity might affect the measurements. "Are you going to be a patient here?" she asked as she entered the findings on his chart.

"No. I'm applying for a job—as a scientist."

"Really? You look so young."

"I just graduated from the University of Pennsylvania, magna cum laude in biology."

"Wow, that's impressive." She lingered, though her work was done. "I'd love to see your lab some time."

He laughed. "I haven't been hired yet, but if I am, I promise to show it to you. What's your last name, Emily?"

"Jenkins, Emily Jenkins."

Tommy was hired, but not as a scientist. His initial responsibility was washing and autoclaving the petri dishes and flasks in which tubercle bacilli would be grown. He impressed Dr. Petroff, the senior scientist in the lab, and within a month Tommy was plating the bacilli on dishes and growing them in flasks. He remembered his promise to Emily and soon gave her a tour of the lab. Afterward, he walked her back to the student nurses' dormitory and just before they parted, with his heart pounding, asked her for a date. She agreed, and the next Saturday he took her for an ice cream soda in the village. Returning from their second date, they stopped to sit and talk on the alabaster bench by Dr. Trudeau's statue. Tom put his arm around Emily and soon they were kissing. They were interrupted by four male patients rushing back from the village just before curfew, more than a little drunk. They intimidated the young couple, first shining the light on Tommy, asking what he was doing there. He told them about his job. Then they flashed the light in Emily's eyes, warning her, "Watch out for these scientists. They can do devilish things." The men laughed, but Tommy was mortified.

A few weeks later, Norman Bethune embraced and kissed Emily as she assisted him back to Lea Cottage after his artificial pneumothorax. Tommy had invited her to go Christmas caroling in the village, but she was not ready to take up with a mere boy again—she guessed he was only a year or two older than she and only an inch taller. Compared to Bethune's resonant baritone, Tommy's voice, she thought, had not completed its descent from puberty. His cheeks were also boyishly smooth and she was sure he could not sport a moustache—at his entrance physical, she had noticed he didn't have a hair on his chest, though his muscles were well developed.

In January, Tommy invited Emily to an ice-skating party on Lake Flower. Beginning to realize that Norman Bethune was a closed chapter in her life, she accepted. Neither of them were good skaters, but Emily always managed to avoid falling into his arms when she slipped. She made it clear then and on the next few dates that she was not ready to be kissed again.

Sometimes they would walk into the village to see one of the new talking movies, stopping for a hot chocolate afterwards. Gradually, Emily grew to like Tommy. He listened with interest and amusement when she talked about the patients, including Dr. Bethune—his song and dance routines, how he got the nurses to serve him tea on a silver service he had brought to Trudeau—never revealing the momentous kiss or her modeling.

On an unseasonably warm evening in April, they crossed over the river at Pine Street and walked to nearby Moody Pond. They took off their jackets, spread them on the damp ground, and lay on them gazing at the myriad stars. Tommy turned to her and gently kissed her lips. He was pleasantly surprised when she put her arms around him, pulling him closer. He was more surprised when her tongue gently parted his lips. Back in the fall, her kiss was nothing like this. He wondered where she had learned to deep kiss but concluded no good would come from asking.

Emily graduated from the Trudeau School of Nursing in June 1928 and was immediately hired as a full-time nurse. She and Tommy were now known as a couple. During the summer of 1929, Tom—he now preferred it to Tommy—told Dr. Petroff that he was going to apply for a graduate program in microbiology to earn a Ph.D. Petroff had come to rely on Steele to isolate and characterize different strains of the tubercle bacillus; Tom had developed new techniques to facilitate his work and also co-authored two papers with Petroff. A few days later, Petroff called Tom into his office and offered him a staff position and a substantial raise, on the condition that he would postpone leaving the lab. Tom talked Petroff's offer over with two people, Emily and Hal Hungerford. Emily had begun to feel that marrying Tom would not be the worst thing and that he would go much further with a Ph.D. When Tom told her about Petroff's offer, she wavered, finally telling Tom he had to decide for himself; she didn't want him blaming her for his decision if it didn't work out.

Hal, over a decade older than Tom, had also been working in Petroff's lab and became friendly with Tom. He pointed out that if Tom was already worth so much to Petroff he surely would go much further with a Ph.D., and encouraged him to leave. While he was deliberating, the stock market crashed at the end of October. Worried that he might not get into graduate school or find another job, and that Emily might not wait for him even if he succeeded, Tom accepted Petroff's offer. Emily Jenkins and Thomas Steele were married in 931. Tom never obtained a Ph.D.

PART TWO

1953: Winter and Spring

Chapter 4

"There's a gentleman from the Federal Bureau of Investigation to see you," Greta Andrews announced.

Brandon Warner stopped placing medical books on the shelves of his office and stared at his secretary. "Did he say what it was about?"

"He said he could discuss it only with you."

Warner put the books he was holding on one of the shelves, dusted his hands off, and said, "Show him in." His office was dingy and had not changed much since Edward Trudeau, founder of the sanatorium for tuberculosis that now bore his name, had occupied it. Dimly lit by a desk light and a solitary floor lamp topped with a fluted silk shade yellowed with age, the office on this February morning lacked the cheery sunlight that often flooded through the tall southwest window on winter afternoons. Becoming aware of shovels scraping snow off the paved sidewalk below, Warner walked to the window, gazing across Park Avenue to snow-covered Mt. Baker close by and twin-peaked Mackenzie farther away. When the door opened, he turned to face the agent.

"Dr. Warner, thanks for seeing me without an appointment." He pulled his wallet out and flicked it open to his badge. "Larry Crane, FBI."

"It must be an urgent matter that brings you up this way, unannounced, before the roads have been cleared."

"With chains it wasn't difficult." He ignored Warner's reference to an urgent matter. "We're seeking your cooperation, Dr. Warner."

Given his tendency to accommodate, Warner responded, "I'll do whatever I can to help," though he immediately regretted making this commitment before he had learned more. Guiding Crane around the cartons yet to be unpacked, Warner offered him a chair in front of his glass-topped desk and then settled into his swivel chair behind it, apologizing for the mess. "I was promoted to director in January and I'm still moving in," he added.

"Have you been at the Sanatorium for long?"

"Since 1947, first as associate medical director, now executive director."

"Have you ever heard of Norman Bethune, doctor?" Crane asked, leaning slightly forward as he spoke. He was wearing a three-piece pinstriped suit, neat tie under a pointed white collar, highly polished wing-tipped shoes planted flat on the dull oak floor. (One of Warner's first changes had been to get rid of the threadbare carpets.) In contrast, Warner wore a V-necked sweater over an open-collared plaid shirt and dark corduroy slacks. He thought for a moment before replying. "No, I haven't."

"He was a patient here in 1926 and again in 1927."

"What do you want with Mr. Bethune?"

"Actually, it's Dr. Bethune—an M.D."

"Is he wanted for some nefarious business?"

"It depends how you define 'nefarious.' Bethune declared himself to be a member of the Communist Party of Canada in 1937."

"Oh, I see. Had he been spying on Americans?"

Crane's answer was evasive. "There's no evidence that he

tried to steal state secrets like the Rosenbergs. But if you count him as a foreign agent trying to recruit Americans to join the Communist Party here, or as one who was recruited by Americans to join the Party in Canada, then he was part of the vast communist conspiracy."

When Crane did not immediately continue, Warner asked, "You said you wanted my cooperation. How?"

"We have reason to believe Bethune was a Communist when he was a patient here."

"Have you asked Bethune when he became a Communist?"

"It would be difficult, even if he were to cooperate; he died in 1939."

"Oh, I see." Warner drummed his fingers on the glass desktop. "What do you want from me?"

"We'd like the names of patients and staff that Bethune associated with when he was here."

Although Warner could not explain why, his stomach contracted. He stood, followed quickly by the agent. "I'll see what I can do," Warner said, not fully realizing that he was implying a commitment.

Crane reached for his wallet. "Here's my card. Let me know when you have something. Good day."

Warner sat at his desk, picked up a pencil, and absent-mindedly twirled it, sorrier by the minute that he had agreed to accept the promotion from associate director, knowing that he would preside over the closure of the Trudeau Sanatorium. The number of admissions to Trudeau had started to decline due to the use of streptomycin, discovered by Dr. Selman Waxman to effectively treat tuberculosis. When the Sanatorium closed, the village of Saranac Lake could sink; jobs would be lost, guest houses and fine stores closed, cure cottages no longer needed to house tuberculosis patients too sick to be admitted to the Sanatorium.

The chairman of the Trudeau Board, Dr. Fred Todd, was also putting pressure on him to get Arnold Springer, director of the Saranac Laboratory, to prepare the papers of last year's research symposium for publication, and Springer was resisting.

And now Agent Crane. Warner had paid little attention to Senator Joseph McCarthy waving lists of alleged Communists, scaring much of the country. But after Crane's visit, he'd have to be more attentive.

Near its zenith, the sun had emerged from the fleeting clouds and was melting the icicles that had formed above Warner's windows. He became aware of the constant dripping on the cleared pavement below. Putting his pencil down, he again walked to the window. Looking out at the mountains, at patches of green where the sun had melted the snow on the pine and spruce boughs, Warner found a semblance of serenity. The contraction in his stomach had given way to a growl of hunger. After lunch, he'd take the obligatory first step and find out more about Norman Bethune.

Without putting his galoshes on, Warner walked the quarter mile along Park Avenue, the broad street that led into and out of the Sanatorium's buildings, to his home. Predictably, Janet made him remove his shoes before he entered.

"I thought you'd tire of unloading books before now, Brandon. Did something come up?"

"I had a visitor."

"Anybody I know?" Janet had a knack of subtly getting information from him.

"Do you know anybody who works for the FBI?"

She was bringing the sandwiches she'd made to the kitchen

table but stopped in her tracks and grinned. "Is there something about you I don't know?"

They had met in high school in Buffalo and married while he was a student in the medical school there, after she had obtained a B.A. from Teachers College at Columbia. His medical education was interrupted by bouts of tuberculosis, which helped formulate his lifelong interest in pulmonary diseases. She got a job teaching history and economics at their alma mater and helped pay his way through medical school, and for his hospitalizations. With their young son, John, they moved from Buffalo to Saranac Lake in 1947 for Brandon's new job. His salary could support the family and Janet had stopped teaching, but she retained an interest in the social sciences and read the daily newspapers more avidly than Brandon, preoccupied as he was with his responsibilities at the Sanatorium.

"No. This agent came to see me in my capacity as director. He wanted information about a patient who was here in the 1920s—Norman Bethune, a doctor."

Janet put their plates on the table and went to the stove where the teakettle had started to whistle. "That name sounds familiar, but I can't place it."

"This Bethune was a Communist, who died in 1939. The agent wanted names of people who knew him."

"And you agreed to cooperate?"

"Do you think that was a mistake?"

Janet poured their tea and brought the cups to the table. Brandon had started his sandwich before she sat down. "Wait a minute." Furrowing her forehead, thinking deeply for a moment, she said, "I recall Emily Steele mentioning that name; a doctor who was a patient here when she was a student nurse at Trudeau in the 1920s. She seemed sort of wistful about him."

Janet was a loyal American, from a family going back generations, but as a teacher in Buffalo during the Depression she was appalled when kids came to school hungry, often in rags. When the New Deal made it easier for unions to form, she joined the Congress of Industrial Organizations, not so much to organize teachers but to help get factory workers a "New Deal." She knew Communists in the CIO, even had them to dinner, where Brandon met them, but neither had joined "the Party," as it was referred to in the 1930s. As a medical student and then as a house officer, Brandon saw rampant poverty touch the lives of many of his patients but never connected his tuberculosis to the ills of society.

"You Whack!" Janet exclaimed. Brandon looked at her quizzically. "The House Un-American Activities Committee, H-U-A-C. The FBI must be working with it. Or maybe with McCarthy or that other Senate investigating committee. They want names. Why were you so accommodating, Brandon?"

"When the FBI comes up here at the tail end of a blizzard and asks for your help, it's hard to refuse."

"If you give this agent names, the FBI could make their lives miserable. If they don't give more names, then they're suspect."

He took a final gulp of tea and put his cup down. "And if I don't give him names, then I—we—are suspect. It's a slippery slope."

"Maybe you should discuss cooperating with your colleagues."

"Fat chance they would tell the FBI to do its own investigation."

"You won't know until you try. They're your friends, Brandon. You're just asking their opinion."

"Maybe, but let me find out more about this Bethune first." He headed toward the door.

"Remember to call for John at Mt. Pisgah, dear, and wear your galoshes home; it's supposed to snow tonight. And don't leave your overcoat in the office."

Instead of returning to his office on the first floor, Warner climbed the stairs to the office of the registrar, Sally Putnam. "Good afternoon, Sally," he greeted her. "I got a request this morning for information about a past patient here."

"Was it from the gentleman driving that new black Buick?"

"I didn't see his car, but sounds like it could have been."

"What was the patient's name? When was he, or she, here?"

"Norman Bethune. 1926 or 27."

"Long before my time."

"You probably weren't even born then."

"I'm not that young, Dr. Warner, but thank you for the compliment. Let me look in the card file first." She scurried back to banks of wooden cabinets holding drawer after drawer of five-by-seven-inch cards. She walked behind one bank and raised her voice so Warner could still hear her. "Back then, one drawer could barely hold all the cards of patients admitted in a single year. Not anymore; every year the number gets smaller."

Bethune, Henry Norman	Date of birth: March 4, 1890
411 Selden Street	Place: Gravenhurst,
Detroit, Michigan	Ontario, Canada
Next of kin: Frances Penney Bethune (wife) Occupation: Physician	
Date of admission: December 16, 1926 Date of discharge: March 24, 1927 (against advice) Cottage: Robbins	
Readmitted: July 16, 1927	

"You don't have to tell me," Warner muttered.

"1926. Within the year, they're organized alphabetically by last name," Sally continued. "Let's see, Bell, Bernstein, Bethune." She pulled out the drawer, placed it on the counter before Warner, and rotated it so Warner could read the contents of the card.

"Hmm, says he was readmitted in July 1927. Let's see if you can find a card on Bethune in 1927."

Sally returned with a second box and Warner soon found Bethune's second card. "Readmitted July 16, 1927. Cottage: Lea. Still lists Frances Penney as next of kin but now says divorced. Discharged: December 10, 1927, in remission." "In remission, in six months? Quite remarkable!" He jotted down the information on a pad Sally provided and put it in his coat pocket. "Had you heard of Norman Bethune, Sally, before I 'introduced' you?"

"No, doctor, I hadn't."

"I don't suppose there's anybody on the staff today who was here twenty-six years ago, is there?"

"Dr. Wren keeps reminding us he's been here forever. Maybe he was."

"Well, thanks very much Sally. Sorry to trouble you. I've got to get back to my office."

As he walked downstairs, Warner was rather pleased. He thought he knew as much abut Bethune's background as the FBI and could probably find out more without arousing suspicion. He rang up Edgar Wren. Now in his sixties, Wren had the longest tenure on the medical staff.

"Edgar, Brandon Warner. I had occasion to look up a patient here in 1926, Norman Bethune. He was readmitted in July 1927 and was discharged 'in remission' six months later.

I thought that remarkable. Are you familiar with Bethune? He was a physician."

Wren took a few seconds before he answered. "Norman Bethune. I knew him well. I'm just seeing my last patient here. Why don't I come over to your office in a few minutes and tell you about him?"

It was past five o'clock when Wren finished describing to Warner how he had performed his first artificial pneumothorax on Norman Bethune, primarily at Bethune's request. "He pioneered pneumothorax, and before streptomycin came along it was the principal treatment for unilateral pulmonary tuberculosis, but of course you know that. Beth also invented some thoracic surgery instruments that are still in use today. You do know what happened to Norman Bethune after he left the Sanatorium?" Wren asked.

"Did he go to work with Dr. Archibald?"

"Yes, and then became a prominent thoracic surgeon in Quebec, but it's his history afterward that made him famous."

"You mean his being a Communist?"

"So you know he went to Spain and then China, where he died?"

"No, I didn't know that. In fact, I had never heard of Norman Bethune until this morning, when an FBI agent told me Bethune declared himself to be a Communist, uhh, I think in 1937. The agent wanted to know whether he was a Communist when he was a patient here."

"I doubt it," Wren replied. "The only suggestion he might have been a Communist," Wren laughed, "was that he broke all the rules. He was a reprobate, a womanizer, and a heavy drinker when he could get his hands on a bottle. We never talked politics. Apparently, he changed drastically in the Thirties."

The lamps were lit in Warner's office but outside total darkness had descended and a shadowy gloom filled the room.

"In 1936," Wren continued, "Bethune resigned his appointment as chief of thoracic surgery at Hôpital du Sacré Coeur in Quebec and volunteered his medical services to the Spanish Republic in its defense against Franco's insurgents. In Spain, he put together a team that was able to type and crossmatch donors' blood, place the packets of blood in refrigerated containers, and ship them to the battlefronts in ambulances outfitted to give transfusions. The quick availability of blood saved many lives. Even so, word got around that Beth didn't get along well with the Spaniards and he returned to Canada in 1937, spending most of the year touring the country to raise money for the Spanish Republic and declaring he was a member of the Communist Party of Canada.

"In 1938, he left for China to help Mao Tse-Tung's Red Army establish mobile hospitals, in which he operated on Japanese prisoners as well as Chinese soldiers. He also started a field medical school to rapidly train Chinese doctors to serve on the battlefront against the invading Japanese."

"Sounds like a man for all seasons," Warner commented.

"The story is almost over," Wren continued. "Bethune cut his finger while operating behind Japanese lines in November 1939. The cut got infected, his finger became swollen, then gangrenous. The Chinese were unable to smuggle sulfa drugs through the Japanese lines. Bethune's Chinese colleagues tried to persuade him to have his finger removed, and then, as the infection spread, to have his arm amputated. Confident he would recover, and expecting to operate again, he refused. His consciousness fluctuated and he died less than two weeks after he cut himself. Instantly, he became a hero in China and word quickly spread back to Canada. It wasn't long before word got to us here at Trudeau about his martyrdom."

Brandon looked at his watch. "Oh my god! Janet's gonna be mad. I was supposed to pick up John and his friend from their ski lesson an hour ago. They must be home by now; I hope so anyway." He picked up his galoshes and they walked out together. The cold air reminded Warner that he needed his coat and they parted in front of the administration building. Warner went back inside for his coat, and when he came out again Wren had disappeared into the darkness.

Janet met Brandon at the door as he dropped his galoshes in the snow room. "Did John get home all right?" he asked.

"No thanks to you, but am I right in guessing there were extenuating circumstances?"

He hung up his coat and kissed her. "You are prescient, Janet." John was doing his homework upstairs, and the couple went into the living room where Brandon prepared martinis. As he was telling her what he had learned from Edgar Wren, she struck her forehead with the palm of her hand. "Now I remember. That's why Emily Steele brought him up; we were talking about famous patients. I also remember what Emily said: 'You could have knocked me over with a feather when I learned he was a Communist. He behaved more like a prince when he was here. I thought he might have been looking for a princess.'"

Sipping their drinks, they were silent for a few minutes. "Now what?" Janet asked.

"More consultations, as you suggested."

"Then what?"

"Let's wait and see what they have to say."

Only a light dusting of snow fell that night, and by the time Brandon had finished his breakfast the sun was shining brightly. He did not take his galoshes but he put his coat on and walked briskly to the administration building. He asked Greta to call Sally Putnam, Edgar Wren, Tom Steele, and Arnold Springer to come to a meeting in the conference room adjoining the medical library at eleven o'clock. Steele was the director of the Trudeau Laboratory; its research dealt with the tubercle bacillus.

They all came except Springer, who was out of town. Warner thanked them for coming on such short notice and came right to the point. "As Ed Wren already knows, I was visited yesterday by Larry Crane, an agent of the FBI. He wanted to know if I was familiar with Norman Bethune. Thanks to Sally and Edgar, I am now. Bethune was a patient here in 1926 and '27 and, according to Agent Crane, he was a member of the Communist Party of Canada in 1937. He has become quite famous in China and Canada, Dr. Wren tells me."

"Infamous might be a better term," Tom Steele interjected.

"Did you know Bethune, Tom?"

"I knew of him," Tom answered without elaborating. "What does the FBI want to know about Bethune?"

"Whether he was a Communist when he was here. I've asked you all here to get your views on cooperating with the FBI and giving it the names of people at Trudeau who knew Bethune."

"Well, I'm at the top of the list," Wren quickly replied with a nervous laugh. "But Bethune and I never talked politics."

"You're only one person, Edgar," Tom Steele replied. "Maybe there were others here in the 1920s who were Communists. Maybe one of them indoctrinated Bethune." He turned to Warner. "What you should do, Brandon, is conduct your own investigation—find out who knew Bethune, and if there's any indication he was a red back then, give the FBI what you find."

"I've got my hands full as it is, Tom. And I certainly don't want to begin an investigation without you backing me up."

Sally looked up from the steno pad on which she was taking notes. "If we conduct our own investigation, couldn't that stop them from asking to see our patients' records? They could subpoena them if we refuse. I don't see what's wrong with turning over the names of people who we can document were close to Dr. Bethune when he was here. Dr. Wren for instance, or Dr. Bethune's cottage mates."

"None of you are worried that we might be hurting innocent people by giving their names to the FBI?" Warner asked.

"On the other hand," Steele argued, "we might be exposing a hidden communist ring—doing our patriotic duty."

Abruptly, Warner stood. "Well, thanks for your input. The meeting is adjourned."

Tom Steele stayed behind, closing the door after the others had left. He was a compact man of average height, about the same as Warner. Tom had a round, pleasant face, though he seldom smiled, and was bald. Warner was leaner and had shaggy brown hair, usually in need of a haircut. "Brandon, there's another matter that seems much more immediate," Tom began. "People on my staff—and, I'm told, on the medical and nursing side—are hearing rumors that the Sanatorium is a sinking ship, but one they don't have the luxury of deserting. Many of them have been in the Adirondacks for three generations or longer and are reluctant to leave. When is the administration going to acknowledge a problem?"

Warner sighed and pointed to the armchair and Steele sat down. "I guess it's too much to expect that rumors won't start flying."

"Not when people retire and you don't replace them, when you seem to have put a freeze on new hires, and when there are empty beds. Do you think we're blind or just stupid?" Steele asked aggressively.

"I knew it would be obvious to you," Warner admitted. "Streptomycin—"

Steele cut him off. "Streptomycin! It's ironic that the only reward I get from Selman Waxman for providing him with different T.B. strains to measure the drug's effectiveness is to have this place close down and lose my job." He took a handkerchief out of his back pocket and blew his nose. "Are the trustees aware of the problem?"

"Of course. They thought it would cause a panic if we announced we were closing without having a plan to save as many jobs as possible."

"As head of the Trudeau Laboratory, didn't I deserve to be in on the plan?"

Warner knew the answer to Steele's question was yes. But the prominent scientists whom he looked to for advice on the future of the Trudeau looked down on Steele, not least because he lacked an advanced degree. He was not in the "old boys' club" and Brandon didn't want to offend them. Tom seemed to have a chip on his shoulder, but the people who worked for him loved him and he was loyal to them.

Warner knew some of Tom's past history. He had risen from dishwasher in Strasimir Petroff's lab to director of the entire laboratory. He maintained a repository of different strains of tubercle bacilli, many cultured from the Sanatorium's patients, but increasingly from centers around the world.

"Had I been in charge then," Warner explained, "you would have been included in the planning. The only excuse I can offer is that the trustees hoped a solution would be found quickly that would preserve the Trudeau as a preeminent research institution for tuberculosis and other pulmonary diseases. They didn't want to ring alarm bells."

"I take it no solution has been found."

"The Board of Trustees thought that a collaboration with a university and medical center would be mutually fruitful, but those prospects have fallen through."

"So what's next?"

Warner could have cut off the discussion by commenting, *I'm not at liberty to say*, but he continued, "We're trying to sell the Sanatorium, the land and buildings—"

"That means my lab goes—"

"Let me finish, Tom—and use the proceeds to build a Trudeau Institute elsewhere in Saranac Lake entirely devoted to research. You'd have more laboratory space, state-of-the-art equipment, and a bigger staff." Warner dreaded Tom's next question.

"Who would be the director?"

"The Board of Trustees believes a prominent scientist with administrative experience at a major university would best maintain the stature of the Trudeau."

Steele sat quietly for a moment. "I concur. For as many years as I've got left, I just want to continue my research."

Visibly relieved, Warner smiled. "That's what we all want, Tom." He stood, followed quickly by Steele.

"Is there a prospective buyer?"

Again Warner hesitated. "In strictest confidence, Tom, the

Corporate Managers of America."

"Can the Sanatorium hold on until the deal is concluded?"

"We may have to close it before then; we're losing money with the diminishing number of admissions. In any event, your lab will keep operating."

"My people are very worried that they'll wake up one day without jobs and little or no savings. Will the Foundation provide severance pay?"

Warner realized the justness of Tom's question. He stood. "We'll work something out, Tom, I can assure you."

"Well, I hope you and the trustees know what you're doing," Steele said, his hand on the door knob. He turned to face Warner, changing the subject. "And if you think refusing to cooperate with the FBI is going to help Trudeau, you're sadly mistaken."

⸺

Shortly after Warner returned to his office from lunch, Sally Putnam came down the stairs from her office. "I know how busy you are, Dr. Warner, so I did a little fishing of my own. In another file I was able to see who the other patients were in Lea Cottage in 1927 with Dr. Bethune. Three of them were physicians and I thought you might know them." She handed him a slip of paper with their names.

"My god, Sally. If there was a *Who's Who in American Medicine*, they'd all be in it."

⸺

"Tom Steele said it would be our patriotic duty to cooperate with the FBI," Warner told Janet that evening as he smoked his after-dinner pipe. "He suggested we conduct our own investigation."

"What about the others?"

"Edgar Wren said he never talked politics with Bethune when he was a patient here. Sally's worried if we don't give names, the FBI could subpoena our files."

"Sally has a point. That could be worse—exposing a lot more patients to FBI scrutiny. Seems like your best path, dear, is to try to learn whether Bethune was a Communist when he was here. If there's no evidence he was, then you might get the FBI off your back."

"And if there is evidence?"

"Why don't you wait and see what turns up?"

Brandon sighed. "I'm really sorry I took the promotion. If Johnny were a little bigger, I think I'd resign and get out of here." He reached for his pipe. "Oh, that reminds me, I had a letter from the United Mine Workers. They're establishing a chain of hospitals and outpatient facilities in mining country, West Virginia and Kentucky, and invited me to apply as chief and coordinator of their hospital system."

"Do miners have a lot of tuberculosis?" Janet asked.

"Not that I know of, but they have their own disease—'black lung' from inhaling coal dust most of their lives."

Chapter 5

The next morning, Warner asked Greta to call the three physicians who were patients in Lea Cottage with Norman Bethune. The first she reached was Dr. Alfred Blalock, chief of surgery at Johns Hopkins.

"Dr. Blalock, this is Brandon Warner calling from the Trudeau Sanatorium—"

"Ah, Trudeau! I have pleasant memories of Trudeau, despite the circumstances that brought me there." Blalock, a southerner, waited for Warner to continue.

"I'll be brief. Earlier this week, I had a visit from an FBI agent who asked that we provide him with the names of people who knew Dr. Norman Bethune."

"Norman Bethune!" Blalock surprised Warner with his enthusiastic response. "One of the most brilliant and courageous men I've ever met. Too bad he went off the deep end."

"What do you mean?"

"Became a Communist, ruined his career, and essentially killed himself—operating relentlessly under terrible conditions."

"I'd like to ask you a question that might help us in responding to the FBI."

"Go ahead."

"Was Bethune a Communist when you were a roommate of his in Lea Cottage up here?"

Without hesitation, Blalock replied. "Not a chance! He was more interested in carousing, chasing after the nurses, breaking curfew. Politics never entered into our discussions, and we had many of them. Sure, he was concerned about the well-being of his patients, but so were we all."

"That's very helpful—"

"Did you know, Warner, that Beth almost died from his first artificial pneumothorax?" He didn't wait for Brandon to answer. "That evening, he complained of chest pain and coughed up blood, something he hadn't done for several weeks. He thought, and we concurred, that Dr. Wren had perforated his lung, that his death was imminent. Nevertheless, or maybe because he thought so, he refused to go to bed and continued work on the murals, almost falling off the chair he was standing on with paroxysms of coughing—"

Warner interrupted, "Murals?"

Brandon heard Blalock talking to someone near his phone. "Look, Warner, my secretary tells me I'm late for an appointment. Hal Hungerford can tell you about the murals; he took them with him when he went to Duke. If you need more information from me, don't hesitate to call. Goodbye."

Murals, that's an interesting wrinkle, Brandon thought. Janet had gotten him interested in two contemporary Mexican artists, Diego Rivera and David Siqueiros, whose fiery revolutionary beliefs prompted them to paint inflammatory pictures including several murals. As Warner recalled, Rivera painted the most controversial one in Rockefeller Center in the early 1930s. Nelson Rockefeller, who commissioned the mural, found it too radical for his taste, fired Rivera, and had the mural destroyed. *Was the mural a genre for portraying revolutionary scenes in the 1920s, and was Bethune's mural painted in that vein?* Warner wondered. *From what Blalock said, it didn't sound like it.*

"Dr. Hungerford is out of town this week," Greta reported to Warner. "I arranged a telephone appointment with him next Monday. Shall I try Dr. Davidson?"

"Please do."

When Warner explained the purpose of his call, Louis Davidson, professor of surgery at Columbia University's College of Physicians and Surgeons, had a reaction similar to Blalock. "Bethune was a remarkable individual," he said, "although somewhat tempestuous. He could watch and listen with remarkable patience and absorb everything, but when he found someone or something annoying he could be devastating. Out of the blue, Beth called me before he went to China, must have been 1938. He wanted a refresher course in general surgery to prepare for his work there. With my colleagues, we brought him up to date over a few days."

"Quite something, wasn't he?" Warner commented. "When you, Bethune, Blalock, and Hungerford were together in Lea Cottage up here, did you ever talk about communism?"

"Never," Davidson immediately replied. "Beth had no interest in politics. He liked to show off in front of the nurses and the other patients, but underneath he was depressed. One night in the summer of 1927, after Beth had received the terms of the divorce from Frances, we picked up a bottle of whiskey from a bootlegger and went to the shore of Lake Flower. Beth was drunk when he peeled off his clothes and swam for several minutes, trying, I thought, to drown himself, but the water seemed to revive him. He dragged himself out and said to me, 'Look, Louis, every one of us ought to jump in the lake; we're no damn good to ourselves or anyone else.'"

Davidson paused. "No, Beth was too caught up in his own

problems then to think about communism. All that came in the 1930s. When he visited Columbia in 1938, asking for a refresher course, he was a different person. I had missed the transition. His mind was made up and I could not dissuade him from going to China."

Warner asked Davidson about the murals. "You should speak to Hal Hungerford," he replied.

———◆———

The following Monday, Warner spoke to Dr. Hungerford by phone. Though twenty-five years younger than Hungerford, Warner was casually acquainted with him through the American Thoracic Society, of which Hungerford had been president. In 1946, Hungerford left his post as professor of medicine at Duke to become deputy director of the National Microbiological Institute. When Hungerford had received the prestigious Trudeau Medal from the National Tuberculosis Society in 1951, Brandon had written to congratulate him.

"Dr. Hungerford, this is Brandon Warner at the Trudeau Sanatorium."

"Oh yes, Brandon, nice to hear from you. Ahh hear the Sanatorium is in hard times," he said in his southern drawl. They chatted amicably for a few minutes about the implications of the discovery of streptomycin. "We're funding clinical trials that show the drug has a remarkable effect, but some patients, or rather their tubercle bacilli, are resistant to it." As the conversation ground to a halt, Warner told him the purpose of his call, as he had done with Blalock and T.B's .

"What was the agent's name?" Hungerford inquired.

"Larry Crane." Warner heard Hungerford grunt. "Do you know him?" Warner asked.

"He visited me in January. You see, Brandon, I refused to sign the loyalty oath required of me as a government employee and Agent Crane wanted to know if I was a Communist. My days at NIH are numbered, I'm afraid. What did Agent Crane want with you?"

"Nothing personally. He informed me that Norman Bethune was a patient here in the 1920s and he wanted to know if Bethune was a Communist then."

The line was quiet for almost a minute. Finally, Hungerford spoke. "It's mah fault."

"I beg your pardon?"

"It's mah fault that Crane got to you, or rather to the Trudeau Sanatorium." Another pause. "You see, Crane asked me if I knew any Communists, and I thought I was being clever and not hurting anyone by naming Norman Bethune. After all, he has been dead for fourteen years. I thought I was teaching Crane a lesson by telling him about Bethune, including that he and I were patients at Trudeau in 1927. Turns out, Crane taught me a lesson: Don't name names, not even dead ones."

"That's what he wants from us: names. I haven't replied yet, and I'm hoping I can tell Crane that Bethune's physician friends up here, his cottage mates and a member of the current staff, all say Bethune was not a Communist in 1927."

"I would agree," Hungerford said.

"That makes it unanimous." Warner paused before changing the subject. "In the course of finding out about Bethune, I learned that he had started painting murals around the time he had his first artificial pneumothorax here."

"Drew, not painted, using some sort of pastel crayon."

"I see. At any rate, I wondered whether the murals might

give corroborating evidence that Bethune was not a Communist when he drew them—evidence I could pass on to Agent Crane without implicating anyone else. Do they have any political content?"

Hungerford laughed. "Like pictures of Marx or Lenin? No, nothing like that. They were about his battle with tuberculosis, but they did reflect his disillusion with life as he tried fruitlessly to escape the clutches of infectious diseases. The final panel showed Beth's tombstone and those of his cottage mates, including me, with our predicted years of death. The panel was dominated by a beautiful angel, her wings spread, holding the dead Norman Bethune in her arms."

"What happened to the murals?"

"I took them down and brought them to Duke with me in 1930. I left them there when I came to NIH in 1946."

"Do you think," Brandon asked Hungerford, "you could arrange to have the murals sent back to us here at Trudeau in Saranac Lake?" Bolstering his case, he added, "They were drawn here, so Trudeau could be considered their rightful owner."

"I can do that, Brandon, but the last time I saw them—seven years ago—the chalk had smeared in places, and the laundry wrapping paper on which they were drawn was tearing. God knows what shape they're in now. I'll ask my friend in the Department of Medicine at Duke to ship the original murals to you."

"That would be wonderful. We'll be pleased to cover any costs."

"Well, Brandon, good luck with Agent Crane. Keep me posted, will you?" Brandon thought he was done but after a moment Hungerford asked, "I gather that the Steele lad is still up there with you. We worked in the Trudeau Lab together."

Brandon laughed. "That Steele lad is now about fifty years old. He heads up the Trudeau Laboratory."

"Ah yes, now I recall. You know, Brandon, he should have gotten some of the recognition that Selman Waxman got for discovering streptomycin. It was the strains of tuberculosis maintained by Steele at Trudeau that Selman used to demonstrate that the drug worked *in vitro*. Waxman may have thought he would get away with it because Steele didn't have an advanced degree, though he didn't treat his own postdocs any better. I encouraged Tom to get an advanced degree when we both worked at the Trudeau Lab, but he didn't take advice readily, except from Strasimir Petroff. Well, give Steele my best."

When Warner got off the phone with Hungerford, Greta buzzed, reminding him that in forty minutes he had an appointment at the Saranac Laboratory with Arnold Springer, the laboratory's director. Briskly, he walked back home, went straight to the garage, got into his 1948 wood-paneled Dodge station wagon, and drove down Park Avenue, arriving at the Saranac Laboratory on Church Street in a few minutes. He had asked Greta to make the appointment. When Dr. Springer asked what it was about, she had replied, "Dr. Warner didn't say."

The Saranac Laboratory was built in 1894 after fire destroyed Dr. Trudeau's home and his adjacent laboratory while he and his family were in New York City. Built of stone and steel, the new laboratory was so fireproof that no insurance was taken on it. In 1895, it was one of the first buildings in the village to be electrified. Warner walked up the seven stone steps, entered the vestibule, and from there went into the main laboratory, its walls made of white glazed brick interrupted by huge windows letting in the midday light. The laboratory had indeed stood the test of time and was a beehive of activity, with technicians and scientists engaged in a variety of work. Springer, in his long white lab coat, greeted Warner at the door. "I thought you might have forgotten."

"No, Arnie, I do have to talk to you; a phone call detained me. Greta whisked me out as soon as I got off." He unbuttoned his coat.

"You haven't been here for some time. Let me give you a brief tour." Along the way, Springer showed him the new animal quarters and inhalation equipment. They stopped to chat with staff, who summarized their current work, and then went upstairs to Springer's office.

"I understand you invited me to a meeting last week. Sorry I missed it, Brandon. I was invited to lecture in West Virginia. Is this a follow-up?"

"No. I had a visit from the FBI and I wanted to get advice from you and a few others."

"The FBI?" Springer seemed moderately interested.

"Yes, an Agent Crane drove all the way up from New York City at the end of the blizzard." If Springer stirred in his seat at the mention of Crane's name, Warner did not notice. "He wanted to know whether the Trudeau harbored any Communists."

Springer leaned forward. "What did you tell him?"

"Actually, he seemed most interested in whether there were Communists here in 1927, because a famous Communist was a patient at the Sanatorium then."

"What was his name?"

"Norman Bethune, a doctor."

"Never heard of him," Springer commented.

"I tracked down Bethune's cottage mates at the Sanatorium in 1927. All prominent physicians. None of them thought he was a Communist when he was here."

Springer started to ask another question, but Warner cut him off. "Look, Arnold, I didn't come here to talk about Communists, but, you know, Fred Todd keeps after me about publishing the Seventh Symposium papers. In the year and a half since the symposium, I've received many letters congratulating the Trudeau Foundation on sponsoring it but inquiring when the results will be published." Springer got out of his chair and closed the door to his office.

"Brandon, do you realize what the publication of those papers, especially the ones on asbestos, will do to this laboratory?" Although neither would admit it, there had been tension between them ever since Trudeau's Board of Trustees had rejected Springer's recommendation to make the Saranac Laboratory independent. Instead, the Board appointed Warner executive director, essentially making him Springer's boss. "Some of those papers can only be published with the permission of the corporations that supported the work, and they have been unwilling to grant it."

"That sounds unethical. It may also be illegal."

"If those papers come out under the aegis of the Saranac Laboratory, the lab will be destroyed."

"What makes you so sure?"

"One company warned me that if we used its brand name when we described how dangerous a product was, we risked losing its support. Other companies have asked to review and *correct* some of the papers. Their support could be jeopardized if we publish them as they are."

"Sooner or later, Arnie, the truth will out. Scientists elsewhere are bound to replicate our findings. I know it's difficult to bite the hand that feeds you—" Brandon stopped mid-sentence as a new thought occurred to him. "I've read Dr. Trudeau's autobiography recently, Arnie. Shortly after this laboratory was built, he wrote that as it was to be purely a research laboratory, there should be no 'commercial side' to it."

"Then you'll be writing off the Saranac Laboratory."

"Not necessarily," Brandon replied weakly . "NIH is increasing its extramural grants and we should apply to it for support."

"There's no guarantee we'll get it." Springer, who had been standing, slumped into his seat. "You realize that if the Sanatorium goes under, and this laboratory along with it, the town of Saranac Lake is likely to die; the Trudeau Foundation employs more people than any other organization in the village."

"You don't have to tell me." Warner stood. "I hope I've made the Board's position clear, Arnie. If you need funds to publish the Seventh Symposium, let me know. And you and your fellow scientists here should start looking into new sources of funding. Good day."

———◆———

Before Brandon left for work that morning, Janet had reminded him that she needed their station wagon to transport John and Billy Steele and their equipment to their ski lesson on Mt. Pisgah after school. Although he had done his best to avoid confrontation, he was uneasy after his discussion with Arnie Springer. He vaguely remembered that he had to drop the station wagon off and decided to have lunch at home.

Janet had finished her lunch and was having a cup of tea and some leftover apple pie when Brandon entered. "I'm glad you came home, dear. I was indecently about to finish off the pie. There's some leftover pea soup in the fridge if you want to warm up on that first."

Brandon followed his wife's suggestion, buttered a piece of bread, and sat at the kitchen table where she lingered while he ate. "Arnold's not going to follow the Board's instruction," he predicted. Janet already knew about the problem. "Seems that some of the companies that support his lab are balking at seeing the work published."

"Can they do that?"

"Some of their gifts stipulate that they must review work that their funds support before the researcher submits it for publication. Whether they can prevent publication if they don't like it is another story." He finished his soup and Janet pushed the pie plate toward him and poured tea for both of them. "The bigger problem, as Arnie made clear, is that they may withdraw support from the Saranac Laboratory. I suggested he apply to NIH for grants, but he pointed out—and he may be right—that there's no guarantee he'll get them."

"Isn't there a bigger problem, dear?"

"What do you mean?"

"From what you've told me, asbestos could affect the health of everyone who's exposed to it. That could be millions of people." Brandon did not argue. "Do the companies have the right to withhold that information?" She stopped and thought for a moment. "Well, maybe they have a right legally, but is that ethical?" Again, she paused. "The law should comport with what's ethical."

Brandon finished his pie, drained his cup, and stood. He

realized that he had not used this most potent argument on Springer. His only excuse was that he was just trying to keep the peace. As he put on his coat, Janet held out her hand. He looked at her quizzically. "You're going to have to walk back to the Sanatorium, Brandon." His face brightened and he dropped the car keys in her hand.

———◆———

Emily Steele was waiting with her son's ski equipment when Janet pulled up. The Warners' son, John, and Billy, the Steeles' younger son, were in the sixth grade at the Lake Colby Public School and were best friends. They picked the boys up from school and drove the short distance to the Mt. Pisgah Ski Center for the boys' weekly lesson. After seeing them off, the two women went into the cozy wooden hut for hot beverages. They picked a small round table near the pot-bellied stove.

Though hard to tell under their quilted coats, both women were slim. Janet Warner, a few inches shorter than Emily Steele, looked older despite being the same age. About five feet six inches, Emily had dark eyes, a smooth, ruddy complexion, and black hair that tumbled over her sloping shoulders when she pulled off her ski cap. She carried her height well, with excellent posture that made her seem taller.

Their conversation began with the usual pleasantries about the weather and their families. Then Emily said, "Tom told me about the FBI agent who was here last week asking about Norman Bethune. It worries me, Janet."

"What worries you? He's looking for Communists." Janet remembered that in 1952, the Steeles had an "I Like Ike" sign on their lawn.

"No, that's not it. According to Tom, he wants to know

more about people who knew Norman Bethune."

"I remember you mentioned his name a few years ago. Did you know him?"

Emily sipped her hot chocolate. She paused, took another sip, and answered. "Yes, Janet. I knew him." Her face had a worried expression. "What concerns me, Janet, is that Tom will suspect I had something going with Bethune."

"Did you?"

Emily put her cup down and laughed nervously. "That's a matter of opinion."

"Whether you did or didn't, I don't think that's what interests the FBI." Then she added, "Unless you have reason to believe that Bethune was a Communist."

"No. In the little talking we did, it was never about politics."

"Did you have an affair?"

"No, no," Emily said quickly. "I wasn't even engaged to Tom at the time. I've been fondled and propositioned by some of the men around here—never Brandon—since our marriage, but I am a faithful wife."

"Then what could you possibly worry about with the FBI?"

"It's a long story."

Janet turned to look at the clock on the wall. "We've got another forty minutes before the boys come off the slope." Emily proceeded to tell her how she had met Bethune and modeled for him.

———

Emily turned to look at the clock on the wall of the hut and then across at Janet, who sat absorbed in the story. "We'd better go meet the boys," Emily said. They walked toward the meeting place at the bottom of the slope.

"Did Bethune draw you into the murals?"

"I never saw them until I heard that Dr. Hungerford was going to take them down before Lea was demolished. I was stunned. There I was in one of the panels, the Angel of Death, kneeling on one knee, cradling the dead Norman Bethune in my arms. The only thing Beth changed was the color of my hair, making it as bright as an angel's. He drew my bob cut and the slope of my shoulders perfectly." She stopped walking and turned to face Janet. "Do you see this birthmark?" She held her finger just below a tiny mole under her left eye. "He even drew it into the mural. If Tom ever sees the mural, he's sure to recognize me."

They resumed walking. "You see, Janet, when I thought Beth and I had something going I stopped dating Tom. He must have suspected I had another beau."

The boys had taken off their skis by the time their mothers arrived. Stowing their equipment in the back of the Warners' station wagon, the boys climbed into the back seat, chattering away. The women were silent as Janet steered on to Trudeau Way. Then, quietly, she asked Emily, "So what if Tom finds out?" She looked over at Emily, who was staring straight ahead, her lips tightly compressed, before she answered.

"Tom was so good when we courted; understanding, trying to please me. In many ways he remained that way." She turned to make sure the kids were engaged in their own conversation. "But he soon made it plain that he was the lord and master. I was to be subservient, the good housewife." She paused, thinking of an example. "After the kids were in school, I raised the possibility of returning to nursing. Tom wouldn't hear of it. 'Your place is in the home,' he told me. 'Isn't that why you became a nurse in the first place? To catch a husband? Now

you've got one. Leave it to the younger girls to catch theirs.'"
Thinking she'd been too harsh on Tom, she added, "He's been
a good provider, though he doesn't confide in me very often.
He's great with our boys; never lifts a hand to them, though
he's become impatient lately when Gerald challenges him.
When it comes to me, his one blind spot is jealousy. When I'm
complimented by other men, he accuses me of trying to seduce them and becomes—" she paused, looking for the right
word, "irrational." They rode on silently. "So, what if Tom
finds out?" Emily repeated Janet's question. "I don't know.
Honestly, I hadn't thought about the murals for years until
Tom told me about the FBI coming here. If they're investigating Norman Bethune, they're likely to find out about the
murals. Once Tom sees them, he'll know right away why he
had a winter of discontent in 1928. True, it would end my
worry about his finding out, but God knows how he'll react."
The station wagon came to a stop at the Steeles' driveway and
Emily and Billy said their goodbyes.

Janet was surprised to hear Emily's confession. Tom was
always friendly and polite. He and Emily got along well on social occasions. *You never know what goes on inside a marriage*, she
thought.

———— ♦ ————

Brandon was already home, reading the local newspaper, and
sipping his martini when Janet joined him. She dropped the
car keys in an ashtray and plopped down on the sofa. "Boy!
Did I get an earful from Emily Steele this afternoon."

Putting his paper down, Brandon stood and held up the
icy shaker. "Can I pour you a martini before you tell me?"

"I'd prefer sherry, please." When they were both settled,

she continued. "Did you know that Bethune drew a set of murals when he was a patient at the Sanatorium?"

He surprised her. "As a matter of fact I did. Dr. Blalock mentioned them when we spoke last week. This morning Harold Hungerford at NIH told me more about them. I forgot to tell you at lunch."

"Do they still exist?"

"Yes, so far as Hungerford knows."

"Where are they?"

"At Duke Hospital in Durham."

Janet sighed. "Emily will be pleased to hear they're far away."

Brandon did not ask why Emily wanted the murals far away, and Janet did not tell him. "Not for long if Hungerford follows through," Brandon said, as he poured the last of the martini from the shaker. "I'm sorry to disappoint Emily, but Hungerford is arranging to send us the murals. They might help get Agent Crane off our backs."

Chapter 6

In the years after the death of Dr. E. L. Trudeau, the Trudeau family had gradually expanded the Board of Trustees of the Foundation and transferred oversight of the Sanatorium and the laboratories to it. The trustees sat at the pleasure of Dr. Trudeau's heirs, and the chairman of the Board, Fred Todd, kept them apprised of the Foundation's activities. By 1953, no member of the Trudeau family sat on the Board.

The three items on the agenda for the Board's February meeting that year proved contentious: the imminent closure of the Sanatorium as the number of admissions continued to plummet; the FBI's hunt for contacts of Norman Bethune, a Communist, when he was a patient in 1927; and Arnold Springer's recalcitrance in publishing the proceedings of the Seventh Saranac Symposium, held in 1952.

Shortly before the Board meeting, an editorial in *The Adirondack Daily Eagle* predicted the imminent closure of the Sanatorium and chastised the Board for its indifference to the plight of the Saranac community, particularly the loss of jobs, should this happen. As rumors spread about the closing, a "town-gown" split was developing, with many workers and small businessmen complaining about the "snobbishness" of the doctors and research scientists at Trudeau. That spread to the Board of Trustees, where two Saranac Lake resident members, Archibald Chandler and Walter Reilly, both prominent businessmen, were skeptical that the decline in patients could be due to a new drug.

Over the past few years, the physician scientists on the Board had urged the other trustees to recognize that streptomycin was reducing the number of admissions to the Sanatorium and would eventually lead to its demise. They finally succeeded in getting the Board to look for a buyer for the several acres of Trudeau property. At its February meeting, Fred Todd, professor of medicine at Cornell Medical College in Manhattan, reported that the Foundation had received an attractive offer from the Corporate Managers of America to buy the Sanatorium lock, stock, and barrel. If the sale went through, plenty of jobs would be available.

"Will that mean the demise of the Trudeau Foundation?" a trustee asked.

"No, not all," Todd replied. "First of all, the Saranac Laboratory, located in the village, is not part of the sale offer. It will continue to operate. Second, the Trudeau family wants to see the name Trudeau perpetuated in the Saranac Lake area. Third, the proceeds of the sale will give the Foundation the opportunity to purchase new facilities to expand the research of the Saranac Laboratory and the Trudeau Laboratory, which is part of the sale offer as it is within the Sanatorium grounds. We may have a generous gift of land on Lower Saranac Lake that would make a much-expanded Trudeau Research Institute a reality."

With a few minor tweaks, the Board approved acceptance of the offer. It also instructed Brandon Warner to calculate "separation allowances" for all staff members, to tide them over until they could find new jobs once ownership of the land had been transferred to the Corporate Managers of America.

"Thank you, gentlemen. Before we break for lunch, let's hear from Dr. Warner about his visit from the FBI." Fred turned to Warner.

"In January, I was visited by FBI Agent Larry Crane. He told me that Dr. Norman Bethune, a patient here in 1927, was known to be a Communist. I hadn't heard of Bethune, but I subsequently learned that he was a prominent thoracic surgeon in Canada who declared himself a Communist in 1937." Warner quickly filled the Board in on what he had learned about Bethune. "Agent Crane asked me to provide names of people close to Bethune when he was here. The question I have for the Board is whether to cooperate with the FBI."

"Our country faces a communist menace," Walter Reilly pronounced. "It's our duty to cooperate with the FBI to root out Communists wherever they are."

"It does seem a little far-fetched," a scientist trustee commented. "So what if Bethune was a Communist in 1927? That was twenty-six years ago. The Great Depression and World War II intervened. Doesn't the FBI have better things to do?"

"Do you think the FBI is after the Trudeau Foundation?" Todd asked.

"That never occurred to me," Brandon answered. "I thought their investigation was, like Mr. Reilly said, to root out Communists. Sally Putnam, our registrar, identified three of Bethune's cottage mates at Trudeau in 1927; they are all prominent American physicians today. Neither they, nor Dr. Edgar Wren, who operated on Dr. Bethune in 1927 and is still on our staff, believe he was a Communist in 1927."

"Have you given their names to the FBI?" Todd asked.

"I wanted the Board's approval first." He paused. He had discussed what he would say to the Board with his wife, Janet.

Now he presented her argument. "By giving their names, the Foundation could subject them to unnecessary harassment by the FBI or by congressional committees with which the FBI cooperates."

"But if the Foundation doesn't give their names," another trustee noted, "isn't it opening itself up to greater scrutiny? Might it not be accused of harboring Communists? If you don't give the FBI the names, can't the FBI come up here, subpoena the Sanatorium's records, identify those three, and maybe others who might have been Communists then—and might still be if they're alive?"

"That seems to be a real possibility." Archibald Chandler spoke for the first time during the discussion. "Our job as trustees is to protect and promote the Foundation. I think you should cooperate with the FBI, Warner. What are a few names compared to preserving the Foundation?" Chandler, a retired banker, was the oldest and longest-serving trustee.

"With all due respect, Mr. Chandler," Todd replied, "if we cooperate we are fostering the witch hunt that is already proceeding at full throttle in this country. We are essentially a hospital and a health research facility. We're not engaged in political activity. If we instruct Dr. Warner not to supply names and the FBI does subpoena our records, we as a Board should resist that effort legally."

Warner surprised the Board. "There may be a way out of this dilemma. I learned from Bethune's cottage mates that he drew a series of murals on paper he had tacked up on the walls of their cottage while he was a patient here. One of them, Dr. Harold Hungerford, took them with him when he left the Adirondacks to join the faculty at the new Duke Medical School, where they are now. I would like the Board's permission to request that Duke return the murals to the Foundation, their rightful owner. They might provide a direct expression of Bethune's ideology at the time he drew them. If the murals fail to provide evidence he was a Communist, we convey that to the FBI, giving them an opportunity to see the murals for themselves. That should end the investigation without having to release names or subject the Foundation to further inquiry."

"And what if they show communist sympathies?" Roger Anderson asked. He was the chairman of the Clearview Coal and Ore Corporation, headquartered in West Virginia. "Then what?"

"From what his cottage mates have told me about the murals, that seems highly doubtful. The murals are about Bethune's personal fight against infectious diseases, especially tuberculosis."

"Well," Fred Todd said, "Brandon's request to seek the murals gives us some breathing space if nothing else. Any objection to his requesting the murals from Duke?" There were none and the Board adjourned for lunch.

———————

Roger Anderson had arranged for the Trudeau station wagon to take him to the Saranac Laboratory to have lunch with Arnold Springer. From the lab, the two men walked to the Pale Moon Tea Room on Broadway. Springer had been consulting for Anderson's coal company for several years and the two had become friends.

"Looks like the visit I suggested is beginning to pay off," Anderson began as they ate. Springer seemed puzzled. "I'm talking about your visit to the FBI in January."

"Oh, that visit. Yeah, when Brandon came to prod me

about the Seventh Symposium he mentioned that Agent Crane, the one who I had spoken to in Manhattan, had visited him. According to Brandon, Crane seemed more interested in a commie who was a patient here in 1927 than what's going on here today."

"Too much of a coincidence, Arnold. The timing, the same agent. Looks like your visit sparked Crane's interest. I don't think the FBI would be spending taxpayer money just to learn more about commies in 1927. Its interest may play to our advantage. And none too soon." Springer looked inquisitively at Anderson. "This afternoon, the Board will be discussing your reluctance to publish the Seventh Symposium. It's not inconceivable the trustees will vote to put the screws on you to prepare it for publication."

"And if I don't?"

"Hard to say. Depends how vindictive Fred Todd is. He might ask Warner to fire you."

"I'll resign before I publish all that stuff. The Board should realize publication could be suicidal for the Foundation."

"I'll do all I can this afternoon to protect you, or rather the papers from the Seventh Symposium." Anderson looked at his watch and stood. "But if I fail, we may get a little help from the federal government," he said with a cynical smile. He beckoned the waiter and paid the bill. "We may have to give the FBI's investigation a nudge." They walked briskly back to Springer's lab, where the shuttle picked him up at 1:30 p.m.

———◆———

Chairman Todd reconvened the Board meeting at precisely two o'clock. "We have one more item before we go into executive session. The sooner we get done, the more time you'll have before cocktails." He turned to Archibald Chandler. "And I want to thank Dr. and Mrs. Chandler for hosting the reception this evening. We'll now discuss Dr. Springer's apparent unwillingness to prepare last year's Saranac Symposium on Inhaled Dust Diseases for publication. Dr. Warner, can you bring us up to date?"

"I met with Dr. Springer within the last month. He told me that the corporate sponsors of some of the research reported at the symposium had not been pleased with the results and would be unhappy to see them published."

"What is the basis of their displeasure?" Trustee Chandler asked. "Do they dispute the validity of the findings?"

Dr. Todd interceded. "Not at all. It's the validity that worries them. The findings may expose them to liability lawsuits because their product, asbestos, is more dangerous to human health than previously suspected."

"That sounds like a conflict of interest," Chandler concluded.

"It's not quite as simple as that," Roger Anderson replied. "Although my company is not involved in the mining or manufacturing of asbestos, I would like to remind the Board of the tremendous importance of this remarkable mineral. It is used in everything from kitchen potholders to the pipes that insulate our homes, businesses, and schools. It is unique in its ability to prevent fire. Imagine the loss of life from fire if the companies that make it are forced to cease production because of liability suits."

"But if those who come in contact with it," Todd interrupted, "not only the workers who mine and manufacture it, but the people who are exposed to even small amounts of asbestos fiber, are at risk for cancer or lung disease—that is what these unpublished experiments show—as many lives could be lost as from the potential fire, Roger."

"Still sounds like a conflict of interest to me," Chandler concluded.

Walter Reilly, the owner of the only medical, surgical, and scientific supply company in Saranac Lake, turned to his good friend Chandler. "I don't know, Archibald. If these companies withdraw support, the Saranac Laboratory might go under. With the Sanatorium up for sale, *The Daily Eagle* might be right. The economy of the village will suffer."

Another physician scientist on the Board pointed out that rumors about the suppression of the papers were beginning to spread among the medical-scientific community. Unless they were squelched, he said, no reputable physician scientist would accept a position to head the new Trudeau Institute once land and funds were procured.

"Dr. Springer, who heads the lab now, would make an excellent scientific director," Roger Anderson commented.

A moment of silence ensued as the trustees looked at Warner, seated next to Todd at the head of the oval table. The trustees had selected Warner to direct the Sanatorium, with the Saranac Laboratory underneath him.

"I'm sure Dr. Springer could do a fine job," Warner replied, "but the Board should know that in our recent conversation he defended the laboratory's reliance on private donations from our grateful patients, which are likely to decrease once the Sanatorium closes, as well as from prominent corporations."

Walter Reilly asked, "If not for industry support, how else would the research get done?"

"Grants from the federal government, Walter," Todd replied. "In the last few years, Congress has committed the federal government to a major expansion of research."

Roger Anderson quickly asked, "Would we rather have government telling us what to do than industry?"

"That's not the way the system works, Roger," a scientist interjected. "Springer, or any scientist applying for federal funds, would have to apply for a research grant, and his application would have to be approved by a committee of his peers, most of them outside the government."

"Besides," Todd added, "the government has no stake in a particular outcome of the research. The intent of NIH is to advance knowledge in the belief that the more we know, the better the public's health will be."

Chandler turned to Todd. "What do you want us to do?"

"I'd like the Board to authorize Brandon Warner as executive director of the Foundation to take whatever action is necessary to arrange the publication of the Seventh Saranac Symposium."

"So move," said Chandler. The motion was seconded, and it was carried by one vote. With the exception of Chandler, all the business members opposed the motion.

———

When the Warners arrived at the Chandlers for cocktails after the meeting, most of the Board members were already present. Tom and Emily Steele—invited because Tom was director of the Trudeau Laboratory—were also there, having arrived shortly before the Warners. As they took off their coats, Brandon seized Tom's arm. "I've been meaning to tell you, Tom, Harold Hungerford sent his best to you. He worked in Petroff's lab with you in the 1920s."

Tom's face lit up. "Hal Hungerford? A southerner, I remember him well. Urged me to get a Ph.D. but Petroff wouldn't hear of it. I looked up to Hal. Great guy." They walked to-gether to the makeshift bar.

Janet Warner was about to greet Emily Steele when Archibald Chandler beckoned Emily into the living room. Ramrod straight, six feet tall, his white hair neatly parted on the left, Archibald escorted Emily toward an elegantly framed picture on the wall of the deeply carpeted, expansive room. Janet was amused to see his hand, initially on Emily's back, slowly and gracefully descend below her waist, stopping in what Janet considered an "indecent" position. Emily took a delicate step closer to the print to tactfully elude Chandler, but so did Chandler and his hand. Janet joined them. "I see you've got a new addition to your collection, Archibald."

Because of their mutual interest in art, Janet and Archibald had become friends soon after she and Brandon had come to Saranac Lake. Chandler had told her that he came there for his tuberculosis in 1913 when he was thirty-five years old and heir to a small fortune in banking, which he then made even bigger. A competitive skier before and even after his successful stay at Trudeau, he was able to manage his banking empire from a mansion he built on Park Avenue, close to the Sanatorium. He branched out into bobsledding and managed the U.S. Olympic team in 1924 at Chamonix, the first winter games.

"Ah, Janet, how nice to see you." Chandler politely kissed her cheek.

"Hello, Janet," Emily said. "I was just about to head to the bar. Will you join me?"

Before Janet could answer, Archibald said, "Hold on, I want to get Janet's opinion on this acquisition. I'll only detain her a minute." Emily smiled at them both and sauntered off. "Look at this 1945 limited edition etching of Don Quixote done by Salvador Dali. Cost me a pretty penny but it's worth it, don't you think?"

"I'm not an art appraiser, Archibald, but it is stunning. Quite different from most of your collection."

"Perceptive of you, Janet, but I'm not surprised. You have a good eye." He turned to face her, his hands at his side. "You won't believe this, but I learned today that a piece of art by a patient at the Sanatorium might be worth something if we can get hold of it."

"Really?"

"Hasn't your husband told you about it?"

"Brandon's not as interested in art as I am."

"He does seem interested in this one. Actually, it's more than one. It's a set of murals that decorated the walls of the Sanatorium's Lea Cottage before it was torn down. The Board authorized Brandon to retrieve them from Duke Medical School."

"Are they really good?"

"I don't know, but it's the artist that makes them famous."

Innocently, Janet asked, "Who is it?"

"It's a damned Communist, a doctor to boot. Norman Bethune's his name. One of the doctors on the Board told me he died a martyr in China and is a national hero there." At that moment, Caroline Chandler, almost as tall as her husband and also ramrod straight, though her face was more lined than his, interrupted them. She greeted Janet before turning to her husband. "Darling, you must bring up a few more bottles of Chardonnay from the cellar." She turned to Janet, "Will you excuse him, Janet?" Janet smiled her assent and turned to the bar where she caught up with Emily.

"I see what you mean, Emily."

"What are you talking about?"

"The way men fondle you."

Emily looked puzzled for a moment and then smiled. "Oh. Archibald. He means no harm."

"He told me something that might interest you." Emily looked at Janet inquiringly. "Seems the Bethune murals will be coming back to Saranac Lake soon. When Archibald Chandler wants some artwork, he usually gets it."

Stunned, Emily took a step toward Janet, spilling some of her drink on Janet's dress and quickly brushing it off with her free hand. "I'll die if Tom sees the mural."

"Aren't you being overly dramatic?"

Emily clutched Janet's arm. "You don't know Tom."

The following morning, Brandon met with Fred Todd before he returned to the city. "Yesterday's meeting was the most divisive one I've attended since joining the Board five years ago," Todd told him. "The trouble started when we discussed your proposal on dealing with the FBI. Although we unanimously agreed to have you obtain the murals, the debate revealed some deep divisions. When we went into executive session, one of the business trustees suggested that you were subverting the Trudeau Foundation and wouldn't be surprised if you were a Communist. I noticed two of his allies nod their heads at the suggestion." Brandon laughed at the accusation. "Yes, I know," Todd continued, "it's absurd, but the mood of the country being what it is, we may not be able to ignore it, if the allegation becomes public."

"Do you want me to resign, Fred?"

"No, I don't, but when you hear what I'm about to ask you

to do, you might find your job here very unpleasant. I need you, Brandon; don't abandon ship now." Brandon waited for Todd to continue. "First, once the Corporate Managers of America agrees on the deal, I want you to publicly announce that the Sanatorium will close. Second, you must insist that Arnold Springer prepares the Seventh Symposium for publication."

"And if he refuses?"

"Fire him or get him to resign. I know that what I'm asking, Brandon, will earn you some more enemies. I'm not sure the Board will continue to back you up, but I will personally."

"One more thing Fred. Do you think I should notify Agent Crane that we're trying to get the murals?"

Todd thought for a moment. "Has he been pressing you?" Warner shook his head. "No, let sleeping dogs lie. If he makes inquiries, you can tell him how the Foundation is proceeding."

Chapter 7

Removing her stockings while sitting on the edge of their bed the night of the Chandlers' reception, Emily asked Tom, "Do you think I've changed?"

He had just come from the bathroom, already in his pajamas. "Changed? From when? In what way?" He looked her up and down. "You're more serious than you used to be. I'd like it if you'd lighten up. I'm the one who has to worry, not only about my work but keeping you and the boys clothed and fed."

"I'll try," she said with a forced laugh. "What I meant was, uhh, my appearance, my, uhh, looks."

Standing in front of her, he lifted her off the bed by her arm, turned her around, undid her bra and pulled her panties down, then turned her back around—she offered no resistance—and removed his pajama bottoms. Admiring her for a moment, he grasped her shoulders and leaned forward so they both fell on to the bed. Instantly, he was inside her. Without waiting for any sign that she was aroused, he quickly satisfied himself. A few minutes later, after she returned from the bathroom, he said, "Yeah, you've changed. You don't put out the way you used to."

Maybe he was drunk, Emily thought. *Tom certainly didn't pick up that I wasn't in the mood.* She was looking for excuses. *Maybe he thought I <u>was</u> in the mood. Of course, he didn't understand the reason for my question.*

Emily did not sleep well that night. Nevertheless, she was

up the next morning to make breakfast for Tom and the boys. After Tom left for work, and the boys for school, and with her morning household chores completed, Emily removed the first and the last family photo albums from the large mahogany bookcase in the living room. She set the recent one next to her on the sofa and opened the older one on her lap. The first few pages contained old photos of varying sizes of her parents and also of Tom's. Tom had bought a Kodak Box Brownie soon after he came to Saranac Lake and there were a few pictures of Emily from the early fall of 1927, in her student nurse's uniform; some more from 1928 after they had started to date again, including her graduation from nursing school; and lots from 1929, when they became serious lovers, even a few in which she had posed in a bathing suit on the beach at Lake Colby. In all these photos, her dark hair was closely cropped. The bathing suit photos showed off her figure, sloping shoulders, shapely legs and thighs, full breasted—more than was fashionable at the time—but no revealing cleavage. The last photo in the album was an eight-by-ten glossy of their wedding, the bride and groom in full nuptial regalia. She had spent a good part of her savings on the gown and although it revealed her shoulders and full bust, billows of silk hid everything below her narrow waist. In the picture, she was standing to the left of Tom, gazing up at him (though he was just an inch taller), as the photographer had instructed, the left side of her face toward the camera, the mole below her left eye visible.

She laid the album down and picked up the recent one, still with empty pages, a bunch of new photos tucked in, waiting for her to paste them. Taken with an Argus C3, which Tom had bought after the war, they were sharper than the older pictures, and many were taken closer up. Most were of the boys at home and on vacation, Emily no longer the center of attention. When she was in a photo, her face was usually serious, worrying—seldom smiling. The striking difference was her hair, still black but falling to her shoulders, making her face rounder but certainly not jolly. In one photo, she and the boys were in bathing suits, again on the beach at Lake Colby. Compared to the shot from twenty years earlier, the costume had changed more than her body. She had worked hard to stay slim, watching her diet carefully and limiting her intake of hard and soft drinks. Pleased though she was, the similarity of the photos troubled her. She worried that the murals would come back to Saranac Lake, as Janet predicted they would. If Tom were to see them, the secret she had kept since before their marriage would be revealed. Tom's roughness as she had prepared for bed, not the first time, had added to her disquiet.

As she returned the albums to the bookcase, she examined the possibilities. She could wait until the murals arrived back at Saranac Lake. *More than likely, Tom will see them when his colleagues do and someone is bound to say, "That angel looks familiar." And Tom will recognize me, he'll be furious, and in that one look at the murals he'll know why I stopped dating him in 1927. God knows what else he'll think … or feel … Maybe less of a man? But what if, before the murals arrive, I tell him that I posed for Beth? Sure, he'll take it out on me, but at least he'll be prepared when other men see his wife half naked.*

She went up to their bedroom, took off her housecoat and nightgown, and stood naked in front of the full-length mirror on the closet door. Her skin was smooth, her breasts firm, nipples pink. She knelt on her left knee, interlaced her fingers and held them on her right thigh as if cradling a baby. Then she tilted her head downward as if looking at a creature in her arms and smiled beatifically, finally stealing a glance at her face in the mirror. Confident that she remembered the mural accurately, she knew it was an exact likeness, except that her hair was longer now and not angelic silver.

She glanced at the painting to the left of the closet, an oil color of a reclining nude, her head thrown back so her facial features were not clearly visible. Tom, an amateur artist, had demanded she pose in 1934—after they were married, but a few years before their first son Gerald was born. As Gerald entered puberty, he became interested in the painting. She explained to him that artists frequently painted nude females to improve their style. "It's not you, is it, Mom?" Gerald had asked. "Do I look like a model?" she scoffed, quickly changing the subject before he could answer one way or the other. In actuality, she preferred Beth's drawing.

She stood and opened the closet, deciding what to wear. While dressing, she concluded that Tom's anger could be assuaged without causing him embarrassment if she told him herself, being careful to choose the right circumstances. To lay the groundwork, she began to join him for his customary cocktail in their living room before dinner and often felt a little tipsy by the time she returned to the kitchen to finish cooking. Part of her plan was to be as loving as possible.

In a matter of days, she discovered that she looked forward to the cocktails. During weekdays over the next few weeks, she often took a drink before the boys came home from school.

The right circumstances came a few weeks later on a Saturday, the first day of spring. Usually, that did not mean much in the Adirondacks, the hardwoods still bare and not in bud, the lakes still frozen. This year, however, the trails were thawing, puddled with melted snow from a blizzard the previous Thursday. By Saturday, the sky was cloudless, the temperature an unseasonable seventy, and the air still. "A day like this is too good to spend in the lab," Tom announced at breakfast. "Let's go for a walk." The boys, old enough to show signs of independence, announced they had other plans, so after the meal Emily and Tom put on light jackets and walked up Park Avenue, through the Sanatorium toward Mt. Pisgah. Tom was in a good mood, confident that his laboratory would not go the way of the Sanatorium, and pleased, as he told Emily for the first time, that the Board of the Saranac Lake Free Library, to which he had been appointed at the beginning of the year, had asked him to serve as chair of its Art Committee. "The library is planning an expansion and I think it would be fitting to adorn the walls with work from local artists."

Emily thought there could not have been a more propitious moment.

"Janet Warner," she started, "told me last week that some murals Norman Bethune drew when he was a patient here are likely to come back to Saranac Lake from Duke Medical School."

"Bethune, the Communist who the FBI is after?" She nodded. He stopped, listening as a sparrow called to its mate. "Oh yes," he remembered, "Brandon thinks the murals might settle the question of whether Bethune was a Communist when he was here." They resumed walking. "I never saw the murals. Did you?" They had walked through the Sanatorium and were on a stretch of Trudeau Way without houses, the macadam strand bordered by still-leafless birch and maples, with newly plowed fields beyond them.

"Yes, as a matter of fact, I did." Something in the way Emily said this prompted a sideways glance from her husband. Her heart started to pound and she forced herself to keep walking at a regular pace, eyes straight ahead. Neither of them spoke until Emily blurted, "I modeled for one of the murals." Abruptly, Tom stopped. Perhaps oblivious to his halt, or perhaps to put space between them, Emily continued walking. When she heard him say in a louder voice than usual, "You modeled for Norman Bethune?" she turned, walked backward a pace, and then stopped.

"Yes. For the Angel of Death."

"Then at least you were fully robed."

"Not exactly." Tears were welling up in her eyes.

"What do you mean, 'not exactly'?"

"Beth, uhh, Bethune gave me a sheet to drape over one shoulder."

At first, she thought he might not have heard her. Then his face contorted, and as he slowly walked toward her she could see his nostrils flaring. Her tears came in a gush. Protectively, she held her arms out in front of her. He pushed them down and grabbed her by the shoulders, oblivious to their surroundings. "What did he do to you?" he glowered.

"Nothing," she sobbed. Then, realizing she was not telling the whole truth, "He kissed me." Roughly, Tom pushed her away so hard that she stumbled and would have fallen on the asphalt had she not got her legs to move forward, righting herself as he stormed past and kept going without turning back.

She stood on the side of the road, pulled a handkerchief from her pocket, blew her nose and dried her cheeks. Rather than follow, she turned back and arrived home an hour after they had left. *Thank God that's over*, she thought, hopeful that the storm had passed. She went to the liquor cabinet, poured a shot of Scotch, and gulped it down.

Tom came in while she was fixing lunch in the kitchen. He

hung up his jacket and went into his study. A few minutes later, when she was putting plates on the table, she heard him walk into the living room. "Emily," he ordered, "come in here."

She could have said no, but she was trained to follow his commands. He was sitting in his club chair. Momentarily, she stood before him awaiting his command, but when he did not speak and was staring off in space, she gained a bit of control and sat on the sofa opposite him.

"We will never talk about this episode again, and until I say otherwise you will sleep in the guest room. I do have one question for you." She knew what he would ask. "Are you recognizable in the mural?"

"I think so."

"Your hair was shorter then."

"That's true, but—"

"That's all I wanted to know." He got up and returned to his study.

———

The following Monday morning, Tom Steele stopped at Brandon Warner's office on his way to the Trudeau Laboratory. He reminded Brandon that he was on the Saranac Lake Free Library's Board and just the previous week had been asked to head up its Art Committee. "You know, Brandon, the library is planning a major expansion and I'm on the lookout for locally painted works of art to cover its walls above the bookshelves. It occurred to me that the murals drawn by Bethune would be a good catch. Emily tells me you're trying to retrieve them from Duke Medical School."

"Yes, Hal Hungerford said he would try to get his successor at Duke to send them. It must have slipped his mind. I'll have to remind him."

"Well, I know Hal's successor at Duke. I could tell him the library is eager to get the murals back to Saranac Lake. I think that would raise fewer eyebrows than your telling him we want them to show to the FBI."

Relieved to have one less chore, Brandon happily agreed to Tom's proposal. "Let me know when they arrive."

———

The sun and warmth of that first day of spring proved to be a brief fling. March went out like a lion with another blizzard. The relief Emily had hoped to feel after telling Tom was short-lived. He no longer showed interest in having cocktails with her and often came home just in time for dinner, though she continued the ritual by herself. For a few days, she tried to engage him at dinner but quickly realized that he was communicating exclusively with his sons.

Happily for the boys, the weather stayed cold after the late blizzard, prolonging the ski season and their after-school lessons. On Monday April 6, Janet stopped at the Steeles' house to pick up Emily and drive together to the Mt. Pisgah Ski Center. She was surprised that Emily was not outside waiting for her. She parked the car and rang the bell. After a few rings, Emily came to the door, disheveled, her face puffy and her hair uncombed. "Oh, Janet," she said, "I must have fallen asleep. I have a terrible headache. Would you mind picking up Gerald and Billy from school and dropping them off here when they're done?"

"Not at all, I'll be happy to." She turned to go, then turned back as Emily started to close the door. "Emily, is everything all right?"

"Why shouldn't it be?" Emily smiled weakly.

"Have you told Tom?"

"Told him?" she asked, with feigned innocence.

"About the murals."

Emily sighed. "It made matters worse." Janet grasped Emily's arm, but she pulled away. "You'd better go or you'll be late for the boys." Janet smelled alcohol on her breath.

Chapter 8

By the time Larry Crane returned to Saranac Lake in his black Buick, spring had really arrived. The ice had melted, the trees were in bud, and mosquitoes and black flies had begun their assault on humans who couldn't wait to peel off the layers of clothing that had protected them from the cold. In contrast to his first trip at the tail end of a blizzard, this time he arrived in sunny, warm weather on Tuesday morning, May 19.

"Agent Crane from the FBI is here to see you," Greta announced. Again, he had arrived without an appointment, his power such that he was confident Warner would see him.

"I wonder what progress you've made in learning about Dr. Bethune's contacts here?" Crane began, after they were comfortably seated in Warner's office.

"I've identified three of Bethune's cottage mates," Warner replied without naming names. "They all knew what became of Bethune, but none of them thought he was a Communist when he was a patient here."

"Have you questioned anyone else?"

"Not yet, but his cottage mates told me that he drew a series of murals when he was here. Tom Steele, director of the Trudeau Laboratory, is trying to get them returned to us from Duke Medical School. That was quite a while ago. Let me see if he's received them." He dialed Greta on the intercom.

While they waited, Crane asked, "Does Steele have a special interest in the murals?"

"He's on the Board of the Saranac Lake Free Library and head of its Art Committee. The library will soon be expanding and would like to show the murals."

Greta had Steele on the phone in thirty seconds. "Tom, Agent Crane of the FBI is here and wants to know if you've received the Bethune murals from Duke." After an unusually long pause, Warner replied, "I see. Well, let me know as soon as the library gets them."

Crane raised his hand, wanting Brandon to say something else to Warner before he hung up. "Ask Dr. Steele if he has a few minutes to talk with me." Warner relayed the request and got an affirmative reply. After Warner hung up, Crane asked, "How long has Dr. Steele been at Trudeau?"

Warner ignored Crane's calling Steele "doctor." Dialing Greta on the intercom again, he asked, "Will you find out how long Tom Steele has been at Trudeau? Ring me back when you have the information."

"How did the murals get to Duke anyway?" Crane asked.

"Dr. Harold Hungerford, one of Bethune's cottage mates at the Sanatorium, took them off the walls of the cottage before it was torn down and took them with him when he joined the faculty there."

"How do you know this?"

"Dr. Hungerford told me himself. He's now the deputy director of the National Microbiological Institute at NIH."

Greta buzzed back to say that Steele was first employed at Trudeau in 1927.

Crane surprised Brandon. "I know Dr. Hungerford's current position." He leaned over to pull a document from his briefcase and handed it to Warner. "Take a look at this."

It took Brandon a few seconds to realize it was Hungerford's unsigned loyalty oath; he had forgotten that in their phone conversation in January Hungerford had told him he had refused to sign. He looked inquiringly at Crane. "So?"

"You just told me, Dr. Warner, that none of Bethune's three cottage mates said he was a Communist. Dr. Hungerford was one of them, was he not?" Brandon nodded. "Do you expect me to believe that a person who refuses to say whether he was a Communist can be trusted to tell you honestly that a person of interest was not a Communist?" Before Warner could answer, Crane asked him, "Are you now, or have you ever been, a member of the Communist Party of the United States?"

Brandon looked at Crane for several seconds. "What authority do you have to ask that question?"

"I don't have the authority since you are not an employee of the federal government, as Dr. Hungerford is. I am, nevertheless, trying to make life easier for you. You have written that you could not find Communists at Trudeau in 1927. Dr. Hungerford was here in 1927, and you have admitted that you have spoken to him about murals drawn by an avowed Communist. Now you're procrastinating to avoid telling me whether you are or were a Communist. If you persist, I cannot take your opinion about Norman Bethune's political affiliations in 1927 in good faith, or your opinions about Dr. Hungerford's affiliations, then or now."

"I don't know a damn thing about Harold Hungerford's political affiliations," Warner answered, his voice rising slightly. "All I know, as I wrote you, is that neither he nor the others I spoke to thought Bethune was a Communist in 1927. They are among the most prominent physicians in American medicine." Warner realized he was starting to perspire.

"All right, Dr. Warner, I'll withdraw the question. But don't be surprised if you receive a subpoena to appear before the House Un-American Activities Committee. The Committee could ask you the same question and if you refuse to answer you could be cited for contempt. You know what could happen if you are convicted?"

Brandon blanched. "Prison," he said quietly. Fleetingly, he had a frightening vision of standing behind bars in a striped prison suit. Never had he thought he might be sentenced to prison like a common criminal.

Crane put the paper back in his briefcase and stood. "Can you steer me to Dr. Steele's laboratory?"

Brandon did so and then told Crane, "By the way, Tom Steele doesn't have a doctorate. He's a very smart guy who has gotten international recognition without one."

"Thanks for telling me. After our little exchange just now, I'm very eager to see those murals."

After Crane left, Warner asked himself, *Now why did I tell Crane that Steele wasn't a doctor? Was it because it rankled to hear Steele referred to as "doctor," or was it to sing his praises?* After having this banal thought, Warner realized he had more important problems than Tom Steele's credentials.

———

Tom had lied to Brandon Warner when he told him the murals hadn't come. Toward the end of April, a clerk at the Saranac Lake Free Library had informed him that a large parcel had arrived from Duke University. He had driven down to the village to pick it up that same day but had stashed the package—a tube, about three feet long and four inches in diameter—in the back of the coat closet in his office.

When Brandon had given him the go-ahead to request the murals, Tom had no plan beyond wanting to look at them and see for himself whether the Angel of Death bore a close resemblance to Emily. If there was no resemblance, he'd simply pass the murals on to Warner. *If there was a resemblance*—his thought stopped there. It was this problem that kept him from opening the parcel.

His anger at Emily had not abated. Although he realized she had not been his property when she'd posed for Bethune, he was tormented that the woman he married was "spoiled goods"; she had been intimate with another man.

Crane's visit caught Steele by surprise. As he waited for his arrival, the thought crossed his mind that there was no harm in showing the murals to Agent Crane, who did not know Emily. Consequently, he would not recognize her as the Angel of Death. But unless Crane took the murals, which he had no right to do, Steele's colleagues would see them sooner or later and Emily's secret would be out. Still uncertain what he would do in that case, Steele walked from the microscopy room, where he had been working, back to his office to greet Agent Crane.

"I'm sorry to disturb your routine, Dr. Steele, but I've just come from a meeting with Dr. Warner, who told me that you're the one who is retrieving the murals drawn by Norman Bethune from Duke."

"Yes, I thought I could help him out that way." As he spoke, he realized that framed photos, one of his two sons and another of Emily, were sitting at the edge of the desk, facing him but partly visible to anyone sitting opposite. He nudged the frame of Emily's photo out of Agent Crane's line of sight.

"You have an interest in art?"

Steele smiled for the first time. "I've been appointed the head of the Art Committee of the Saranac Library and I am an amateur painter." He pointed at a small watercolor on the wall alongside his desk. "That's one of my recent ones." Crane got up to look at it.

"A local landscape? Or should I say waterscape?"

"It's the Saranac River at its source from Upper Saranac Lake. I painted it from the side of a wooden bridge. under which the river flows and immediately spreads out through a marsh of reeds, losing speed and meandering to Middle Saranac Lake."

As Crane went back to his seat, Steele saw him glance at the photographs on his desk.

Crane changed the subject. "Warner tells me you've been at Trudeau for over twenty-five years."

"That's true. Came here to clean petri dishes in Dr. Petroff's lab, ended up as a co-scientist, and now I'm director."

To corroborate Dr. Warner's last bit of information, Crane asked, "Did you get an advanced degree along the way?"

Steele, who had been asked this question many times, had a prepared answer. "Dr. Petroff didn't want me to leave. I had mastered culture techniques and made some important observations correlating strains of tubercle bacilli with virulence in guinea pigs. Initially, Petroff advised me to get a Ph.D., but after a while he said I was too valuable to leave and get one."

"In your early years at Trudeau, did you come in contact with Dr. Norman Bethune?"

"He was a patient when I worked in the laboratory. Our paths did not cross."

Crane glanced pointedly at the photographs on the desk. "Are you married, Dr. Steele?"

"Yes, with two children." He made no effort to show the photos to his visitor.

Crane picked up the photo of the Steeles' two boys. "Handsome lads," he commented. He put the frame down and picked up the other one. "And this beautiful woman is your wife?" Steele nodded, but did not smile. In the photo, Emily was standing, wearing a tight-fitting knit dress that came to her knees. She had a faint Mona Lisa smile and deep-set black eyes that matched the dark hair framing her pale face. Still admiring the picture, Crane asked, "Did you meet her here?"

Matter-of-factly, Tom replied, "She was a student nurse here."

"Did she have contact with Norman Bethune?"

Before he realized what he was saying, he blurted, "You'd have to ask her."

"You do know why the FBI is so interested in Bethune?"

"Yes, Brandon Warner said you were looking for people who knew Bethune when he was a patient here, on suspicion they might be Communists. I urged Brandon to conduct his own investigation, turning over names of people who knew Bethune."

"Was it possible that one of them might have been a Communist?"

"I suppose it's possible." He paused for a moment. "They're all prominent physicians now."

"That doesn't preclude them from being Communists—then or now."

"No, I suppose it doesn't." Steele looked at his watch. "I hope you won't be too much longer. I have a lab meeting in five minutes."

"Do you know Dr. Harold Hungerford, one of Bethune's cottage mates?"

"Yes. We have a mutual interest in T.B. He's at NIH now."

"Do you have any reason to believe he is a Communist?"

"None whatsoever."

"What about Brandon Warner? Is he a Communist?"

Steele looked at Crane intently. He took a few moments to answer. "We seldom talk politics around here, Mr. Crane. And anyone on the left is not going to waste his time talking to me. I wear my views on my front lawn. Had an 'I Like Ike' sign out last year and have a reputation as a rock-ribbed Republican."

Crane got up. "Thank you so much for your time, Dr. Steele. I may want to talk to you again."

"I'm not going any place."

———◆———

Crane scratched his head as he left Steele's office. *Was Steele trying to hide his wife's photograph? Out of what? Jealousy? Did he think I might make a move on her? That didn't seem likely.*

He walked into the visitors' lobby of the Ludington Infirmary and spotted a telephone booth. Outside the booth, the North Country telephone directory, a slim volume compared to Manhattan's, dangled from a metal chain. He found the Steeles' address on Park Avenue, the same street that ran through the Sanatorium grounds, eventually changing into Trudeau Way. Postponing lunch, he drove the short distance to the Steeles' home, parking a few houses away. Leaving his briefcase in the car, Crane walked back toward their house. The neighborhood was neat and stately, with tall trees on lawns of green grass not yet high enough for mowing.

Like many of the others, the Steeles' walkway was fitted with irregular pieces of grey slate thinly separated by a lighter grout. Crane pushed the doorbell, heard the chime deep within the house, and waited. He rang again. Through the window panels next to the door, he saw a woman in a bathrobe approach and peer out. Her black hair, with a few streaks of gray, was uncombed, her eyes puffy. She did not open the door. Instead of shouting, he took his wallet out and flashed his badge next to the window. The door opened.

The woman had a resemblance to the photograph on Steele's desk. "Mrs. Steele?" She nodded, holding the collar of her bathrobe to her throat. "Agent Larry Crane, FBI. May I come in?"

"My husband's not home," she said in a husky voice that surprised him.

"I've just talked to your husband in his laboratory. I wanted to have a few words with you."

"Did he send you?" she asked suspiciously.

"No, not exactly." She stepped inside, letting him enter, and showed him into the living room. A solitary, half-empty glass and an open bottle of sherry stood on the coffee table in front of a damask sofa. She showed Crane to the club chair that was her husband's favorite.

"Would you care for a glass of sherry, or perhaps something else?" she asked.

"No, I don't drink when I'm on the job," he said pointedly. She sat on the sofa, drank from her glass, and then refilled it. "As your husband may have told you, the FBI is trying to learn more about people at the Sanatorium in 1927 who may have known Dr. Norman Bethune when he was a patient here." She took another sip of sherry, her hand trembling slightly, then set the glass on the table and put her hands on her lap, one holding the other. "Your husband said he had no contact with Bethune but that you might."

"Me?"

"You were a student nurse here at the time?"

"Yes, that's true," she said quickly.

"Was Bethune ever a patient of yours?"

Silent for a moment, she started to reach for the wine glass but her hands were shaking so badly she quickly put them back in her lap. "Yes. When Dr. Wren performed artificial pneumothorax on Dr. Bethune, I was the nurse in the room."

"Was that the only time?"

She hesitated. "Well, after the procedure I assisted Dr. Bethune back to Lea Cottage, where he was living."

"In the operating room, or on that walk back to his cottage, did you and Dr. Bethune talk?"

Quickly, she reached for the wine glass and held it firmly in both hands before draining it. "I guess so. I don't recall exactly."

"Nothing political?"

"No," she replied emphatically.

"Did he mention the murals he was drawing on the walls of his cottage?"

Emily closed her eyes for a moment before she answered. Suddenly, she felt very hot; the room spun momentarily. Confused, she heard herself lie. "He may have, I don't remember."

"Have you ever seen the murals, Mrs. Steele?"

"Yes. I went to look at them a few years later, before Lea Cottage was going to be destroyed."

"For what reason?"

"Well, they were the topic of conversation and I was curious." She poured herself another glass of sherry. "Are you sure I can't get you something?" she asked Crane.

"No, thank you. In fact, I just have one more question."

He watched as she took a sip from the filled glass. "What were the murals about?"

"You haven't seen them?"

"No, your husband is expecting them to arrive any day—"

"What?" she asked, sitting forward on the sofa, noticeably alarmed.

"Are you all right, Mrs. Steele?" She nodded, smiling weakly, and Crane continued. "Yes, he's requested them from Duke University. I guess he didn't tell you."

Half aside, she said, "No, he doesn't tell me anything these days." She looked blankly at Crane, trying to remember his question. "Oh yes. The murals portrayed the story of Beth— uh, of Bethune's life from womb to grave. It was one long battle against infectious diseases."

"I see." Crane smiled sympathetically as he stood. Unsteadily, Emily stood and walked alongside him back to the front door. Just before they reached it, she stumbled and would have fallen if Crane had not put his arm around her. She looked up at him, her eyes filled with horror—*or maybe fear*, as Crane thought later. "Thank you very much, Mrs. Steele. You've been very helpful." Crane had a late lunch in Lake Placid and started the drive back to his office in Manhattan.

After Crane left, Emily returned to the sofa and poured herself another glass of sherry. Trying to sweep the cobwebs from her mind, she reenacted his questioning. *Crane's questions about contacts were to do with Bethune as a patient. That was not the relationship when I posed semi-nude for the mural. Which means I did not lie to the FBI.*

———◆———

Agent Crane's visit convinced Tom Steele to examine the murals. He was still uncertain what to do if the Angel of Death looked like Emily, but if she didn't, he would give them to Warner and notify Agent Crane. He hoped no one would ask the clerk at the Saranac Lake Free Library when they had arrived.

Tom attended his lab meeting after Crane left then went back to his office, locked the door, and retrieved the tube from his closet. Clearing his five-foot-long desk, he used his pocket knife to cut through the tape that sealed the metal lid on one end, prying it off with the back edge of the blade. A cloud of colored dust burst from the tube, irritating his nose and throat. When the dust settled, he peered into the tube. It contained several sheets of tightly rolled brown laundry paper, one inside the other. Pinching the sheath between his thumb and index finger, he rotated the tube as he gingerly pulled the papers from it. He laid the still-curled murals on his desk, noting that each one was folded in half. Holding them delicately by their edges, he unfolded them one by one, spreading them out on his desk, the innermost one first and the outermost last. The first one was badly mutilated; two jagged pieces were missing from the drawing of a scroll whose writing, except for the first word, "Norman," was unintelligible. Without the missing pieces, it was impossible to know who was holding the scroll.

The following panels were in better shape. Some of them were not perfect rectangles, with sections cut out to accommodate doors and windows that interrupted the walls on which the murals had originally hung. All the panels had creases from being folded, and he wondered whether his delay in opening the tube might have contributed to the permanency of these folds. The colors on the panels were muted, mostly light brown and white. The pictures were smeared in places. On one, the colors of a large rainbow were limited to brown, pale blue, and white. *Perhaps the other colors have faded*, he thought. Some of the panels had writing on the bottom, often too blurred to make out the inscription. When he laid the last one on top of the others, he noticed his fingertips were covered with chalk.

The panel on top of the pile was the one he was looking for. Dominated by her diaphanous wings, the angel was kneeling on one knee, cradling a dead mortal on her thigh, his limbs long compared to his body, a thin moustache above his upper lip— *probably Bethune himself*, Steele thought. The angel had close-cropped silvery hair, matching her wings. Her face was drawn in profile from her left, the outline of the nose drawn straight down from the forehead without a bridge, just like Emily's. She had a thick eyebrow, prominent lashes, just like Emily's, and, just below the left eye's outer edge, a tiny blemish. *Emily's birthmark*! The angel's gown was draped over her sloping right shoulder, falling in folds across her chest and exposing her left breast, exactly as Emily had described. In Steele's artistic opinion, Bethune had made Emily's neck too thick and had exaggerated the slope of her shoulders so markedly that they disappeared into the angel's upper arms.

Leaving the panels on the table, he went to the microscopy room, returning with a fine camel's hair brush. Delicately, he spread the chalk-like material on the angel's cheek, obliterating the birthmark, then thinning the eyebrow and lashes, and finally smearing the nose's bridge. He rolled up the entire set as tightly as possible and was putting them back in the long tube when the phone rang. With half of the roll still protruding, he put the tube on his desk and bent to lift the receiver from the phone, which he had placed on the floor when he cleared his desk. "Hello?"

"Dad, it's Gerald. Can you come home?"

"Is something wrong?"

"I had to let Billy and me into the house with my key after school. Usually Mom leaves the door unlocked when she's home but not today. The car is in the garage so she hasn't gone out. The guest room door is locked. I knocked on it, but she didn't answer."

"You don't think she's gone for a walk?"

"No, she'd be making dinner at this time. Do you think I should call the police?"

"No, I'm just finishing up here. I'll be home in a few minutes." After replacing the receiver on its cradle, he took the murals out of the tube and rolled them up tighter in order to fit the entire set into the tube. He found the metal cap on the floor, put it on firmly, taped the tube shut, and placed it back in the closet before leaving, locking the main door to the laboratory behind him.

As he approached home on foot, he saw a fire engine, police car, and ambulance, their lights flashing, in front of his house. A knot of people stood on the sidewalk opposite. Janet Warner ran up to him. "Gerald called me a few minutes ago. I hope I didn't overreact, Tom, but I was worried about Emily and called the police."

Tom was infuriated but said nothing. They walked into the house together.

A policeman greeted them. The village was small enough that its police force knew most people by name, especially prominent ones, such as the leaders of Trudeau. "Good evening, Dr. Steele, Mrs. Warner. The firemen had to break down a door to get to your wife." Not waiting to hear more, Steele pushed past the policeman and ran up the stairs. Automatically, he turned left to go to the master bedroom, which was empty. Wheeling around, he saw firemen in their slickers and high rubber boots at the far end of the hall and ran toward them. His boys were not in sight. In the guest room, he pushed aside the men gathered around the bed Emily lay on, mouth agape, arms flung aside, face almost as pale as the sheet. Her bathrobe was open and her nightgown was bunched around her neck.

One of the younger Trudeau doctors, who also worked on the volunteer Fire Department's emergency crew, got up from the edge of the bed, stethoscope dangling from his neck. "Good evening, Dr. Steele. I'm afraid we were too late. I injected adrenalin into her heart, thought I heard a beat but then lost it." Steele did not seem to comprehend. The doctor added, "She's passed away, sir."

"Impossible!" he replied. He moved toward the bed and tried to pull her nightgown down but could not get it below her breasts. The young doctor lifted her body so Steele was able to slide the gown over her breasts and abdomen. The firemen parted as he moved back from the bed, seeming satisfied that he had restored a semblance of decency to his wife, if not life. "Where is Gerald?"

"He and his brother are in the kitchen, sir," one of the firemen replied.

Tom found them sitting at the kitchen table with Janet Warner. They looked up at him expectantly, not sure what had happened upstairs. He stared down at Gerald. "Why did you call Mrs. Warner, Gerald? I told you I'd be right home."

He looked dully at this father. "I thought Mom had been acting strange lately, and in the living room I found a shot glass and an empty bottle of Scotch. Mom never used to drink, Dad."

At first, Janet thought Tom's question indicated that Emily was alive. Then Billy asked, "Can I go upstairs to talk to Mommy?"

Still staring at Gerald, Tom answered loudly, "No, your mother's dead."

Janet was horrified. Tom seemed to be blaming Emily's death on Gerald. *If Gerald hadn't called me, Tom seems to be thinking, Emily would still be alive.*

As soon as he uttered, "your mother's dead," the realization of what had happened hit Tom. He collapsed into the empty chair at the table, dropping his head between his folded arms, and started to weep. Nobody spoke. Sitting next to him, Janet put her hand on his sleeve. Lifting his head, he stared at her blankly, turned to Billy, and said softly, "No, son, you can't talk to mommy. She's passed away."

The boys had never seen their father cry before. That more than his words announced the finality of what had happened. They started to cry. Janet took Billy's hand in her left and Tom's in her right. Opposite her, Gerald held Billy's and his father's hands. They sat in a circle for a few minutes, their sobs finally giving way to silence.

Steele stood up, breaking the circle. He gave a hand to each boy. "Let's go up and say goodbye to your mother."

———◆———

The circumstances of Emily's death required an autopsy followed by an inquest in a windowless conference room in the Saranac Lake Town Hall, which in the warm spring weather became hot and stuffy under bright incandescent ceiling bulbs. The medical examiner for the county, the chief fireman at the scene, Janet Warner, and Tom Steele were called to testify before the coroner of Franklin County. Because he was a minor, Gerald Steele was not asked to appear. The medical examiner fixed the time of Emily's death between four and five o'clock on May 19, 1953. The level of alcohol in the deceased's blood, he said, classified her as intoxicated; the levels of barbiturate were sufficient to cause her death.

Janet Warner testified that she received a phone call from Gerald Steele shortly after five o'clock that day in which he expressed concern about his mother. Lately, Janet reported, her good friend Emily had seemed depressed and had occasionally lapsed in meeting her responsibilities. When Gerald phoned her, she immediately worried Emily had attempted suicide and dialed the phone operator to summon emergency help to the Steeles' home.

Based on Mrs. Warner's concern, the chief fireman at the scene felt justified in breaking down the only locked door upstairs—the door to the guest bedroom—after he found an empty bottle of Seconal on the bed in the master bedroom. He found Mrs. Steele lying supine and unresponsive on the bed in the guest room and summoned one of his volunteers, a physician, to resuscitate her. The label on the bottle indicated that the prescription was for Thomas Steele, with instructions to "take one before bedtime for insomnia."

Tom Steele said he occasionally took Seconal for insomnia but that Emily, his wife, never had trouble sleeping. "Had she been depressed lately?" the coroner asked. Steele said he hadn't really noticed any changes in his wife's behavior. "Do you mean she was chronically depressed?"

"No," Tom replied to the coroner, "I wouldn't say she was chronically depressed."

"Did something happen recently that might have worried

her—for instance, a visitor with disturbing or threatening news?"

"Not that I know of," Tom replied.

The coroner asked Tom why Emily had apparently laid down in the guest room. Tom said he didn't know.

Without hesitation, the coroner ruled the death a suicide. The inquest had taken less than half an hour.

On Saturday, May 23, Emily Jenkins Steele was laid to rest in Pine Ridge Cemetery in the heart of Saranac Lake village.

Chapter 9

Brandon and Janet typically confided in each other, but either through forgetfulness or by intention, not everything was shared. It was not from Brandon that Janet had learned about the Bethune murals, but from Emily Steele and then Archibald Chandler. Brandon hadn't meant to omit telling her; it had just slipped his mind as other matters preoccupied him. Janet, on the other hand, never told Brandon about Emily's fears, not because she had forgotten but because she did not feel right betraying her friend's trust, even to her husband. Walking back to her home after Emily's death, she remembered Emily saying at the reception for the Trudeau Board, "I'll die if Tom sees the mural."

Brandon and Janet talked in their living room until late on the night of Emily's death. Janet, her legs curled under her on the sofa, now felt she could tell her husband that Emily had posed for the mural, and how frightened she had been of Tom's reaction if the murals showed that she resembled the Angel of Death. "Apparently, Tom could be outrageously jealous," Janet told Brandon. "He interpreted her sociability as flirting. He absolutely refused to have her return to nursing after their boys were in school."

"He had reason to be suspicious." Janet shot him a withering look. "What I meant was, Emily still is—or was—a beautiful woman." Brandon paused, scratching his head. "You know, Janet, it's strange that she took her life on the same day that the FBI agent returned for his second visit."

Startled, Janet said, "You didn't tell me he was here today."

"When did I have a chance? Emily's death took precedence." He filled his pipe, struck a wooden match to light it, and took a few puffs. "Agent Crane's visit may have more dire consequences for us than Emily's death." He took a few more puffs and Janet waited for him to continue. "He wanted to know if I had ever been a member of the Communist Party."

"You? Just like that?"

"No, not just like that. From his bag of tricks, Crane pulled out a loyalty oath with Harold Hungerford's name typed in— you know, 'I, Harold Hungerford, do solemnly swear—'"

"Who's Harold Hungerford?"

"He's a prominent physician who now works at NIH. He was one of Bethune's cottage mates here who told me Bethune wasn't a Communist back then. When I spoke to Hungerford about Bethune in January, he told me that the very same agent, Crane, had been assigned to find out why he had refused to sign the oath required of federal employees. This morning, Crane showed me Hungerford's unsigned oath. He asked how I could trust a man, even a prominent physician, who had refused to sign the oath."

"This is terrible, Brandon." Janet rose from the sofa.

"Crane laid all his cards on the table this morning. He withdrew the question about my being a Communist, he said—"

"He had no authority to ask it. You're not an employee of the federal government."

"Crane said, 'Don't be surprised, Dr. Warner, if you receive a subpoena to appear before the House Un-American Activities Committee.' He reminded me I could be cited for contempt if I refused to answer and could go to jail."

"And lose your job and have a hard time finding another one." She came over to Brandon, uncharacteristically sat on his lap, threw her arms around his neck, and kissed him. She liked the taste and aroma of his "Half and Half" tobacco. "I'll have only one loyalty while you're behind bars." He looked at her, puzzled. "To you, of course." She closed her eyes imagining the scenario. "I can see the headlines: 'House Committee opens investigation of Trudeau Sanatorium.' And the lead sentence: 'After putting away ten Hollywood screenwriters and directors, the House Un-American Activities Committee turned its attention to health care, taking special aim at the Trudeau Sanatorium, a hotbed of Communists in the 1920s.'"

"Aren't you being delusional?"

"I don't think so. If they can jail writers like Dalton Trumbo and so scare the Hollywood moguls that they won't dare hire anyone tainted by the Committee, they can do anything. McCarthy's ranting that even the Army's being infiltrated by reds. That makes it all the more likely that any agency—inside government or out—can be targeted. You don't have to be a federal employee to be hounded by HUAC."

Gently, he lifted her off his lap and she returned to the sofa. "This job, Janet, is more than I bargained for. I knew we'd have to close the Sanatorium. Once the deal with Corporate Managers of America is settled, Fred Todd wants me to announce it. And he as much as told me that if Arnold Springer doesn't prepare the Seventh Symposium papers for publication, I have to fire him. And in the executive session of the last Board meeting, he told me that at least one Board member suspected I was a Communist."

"This is scary," she said somberly.

"Do you think I should follow up with the offer from the

United Mine Workers to run their hospital system? We'd have to move to West Virginia."

"There are worse places." She thought for a moment. "If you do, don't make it public until you've got the job. Working for a labor union these days is almost as damning as joining the Communist Party, even if it's as anti-communist as the UMW." She watched as Brandon relit his pipe. "Did Crane come up here primarily to threaten you?"

"He came to follow up on the Bethune case. Despite his accusations and threats, he seemed willing to wait to see the murals Bethune drew. I arranged for him to talk to Tom Steele."

"Why did you do that?"

"A few days after the Board voted to get the murals back, Tom asked if he could retrieve them for me. He had just taken the chair of the Saranac Library's Art Committee and he thought that if the murals had any artistic merit the library might like to display them." Brandon sucked at his pipe meditatively until he clapped his hand to his forehead. "Good god! Now I know why Tom wanted to send for the murals."

"Not to display?" Janet paused. "Oh no. You don't think—"

"Emily must have told him about her modeling for Bethune. He wanted to see if the Angel of Death resembled her." Brandon was so agitated he got up out of his chair and paced around the living room. "It's been two months since Tom offered to get them. Tomorrow morning, I'll call the library to ask whether the murals have arrived. If Tom did request them, they should have arrived by now, and he should have let me know."

"What if they have? You can't bother Tom at a time like this."

"Well let's see if and when the library got them." He glanced at his watch, calculating the hours before it opened.

"It's late, Janet, time we went to bed."

Before Brandon could call the library the next morning, Tom Steele called to say that he had picked up the murals from the library the previous afternoon. "I haven't yet had a chance to look at them," he lied to Warner, "and it will be several more days before I can get back to the lab. I've been thinking it would be good to take the boys camping after the funeral. School's winding down so they won't be missing much."

"Sounds like an excellent idea, Tom." He wasn't sure Tom was asking his permission, which technically he should have, but he added, "Take all the time you want. You've had a terrible tragedy and we're all stunned by it." It was his way of offering his condolences. Tom told him where he could find the murals.

Brandon thought it too coincidental that the murals would have arrived the same day as Crane's visit. He called the library and asked the clerk (who already knew about Mrs. Steele's death and commiserated about it with Brandon) whether the library had received any packages for Dr. Steele recently. "I would be the one to know," she told Warner. "No, not since April, when he received a large packing tube."

"When did he pick it up?"

"Oh, right after I called him."

"That's very helpful," he replied. Hanging up, he called to his wife, "Come on, Janet, we're going to see Bethune's murals."

Brandon was in such a hurry he decided they should drive rather than walk. When they arrived, the usual lab hubbub was muted, the technicians and researchers going about their business sadly and silently. He realized that his arrival was unexpected and that the personnel were waiting for him to say something.

"I'm sure you all know the terrible tragedy that occurred yesterday," he began. "We won't know for sure until we have the medical examiner's report, but it does appear that Mrs. Steele took her own life—for reasons unknown. Tom and their boys are, of course, in mourning. I spoke to Tom a few minutes ago and he is planning to take his boys camping after the funeral so he won't be in to guide your work, probably for the next ten days. Until Tom returns, I'd like Dr. O'Keefe"—he nodded at him—"to assume direction of the laboratory." He paused to look around; a few of the technicians were crying. "I know Emily Steele's death comes as a shock to you, as it does to Janet and me, and that your hearts are with Tom and his sons, as ours are. I will keep you posted on plans for the funeral." He finished and turned, with Janet at his side, to go into Tom's office. He took a step, stopped, and turned back to face the small group. "In our phone call this morning, Tom told me that he had received a package that he had offered to get for me, and he invited me to retrieve it from his office. That's another reason why we're here now." Warner debated whether to say what was in the package and decided not to. He and Janet went into Steele's office and retrieved the tube from the closet. They decided to bring it to the administration building, where they could spread the murals out on the long table in the board room. "I'm glad we have the station wagon. I'd feel awkward carrying it through the street."

"Maybe we should go to the Chandlers' house first," Janet suggested. "Archibald's very eager to see the murals, maybe acquire them. I bumped into him in the village a few days ago and he asked if they had arrived."

Brandon was annoyed. "We're not interested in selling the murals, Janet. The main reason I want to see them is to examine their political content. Can they provide a clue as to whether Bethune was a Communist in 1927?"

"Another reason," Janet added, "is to see whether Emily Steele is recognizable. Archibald's been here longer than we have, and has probably known Emily since she married Tom. Also, he's not prejudiced. We already know that Emily modeled for Bethune; he doesn't."

"You've got a point," Brandon conceded. They drove past the administration building and down Park Avenue to the Chandlers' mansion. The Chandlers had already heard of the tragedy and the two couples somberly talked about it in their spacious living room for a few minutes. Turning to Archibald, Brandon said, "Janet tells me you're interested in Bethune's murals."

"They may be important for historical reasons. Like it or not, this Bethune is a heroic martyr for a good portion of the world's population. If the murals have any artistic merit, they may be quite valuable."

"Tom Steele called me this morning to say that the murals had arrived but he hadn't had a chance to look at them."

"That's exciting. Where are they?"

"In the back of our station wagon. We would like to invite you to join us for our first look at them in the Trudeau board room."

Chandler was out of his chair before Brandon had finished. He turned to Caroline. "This shouldn't take long, dear. I'm sure I'll be back for lunch." He was leading the Warners out the door when he stopped. "Oh, forgot my magnifying glass. I always like to examine a prospective purchase under the glass." He retrieved it from his study and a few minutes later they were in the board room.

Brandon was able to unwrap the tape from one end and the lid lifted off easily. Using the same maneuver Tom Steele had used less than twenty-four hours earlier, he gently lifted the roll out and spread the murals on the table. The last panel, with its tombstones and the Angel of Death holding Bethune's prostrate body, was on top. Janet and Brandon exchanged perplexed glances as Chandler bent over the mural. "Not in great shape, is it?" he asked rhetorically. "How long since they were drawn, twenty-five years or so?" Then he focused his attention on the artistic merits. "Interesting perspective: The angel is so much bigger than the dead man. But Bethune knew how to draw the human figure. It's a pity the angel's face has deteriorated, worse than the rest of the picture."

"Does she remind you of anyone?" Janet asked.

"I don't think so. Maybe if it wasn't smudged. Should it?" Janet ignored Chandler's question. She looked at Brandon for a cue.

"Doesn't remind me of anyone," he told her flatly. "Let's look at the others." They leafed through them, putting each on top of the preceding one so the Angel of Death was on the bottom and the top one was a picture of a dark-faced angel holding a baby, probably Bethune. A vast section of the mural was missing. Several of the panels had writing at the bottom, resembling lines of verse, but only fragments were legible.

"This is strange," observed Archibald, looking at the first mural. "Even though this one is badly damaged, look how sharp the birth angel's features are." He lifted the succeeding murals, glancing at the faces, pointing out to Janet and Brandon how characteristically sharp and neatly outlined Bethune had drawn them, until they came to the Angel of Death. He pulled out his magnifying glass and held it over the Angel of

Death's face. "Hmm. If you look carefully you can see fine brush marks disrupting the eyebrow and part of her cheek." He laid the mural down and repeated the maneuver with several faces on the other panels. "There's nothing like that on the other faces." He handed his glass to Brandon, who, after repeating the examination, handed the glass to his wife. "Someone's tampered with the Angel of Death," Archibald concluded. He looked at Janet and Brandon suspiciously. "What's going on here? Who else has seen the murals?"

"Since they left Duke, no one," Brandon said. "They were sent to Tom Steele, but he hadn't had a chance to look at them." He almost added, "until yesterday," but stopped short, not wanting to incriminate the recent widower. "He was eager to have them to hang on the Saranac Lake Free Library's walls."

"I wouldn't say they're in good enough shape to merit that. If they could be restored and preserved, they might be worth a pretty penny," Chandler said.

"Not enough to help the Sanatorium out of its financial crisis," Warner laughed sardonically. "That would cost a fortune. Besides, the reason we wanted the murals was to see if they showed any evidence of Bethune's communist sympathies." They looked at each panel again.

"All this writing at the bottom of most of them might give a clue," Janet said, "but to me it looks like he's mostly trying to escape from T.B. and other diseases, poor man. It would be nice if there was some record of what Bethune had written."

Chandler agreed with Janet.

Before leaving the board room, Brandon Warner rolled up the murals, fit them back in the tube, and put the cap back on, noticing that the tape sealing one end of the tube was not identical to the tape at the other. *Could Tom have tampered with the tube?* He dropped the tube on the back seat of his station wagon, next to Archibald. After he and Janet dropped Chandler off at his house, they looked at each other across the front seat. "Now what?" Janet asked.

"I'm going to write Dr. Hungerford to see if he can tell us more about the content of the murals."

"If Tom Steele tampered with the Angel of Death" Janet drew a deep breath, "I'd say he is deeply disturbed."

"Look, Janet, unless we can find early pictures of the murals, we won't know whether they were tampered with. Right now, Tom is distraught over what's happened. His concern is with his two sons and how he is going to cope. I'm not about to accuse him of lying to me about when the murals arrived, or of tampering with them. Maybe questions will come up in the future, but I'm not going to ask them now."

"He defaced a work of art."

"A work of art that's already damaged. If we had an earlier photo before the angel was defaced, we might be able to have it repaired, along with the other damaged bits. My concern right now—our concern, I should say—is whether the murals shed light on whether Bethune was a Communist when he drew them. From what we've seen today, I'd say they don't."

Janet sighed but said nothing.

———◆———

Larry Crane did not learn of Emily's death until the following week. The day after he returned from Saranac Lake, he found that Harold Hungerford was still the deputy director of the National Microbiological Institute and phoned him.

"I haven't changed mah mind about signing the loyalty oath," Hungerford told him, "if that's what you're calling about."

"I'm sorry to hear that, but that's not why I'm calling."
Hungerford said nothing. "I want to ask you about Norman
Bethune, with whom you first acquainted me. Dr. Brandon
Warner told me yesterday that he learned from you that the
murals Bethune drew when he was a patient at the Trudeau
Sanatorium were at Duke Medical School and Tom Steele was
trying to retrieve them. How did the murals get to Duke?"

Hungerford did not answer immediately. *Is he debating
whether to tell me?* Crane wondered.

"I brought them there."

"Why?"

Again, Hungerford hesitated. "Otherwise, they would have
been destroyed when Lea Cottage was torn down."

"What were the murals about?" Crane asked.

"Bethune labeled them *The T.B.'s Progress, A Drama in One
Act and Nine Painful Scenes*. Dr. Steele should have them by now.
Why don't you look at them yourself?"

"You're not going to tell me any more?"

"No I'm not, Mr. Crane. I am sorry I ever mentioned Norman Bethune to you."

"Does that mean they show a communist influence?"

"You won't trick me into answering that. Good day sir."
Crane heard the connection click off.

His conversation with Crane jarred Hungerford's memory.
He got up, went to a partly rusted file cabinet that he had
brought from Duke, and opened the bottom drawer. He pulled
out an old folder labeled "Norman Bethune" and leafed backward until he found a reprint of an article, "The T.B.'s Progress"
by Norman Bethune, *The Fluoroscope* 1932; Vol. 1, No. 7.

The article contained black and white photographs of the
panels. The verses were difficult to read, but Beth had included

them in the text so the reader did not have to strain to decipher them. Hungerford read the first verse under the panel depicting Bethune as a fetus in his mother's womb, surrounded by bats:

Look, O Stranger at the danger
To our hero embryonic.
T.B. bats, so red, ferocious
In the breast of our precocious
Laddie, do him in just like his daddy.
His dark cave no barrier knows,
Against this worst of mankind's foes.

Hungerford chuckled, shook his head and said out loud, "I don't think a Communist's biggest fear would be T.B. bats. If Beth was a Communist back then, he sure confused things by making the dreaded bats red." After glancing at the next several verses, he paused longer at the verse under the seventh panel:

Lured by that Siren, Spurious Fame
Who had no heart nor pity
Our hero strives to win a name
In the Canyons of the City

Temptations flourish thickly there
But T.B. bats are thicker,
They swarm about the fetid air,
While he grew sick, and sicker.

A communist influence? Hungerford dismissed the idea that, to Beth, the T.B. bats were a metaphor for capitalists or capitalism. Never in their discussions had Beth suggested such an interpretation.

As he read the last panel, Hal thought, *Would a Communist really end his poem heralding an angel?*

> Sweet death, thou kindest angel of them all,
> In thy soft arms, at last, O let me fall;
> Bright stars are out, long gone the burning sun
> My little act is over, the tiresome day is done.

When Hungerford returned the reprint to the folder, he noticed a large, thick envelope in the drawer. Opening it, he was surprised to see black and white photographs of the murals he had taken before he removed them from Lea Cottage. *I must have sent a copy to Beth, who used them to illustrate the article he wrote in The Fluoroscope.* He put the photos back in their envelope, but instead of putting it back in the old cabinet, he inserted it alphabetically in his active files under "Bethune murals."

PART THREE

1953: Summer and Fall

Chapter 10

The Fourth of July fell on a Saturday in 1953 and the Sanatorium and its laboratories closed Friday, giving all but a skeleton staff a three-day holiday. A few days earlier, Brandon Warner had a showdown with Arnold Springer. "I want to see the edited papers from the Seventh Symposium on my desk when I return from holiday on July 6," he told Springer.

"And if not?" Springer asked.

"If not? With the authority given to me by the Board of Trustees, I will stop your paychecks after July 17." Springer stalked out of Warner's office.

Brandon looked forward to getting away from Trudeau for the long weekend. With Johnny at camp, he and Janet rented a one-bedroom cottage near the outlet of Upper Saranac Lake, a dam over which water fell before flowing through a wooded area to a single-lane wooden bridge about one hundred yards downstream. From the bridge, they could look upstream at the rocky river bed that churned the water into dangerous spume. Downstream, the river widened, meandering calmly through a flat meadow, its banks tall with cattails and other rushes, then—out of sight from the bridge—narrowing as it entered another wooded area, finally reaching Middle Saranac Lake less than a mile from the bridge. At night, under a sky brimming with stars, the moon only a faint crescent, they skinny-dipped off a sandy beach alongside the dam and went to bed listening to the steady roar of the rapids. "Wouldn't it be lovely to own a cottage like this, where we could escape whenever we wanted?" Janet whispered to Brandon as they lay close to each other. When she put her arm around him he did not respond as he usually did. "What's wrong, Brandon?"

"A few days ago, I told Arnold Springer that if he didn't have the papers from the Seventh Symposium on my desk when I got back, his appointment would be terminated."

Janet sat up. "You didn't tell me."

"There's nothing you could have done about it. I was carrying out Fred Todd's instructions."

"What do you think Arnold will do?"

"It will be messy if I have to fire him."

"Well, at least you've got the FBI off your back."

"What makes you think so? I'm still waiting to hear from Hal Hungerford whether the writing on the murals shows Bethune had a communist stripe. If he did, the Foundation may be in real trouble."

Janet snuggled up to him and comforted her husband as best she could. She knew he was right.

———◆———

The fireworks didn't come for Brandon until he returned on July 6. As he sorted through the mail, Greta buzzed to say that Evan Jones, the head technician at the Saranac Laboratory, was on the line.

"Hello, Evan. I hope you had a nice weekend."

"Yes I did, thank you. Have you spoken to Dr. Springer lately?"

"Not since I asked him to get the papers presented at the Seventh Symposium to me." He looked around the desk. "He hasn't done that yet."

"They're gone."

"What do you mean, gone?"

"Not only those papers but some of Dr. Gardner's as well. They were on the table in our conference room when I left on Thursday."

"Have you notified Dr. Springer?"

"I rang his home. No one answered."

"Do you think they've been stolen? We should notify the police."

Jones did not answer immediately. Finally, he said quietly, "I think Dr. Springer's gone too. His personal effects are missing, all but his keys to the lab, which were on his desk."

He's gone, Warner thought with some relief. But when he realized the enormity of what Evan Jones had told him, he was horrified. "Do you know where he lives, Evan?"

"On Helen Street, not far from the lab." He anticipated Warner's request. "I can walk over; if nobody's home, I'll talk to the neighbors."

"Excellent. Call me when you get back." As soon as he put the receiver down, he buzzed Greta. "Get me Dr. Todd, will you please?" *Maybe I should have waited until Evan called me back. No need to alarm him if this turns out to be nothing.*

"Dr. Todd is in conference," Greta buzzed back. "I asked that he call you as soon as he returns." Relieved, Brandon went back to the mail. Toward the bottom of the pile he found a handwritten letter from Dr. Hungerford.

June 26, 1953
Dear Brandon,
    I was terribly saddened to learn of Mrs. Steele's death from your letter last month. I

have sent condolences to Tom. What with
that shock and a phone call from Agent
Crane around the same time, I haven't gotten around to responding until now.

In his phone call, Agent Crane asked me
what Bethune's murals were about. I refused
to tell him, but his visit reminded me that
before I took the murals down from Lea Cottage I had black and white photographs
taken of them. There they were in the file I
keep on Norman Bethune, not the negatives
but good-quality prints. I daresay that, except for the lack of color, these prints come
closer to the murals as Beth drew them than
do the original murals today. My file also
contained a reprint from The Fluoroscope
1932; Vol. 1, No. 7, written by Bethune and
giving a clear exposition of his murals, il-
lustrated with the photos that I had taken
(and apparently given copies to Beth). You
should be able to get the article from the
Trudeau medical library. My own opinion
is that the murals and accompanying verses
are devoid of political content, communist
or otherwise.

Little did I realize when I told him about
Norman Bethune that I would bring
Crane's evil eye to Saranac Lake. So rather
than incriminate other people I have made
up my mind that I will provide no more
information to the FBI. Needless to say, I

have not mentioned the photos or Beth's ar-
ticle in The Fluoroscope to Crane.
   My conscience forbids me from signing
the loyalty oath. I will be out of a job soon.
   Yours truly,
   Hal

Brandon glanced at his watch. *I should have time to walk over
to the medical library, get The Fluoroscope paper and be back before either
Jones or Todd calls*, he thought. "I'll return within a half hour,"
he told Greta. "If either Jones or Todd calls, tell them I'll call
them within the hour."

Hurrying to the library, he decided that the news from
Evan Jones and the letter from Hal Hungerford were both
good and bad. He might have gotten rid of Springer, but official lab records were missing. Similarly, he might be able to
settle the question of Bethune's thoughts when he drew the
mural, but Hungerford might become a victim of the hunt for
Communists. In the library, bound volumes were arranged in
alphabetical order. He quickly found *The Fluoroscope* for 1932
and in number 7, the article by Bethune, "The T.B.'s Progress."

He skimmed it quickly. It contained black and white photos
of the mural, just as Hungerford had described, and easily
readable verses that he and Janet had trouble deciphering in
the murals sent from Duke.

By a rule that he had promulgated, periodicals were not al-
lowed to circulate, but he was so excited that he told the librarian to insert a piece of paper in the volume's place on the
shelf, saying he had borrowed it.

With the book under his arm, he returned to find Greta
speaking on the phone. "Oh, he just walked in. I'll put him

on." She turned to Warner. "It's Evan Jones."

"I'll take it in my office." He put the borrowed volume on his desk and picked up the phone. "What news, Evan?"

"I got no answer at the Springers' but their neighbor was out cutting his lawn. He told me they had rented a moving truck and moved out on Saturday. 'Seemed they were in an awful hurry. Didn't even stay for the fireworks,' the neighbor reported. He had no idea where they were headed. I walked over to the post office, Dr. Warner. The postmaster told me that no one had submitted a forwarding address for the Springers."

"I see."

"What about the lab, sir?"

"Keep it running as best you can, Evan. Continue with any experiments in progress. I've got a call in to Dr. Todd, the chairman of the Trudeau Board. I'll be in touch as soon as we can sort things out. Oh yes, and if you haven't already done so, let the lab's personnel know what's happened. If any of them has more information about Dr. Springer's departure, please call me." As soon as he hung up, Greta buzzed to say that Dr. Todd was on the other line.

Trying to keep cool, Warner greeted Fred Todd, asking if he had a pleasant Fourth of July. Fred replied that he did. "We rented a cottage on Upper Saranac Lake," Warner continued, "beautiful and quiet except for water going over the dam. No fireworks until this morning."

"What do you mean?" Todd asked.

"Arnold Springer and his family moved out of Saranac Lake over the weekend. Evan Jones, his chief technician, phoned a little while ago to tell me. The papers from the Seventh Symposium and the records of some of Dr. Gardner's experiments are gone as well."

The phone was silent for a few moments. "Are you suggesting Springer took them with him?"

"Unless he destroyed them, or someone else took them."

"Which papers of Dr. Gardner's are missing?"

"Those showing that asbestos is capable of causing cancer, again not previously reported." Brandon asked a question of his own. "The missing papers belong to the lab, don't you think?"

"Yes they do."

"Then maybe we should report their disappearance to the police and our insurance carrier."

Fred did not respond immediately. "Let me think about that, Brandon. I don't want us to get into criminal proceedings, at least not until we have all the facts. Is there anything else, Brandon?"

"Yes, there is. I received a letter from Dr. Hungerford this morning. He led me to an article in *The Fluoroscope* in which Norman Bethune described the intent of the murals in 1932. I just read it. It's clear he was not a Communist, or thinking like a Communist, when he drew them."

"Do you think that will satisfy the FBI?"

"Why shouldn't it?"

"Doesn't it strike you as bizarre that the FBI should be spending time and money figuring out whether a Canadian was a Communist over a quarter of a century ago?"

"They are looking for a communist cell up here."

"Yes, Brandon, but why?"

Warner lugged the volume of *The Fluoroscope* home but began his daily report to Janet with news of Springer's departure and the theft of records from the Saranac Laboratory.

"Do you think Arnold could have taken the records?"

"Too much of a coincidence otherwise," Brandon answered, "though I'm not sure he acted alone. Some of the companies that fund the lab, and part of Springer's salary, are worried that if data in the records become public, they'll be swamped by liability lawsuits."

"What will become of the Saranac Laboratory?"

"Unless we find a replacement for Springer, we'll have to close the lab. And that means more jobs lost in the village." He pulled *The Fluoroscope* from his briefcase. "I had to take this journal out of the library in violation of my own rules." He had put a bookmark on the first page of Bethune's article and he laid the volume on Janet's lap. "The verses that Bethune penned in at the bottom of the panels are part of his text. Pure doggerel, no political content. From what I've read about his motivation for drawing the murals, and his descriptions of them, I can't make him out to be a Communist. I'd like your opinion."

While her husband was telling her this, Janet was skimming through the article. Coming to the end, she asked, "Brandon, fetch me your magnifying glass, the one you use for your stamp collection. I want to have a better look at the ninth drawing."

"Did you hear a word I said, or are you still preoccupied with the Angel of Death?"

"I heard every word, and I will read Bethune's paper carefully and give you my honest opinion. But right now I want to see whether the Angel of Death was tampered with in the murals sent to Tom Steele." Obediently, Brandon brought the magnifying glass to his wife. She brought the photograph of the Angel of Death into focus. "Well!" she said, her voice rising with excitement as she handed the glass back to him, "Don't you think she looks like Emily Steele?"

"Yes," Brandon agreed. "The straight nose, the birthmark."

"Seems that Tom altered the mural."

"That doesn't change anything, Janet," he said, exasperated with his wife. "I'm not going to confront Tom. The biggest problem in my lap at the moment is the Saranac Laboratory, which reminds me that I didn't get a chance to tell Tom about Springer's departure. Tom told me a few months ago that he had no interest in running both laboratories, but maybe I should ask him again—at least on a temporary basis."

———◆———

Tom Steele had returned to work in the middle of June, arranging for his boys to spend the summer at the sleepaway camp that the Warners' son, John, went to—Gerald as a junior counselor, getting food, board, and a small stipend; Billy as a camper in the same bunk with John. In the lab, Tom's temper was short and occasionally he burst into tears, retreating into his office. Giving Tom an update, Dr. O'Keefe, his assistant, told him that Dr. and Mrs. Warner had come to the lab the day after Mrs. Steele died and had taken the long tube that Dr. Steele had obtained for him. Steele had not had a chance to speak to Warner since he returned to work.

Brandon phoned Tom at home on the evening of July 6. "Tom, Brandon here." Brandon got right to the point. "You may have heard what I'm about to tell you. I'm sorry if I'm not the first; I just had too much to handle today."

"No, Brandon, I haven't heard anything unusual." Brandon

proceeded to tell him about Springer and the missing papers.

"That son of a bitch," Tom said. Brandon had never heard him curse before. "Those records aren't his property. He had no right to take them. I'd never even think of doing anything like that."

"Hold on, Tom. We have no evidence that Arnold took the papers with him."

"Come on, Brandon. What else could have happened to them over the Fourth of July holiday?"

"We'll try to find out, but the reason I called was to ask if you would be willing to take charge of the Saranac Lab as well as the Trudeau, at least on a temporary basis. Unless we can keep it running, we'll have to close it down."

A long silence ensued. "I can't do it, Brandon," Tom finally said. "Emily's passing stunned me and my boys, and I'm just getting back to speed with my own lab. Besides, I know little about dust diseases and, as I've told you before, I'd rather be working hands-on in the lab than be a damn fool administrator." Realizing that he might have offended Brandon, he added, "Exempting you from the damn fool category, of course. Do you have any other prospects?"

"Not at the moment. Well, anyway, I wanted to let you know. Johnny writes that Billy is doing well at camp."

"I hope so. The house is pretty lonely without the boys." He paused. "And Emily." Brandon thought he heard a catch in Tom's voice.

"Oh, by the way," Brandon said casually, "I did have a look at Bethune's murals with Janet and Archibald Chandler, who's something of an art connoisseur. They're in pretty bad shape, Tom. So I wrote to Hal Hungerford asking if he could shed more light on the verses at the bottom of most panels—I mean about what they said. A reply from Hal that I received today mentioned a paper by Norman Bethune in *The Fluoroscope* in 1932. The paper is in our medical library. It's a narrative description of his murals, including photographs of them, and dispels any notion that he was a Communist when he drew them."

"Photographs?"

"Yeah. Hungerford had photos taken of the murals before Lea Cottage was torn down."

The line was silent for a moment.

"Well, I'd like to have a look at the paper."

"No problem. I'll drop the volume off at your lab tomorrow morning. But please return it to the medical library; it's not supposed to circulate."

———◆———

Tom called back a few minutes later. "Hal Hungerford is your man, Brandon."

"My man? What do you mean?"

"Dr. Hungerford to run the Saranac Laboratory. When I first came to the Trudeau Laboratory, he also worked there. Taught me the ropes. Nice man, southern gentleman, and very smart."

"His work's been on tuberculosis. I'm not sure he's interested in inhaled dust diseases—except as they exacerbate T.B."

"You're looking for an administrator and I hear that's mostly what he's been doing at NIH. I don't know why anyone would want to work for the government, even under a Republican president."

Brandon's mood changed as he realized that Hungerford was a logical choice. He recalled the last line of Hungerford's letter: "I may be out of a job soon." *How ironic*, Brandon thought, *that Tom, the arch-conservative, should be the one to promote the suspected Communist*. Of course, Tom didn't know Hungerford was under suspicion.

"Brandon, are you still there?"

"Yes, Tom. I was just thinking about your suggestion."

⬥

No loyalty oath to sign at Trudeau," Brandon concluded when he described his conversation with Steele to Janet. "It may be the escape hatch that would save Hungerford."

"If he is interested," she asked, "do you think the Board will approve when they learn he refused to sign the loyalty oath?"

"I don't know. I'll see if Hungerford's interested, and if he is, discuss it with Todd."

Warner reached Hungerford on Tuesday morning, coming straight to the point and asking if he might be interested in heading up the Saranac Laboratory. "Ahh might," Hungerford replied. Warner described Springer's sudden departure and the probability that he took laboratory records with him. "That sounds criminal," Hungerford commented.

"Well, we don't have proof yet that Springer did, but if so, I agree."

"Tell me, Brandon, have you discussed the offer with Fred Todd? He's still the chairman of the Trudeau Board, isn't he?"

"Yes, he is, and no, I haven't. I wanted to make sure you were interested first."

"Ahh mentioned in my letter about refusin' to sign the loyalty oath."

"There's no loyalty oath for working for the Trudeau Foundation."

"I'm glad to hear that, but in some people's minds refusing to sign is tantamount to being a Communist. I don't know how Fred feels."

"Are you interested?"

Hungerford did not answer right away. "Ahh'm sixty-three years old, Brandon," he began quietly in his deep drawl, "close to retirement if Ahh live that long. Spent my whole career working on tuberculosis. The Saranac Laboratory's work on pulmonary diseases due to inhaled dusts is only a peripheral interest, but I agree that research in those diseases is best pursued independent of support from organizations that have a vested interest in the outcomes. And I'm familiar with the process of obtaining federal funds, which would be an alternate source. So if you think I'm a viable candidate under those circumstances, yes, Ahh'm interested."

"Then I'll mention your name to Fred and get back to you."

"I won't hold my breath, Brandon, but thanks for thinking of me. Oh, by the way, did you happen to look at that article by Bethune?"

"I did, as soon as I got your letter. It's a big help and I hope it will lay to rest any notion that Bethune was a Communist when he was a patient here."

———◆———

"I think we've got a replacement for Arnold Springer," Brandon Warner told Fred Todd a few hours after he got off the phone with Hungerford.

"Really? Who is it?"

"Harold Hungerford, now deputy director at the National Microbiological Institute at NIH. I spoke to him earlier today and he's interested."

"Hungerford! That's fantastic! He's a leader in the pulmonary community, won the Trudeau Medal from the National Tuberculosis Society, organized the clinical trial of streptomycin—of course you know all this. What made you think of him?"

"Actually, Tom Steele suggested him."

"Isn't he happy at NIH?"

Warner had anticipated this question. "It's not a matter of his being happy. His own action, or rather inaction, is pushing him out."

"What do you mean?"

"As I'm sure you know, federal employees are required to sign a loyalty oath. Hal steadfastly refuses to sign on the grounds that it's none of the government's business—"

"A violation of his constitutional rights," Todd interrupted.

"I didn't discuss his justification, Fred, but I don't think he ever thought it was necessary to declare his patriotism in order to do his job as a physician scientist. I don't believe Hal Hungerford was ever a Communist."

"From what I know of Hungerford, I think you're right. The three physicians on the Board will agree, but I'm not sure about the others. Maybe you should invite him to Saranac Lake to discuss the position. He can meet with Archibald Chandler and Walter Reilly. If we can persuade at least one of them, I think we'll have a solid majority on the Board. We can give up on Roger Anderson. As a matter of fact, I wouldn't be surprised if Anderson had a hand in Springer's sudden departure."

Brandon did not comment on Todd's speculation but agreed to arrange the visit. The Chandlers were in Europe until Labor Day weekend and other Board members were on holiday in July or August. With Todd's concurrence, he scheduled the trustees to meet on Thursday, September 10, and invited Hungerford to come up a few days earlier to stay at the Warners' house on Park Avenue and become reacquainted with the Trudeau and Saranac Lake.

Chapter 11

Tom Steele had spent a restless night and was in his lab when Brandon dropped off the volume of The Fluoroscope on July 7. The reproductions of the murals in black and white were much smaller than the originals but revealed the faces clearly. Even with the naked eye, Tom recognized Emily's features in the ninth panel. Under the magnifying glass, he was shocked to see her face come to life. Quickly, he closed the volume and sat at his desk, staring into space. What have I done? I've defaced the Angel of Death and to what effect? None. None whatsoever. What right did I have to punish Emily? She wasn't mine when she modeled for Bethune. Only my conceit. Now she's gone, and I am to blame. He put his head between his arms and wept. Mutilating the Angel of Death was my second crime. At least I can atone for that one. He walked over to the medical library to return the volume, thinking on the way there and back about admitting his folly.

When he returned to the lab, he phoned the Warners' home. Janet picked up. "Janet, Tom Steele here. Are you and Brandon free this evening? I'd like to come over to discuss something with you … I'd rather not say any more now. Would eight o'clock be okay? … Good, I'll see you then."

Steele had a difficult time concentrating on his work that day; the scientists and technicians often had to repeat their questions before getting a response. After a light supper, he strolled over to the Warners' in the mellow light of the setting sun, reminiscing about how he and Emily would take strolls at this hour, walking down toward Pine Street with the Saranac River below them. They might cross the bridge and have ice cream in the village, coming back up the hill, the fireflies' flashes just visible in the fading light. *What a fool I've been.*

Janet greeted him. "We can sit on the back porch if you like. The mosquitoes don't seem to be attacking yet, probably 'cause we haven't had rain lately." She led him through the house. Brandon was sitting in a rocker on the porch, smoking his pipe and reading the evening paper. He got up as Tom approached. "Can I get you something to drink, Tom?" Janet asked. "I brewed a pitcher of iced tea."

"That would be lovely, Janet." While she retrieved the iced tea and some home-baked oatmeal cookies, Brandon invited Tom to walk across their back lawn to look at the roses that formed the hedge. "These are gorgeous, Brandon. Must take a lot of effort to keep them blooming in this climate."

"Well, yes, it does, but it takes my mind off work and Janet truly loves them." As they walked up to the porch, he pointed to a vase on a wicker table filled with a bouquet of yellow, red, and white roses. Janet decides what she wants to display, I fill the order, and she arranges the flowers. It's a short season."

"Do you cut the grass, too?"

"Unfortunately, but John will be old enough in a couple of years. It'll be worth paying him," he laughed.

They were silent as they climbed the few steps. Then Tom asked about Hungerford.

"Brilliant idea," Brandon answered, "for you to come up with his name for head of the Saranac Lab. He is interested, and Fred Todd wants to pursue it, but we can't nail down the appointment until the Board approves, and they can't meet until the second week in September."

"I'm looking forward to seeing him again," Tom replied, as Janet returned with the pitcher of tea, glasses, and a small bucket of ice.

When they all had their drinks and Janet had taken a seat crosswise on a chaise lounge, Tom announced, "Well, I didn't come here to talk about Hal Hungerford." Janet and Brandon waited for him to continue. "I've come to talk about the Bethune murals." He paused for a moment, sipped his tea, swallowed hard, and put his glass down. "It's not easy for me to do this, and if I get emotional, please forgive me."

Janet put her arm on Tom's sleeve. "We understand, Tom. Emily and I were the best of friends. I know how much you miss her. She loved you."

Tom looked at Janet, wondering if she knew, and then just as quickly dismissed the thought. "So, the murals. In March of this year, Emily confessed to me that when she was a student nurse at the Sanatorium, she was the model for the Angel of Death in Bethune's last panel." He glanced at them. Neither showed any sign of already knowing. As Tom spoke, his voice broke and he suppressed sobs as he continued haltingly. "We had gone out for a walk … It was the first day of spring … I was infuriated … pushed her away from me … banished her from my bed … She slept in the guest room … We seldom talked over the next few months … Then she was dead." He could not contain his sobs and cried openly. Janet went into the house and returned with a box of tissues. After blowing his nose and wiping his eyes, he continued. "I hardly realized that she had begun to drink. As a matter of fact, my son Gerald noticed before I did." He took another drink of the iced tea. Janet refilled his glass.

"Do you know what I was doing while Emily was gulping down the Seconal?" Neither of them answered. "I was mutilating the Angel of Death by smudging her face." They both stirred uncomfortably, trying to hide that his admission was not a surprise. "The morning Agent Crane came to see me in May, he asked if I had known Norman Bethune when he was a patient here. When I told him I hadn't, he asked if my wife had, and I answered carelessly, 'You'd have to ask her.'" He blew his nose and took another swallow of tea.

"I can't prove it, but I believe that Agent Crane visited Emily after he left my lab." Taking a deep breath, he went on. "That visit may have put Emily over the edge, but I was the one who killed her. This wasn't apparent to me immediately—only when the reality of her death had sunk in and I began to ask, 'Why did she do it?' Was my male ego worth her life? I loved Emily, from the moment I first met her." Nobody talked for a few minutes as Tom struggled to regain control.

"When she stopped dating me in 1927, I had no idea it was Bethune who filled the gap. Then, when we started dating again and she brought his name up too many times, I began to wonder. I guess I never really put her interest in Bethune, or his in her, out of my mind, but her telling me about it last March brought it to the fore. Emily and I had a wonderful relationship, or so I thought. Only now do I realize that I demanded fealty from her, not only in our marital relationship but in every aspect of life. 'Love, honor, and obey.' I expected her to take the oath seriously. I had to be the lord and master."

By now, the sun was down. In the approaching darkness the fireflies made their debut. Janet stood, "We should move inside. The mosquitos will start their attack soon."

Steele stood. "I've taken enough of your time. Thanks for

letting me unburden myself. There's no one else I would have felt comfortable with, and besides I owe you an apology for what I've done to the mural, to the Angel of Death. If it can be restored by an expert—he'd have the photo in Bethune's *Fluoroscope* article to guide him—I'll pay for it."

Brandon cut him off. "Don't worry about it, Tom. If you want to display the murals in the Saranac Lake Free Library, the Foundation and the library can discuss sharing the costs of refurbishing and preserving them. They need more work than restoring the profile of the Angel of Death."

"Then you saw what I did?"

"Yes we did, Tom," Brandon replied, quickly reminding Tom that his interest wasn't primarily in the artistic aspects of the murals.

That night Tom Steele had his best sleep since Emily had died.

———◆———

When Tom Steele approached his lab one morning toward the end of July, an unfamiliar black Buick was parked in front. He instantly recognized Agent Larry Crane sitting on a bench in the waiting area, his seersucker suit appropriate for the weather but not for the environs. Crane stood and walked toward him. "Good morning, Dr. Steele. Do you have a few minutes?"

"Do I have a choice?" Tom replied gruffly, showing Crane into his office and offering him the seat in front of his desk.

"I would like to express my condolences on the loss of your wife. I was shocked that it happened on the day I visited her. I had never met her before, but she looked terrible, compared to her picture on your desk. She had finished off at least one glass of sherry and she stumbled when she showed me out."

Steele stared at Crane for a moment. "So you did visit her?"

Crane shifted uncomfortably in his chair. "You told me, if I wanted to know if she knew Bethune I'd have to ask her."

"Yes, it was my fault. I've wondered since whether she'd be alive today if I hadn't said that."

"If you hadn't given me permission, I would have asked you for it. You also mentioned that she was a student nurse at the Trudeau Sanatorium at the time Norman Bethune drew the murals. That led me to wonder whether she took care of Bethune. Mrs. Steele seemed to get agitated when I told her you were expecting the murals to come from Duke."

Keep a grip on yourself, Tom told himself.

"She made a remark that made me wonder whether your marriage was on the rocks. She said, referring to you, 'He doesn't tell me anything these days.' I wondered whether that explained her appearance and behavior, and possibly her death. I was relieved that I hadn't contributed."

"What else did Emily tell you?"

"That she knew Bethune, but that they never talked politics. She seemed very uncomfortable when I asked about Bethune, like she was holding back."

Involuntarily, Steele got up and started to walk around his office. "Emily told me this past March that Bethune asked her to be his model for one of the figures in his mural, the Angel of Death. She and I were not going together when he asked her—that would have been the fall of 1927. When she heard the murals were coming back to Saranac Lake, she worried that I would be very upset when I recognized her in the mural."

"Why?"

"She knew I would be jealous."

"After twenty-six years?"

"Now I know how stupid I was, but that's the reason. Emily knew me better than I knew myself."

"Be that as it may, isn't it possible she and Bethune talked about communism?"

"You're saying she lied to you when she said they never talked politics?" Steele sank into his chair, exasperated. "I don't know, maybe they did. I don't think they talked very much about anything, if you know what I mean."

"Can you tell me where the murals are now?

"Dr. Warner has them."

"Well, I'll go over and have a look at them."

As he got up to leave, Crane reminded Steele that during his previous visit he had said that he knew Harold Hungerford.

"Yes, we worked in the Trudeau Lab here in the late 1920s."

"Did you ever talk politics?"

"Why, do you suspect him of being a Communist, too?

"He has refused to sign the loyalty oath required of federal employees."

"Does that make him a Communist?"

"You can draw your own conclusions, Tom. Good day." Crane did not wait for Steele to respond.

<hr />

For the second time after interviewing Tom Steele, Larry Crane scratched his head. *Steele had not denied that his marriage was on the rocks. But a pre-marital affair twenty-six years ago hardly seemed a rational basis for disrupting a marriage. What was going on? Was he shielding her?* In any event, Crane felt better expressing his condolences to Steele and admitting that he had seen his wife shortly before her death. At least Steele hadn't accused him of killing her.

Crane had a phone call from Arnold Springer just after the Fourth of July holiday. Springer told him he had quit his job as director of the lab and had taken papers from the Seventh Symposium with him. Although he was troubled that Springer could have done such a thing, his conversation with Steele made him more suspicious that Communists had been associated with the Trudeau Sanatorium since the 1920s. He said as much in his report to his chief.

———◆———

Crane's visit put Steele in an angry mood. As a loyal American, he wanted to be helpful to the FBI, but Crane's line of questioning and his insinuations about Emily, that she was "uncomfortable" because she had communist leanings, infuriated him. Crane's final query about Hungerford, whom Steele genuinely liked, irritated him further. He had not thought about loyalty oaths before, but Crane telling him to "draw his own conclusions" made him realize that Crane's entire inquiry was built on innuendo, not evidence.

Later that afternoon, Warner called Tom to tell him that he had shown the murals to Crane. "Did he make any comment about the Angel of Death?" Tom asked.

"Not specifically. He thought the murals were in terrible shape and with so much of Bethune's writing illegible, he said he could not agree that they were free of communist influence."

"Did you mention Bethune's article in *The Fluoroscope?*"

"Yes, I showed it to him. He seemed only mildly interested. Springer's departure and the theft of the Symposium papers seemed more important to him than the murals."

"Did he ask if the Foundation had found a replacement for Springer?"

"He did. I told him the Board was still looking."

"If the Board picks Hal, Crane will have his communist plot confirmed. Crane told me Hal refused to sign a loyalty oath."

"Are you withdrawing your support for Hungerford because of that?"

"It does make me wonder. Maybe he's changed in a quarter of a century. Of course, he's still qualified for the job."

Brandon switched subjects. "Listen, Tom, the reason I'm calling is to tell you I'd like to give the murals, on loan, to the Saranac Lake Free Library. I have no further use for them. If the library is interested in refurbishing them for display, the Foundation will contribute."

"That's kind of you, Brandon. I'll show them to my Art Committee and if they're interested I'll ask the Library Board to contribute to their restoration. But I have to say, right now I'd rather forget about them."

"I can understand."

Chapter 12

On Sunday September 6, Brandon and Janet picked up Harold Hungerford at the Saranac Railway station and gave him a fast tour of the village, driving him down Broadway. "Looks like this Town Hall has survived," Hal commented. "Ahh remember the old one went up in flames in 1926; it was quite a spectacle." They turned up River Road and left on Church Street, passing the Saranac Laboratory. Hal recognized it right away. "Hasn't changed much. Aren't we goin' to stop?" he asked.

"I've arranged for Evan Jones, the technician currently in charge, to have you meet the staff and give you a tour tomorrow. Besides, I don't have a key with me; we keep the lab locked after business hours since Dr. Springer's departure."

"Ahh can wait." As they drove up Catherine Street and on to Park Avenue, Hal commented, "Looks like autumn is makin' its entrance. Do you think there'll be time for me to take a hike or two this week? I'd like to resume my quest of the high peaks, especially this time of the year."

Janet was surprised. "Were you a hiker when you were here?"

"Was then and still am. Did some smaller peaks, Ampersand and Mckenzie. Cascade and Porter were the only four-thousand peaks I managed before I left."

"I'd love to see what the forests look like from the top down," Janet exclaimed. "The best we managed was a drive up Whiteface last fall, which was spectacular, but before I'm too old I'd like to get to some peaks on my own."

"You've got a long way before you're too old, Mrs. Warner" Hal answered gracefully.

"That's nice of you to say, but Brandon would rather stroll around Trudeau."

"And paddle," he added. "We've canoed all the Saranac Lakes."

"Do you think you can manage to get away one day this week, dear, for a climb with Dr. Hungerford?"

"Please call me Hal, ma'am."

"If you call me Janet," she laughed.

"With the Board meeting on Thursday, I've got my hands full," Brandon answered. "But you and Hal can take the station wagon to any trailhead and hike to your heart's content Tuesday or Wednesday. Remember we've arranged a cocktail party for the local Board members and senior staff to meet Hal on Tuesday evening, so don't bite off a bigger mountain than you can chew."

Hal was excited by his tour of the Saranac Laboratory on Monday morning, surprised that the equipment was up to date, and pleased that the technicians were interested in their work. He arranged to come back on Tuesday morning to meet with Evan Jones to go over lab notebooks, the lab's budget, the source of current revenues, and Hal's priorities. "Mind you, Evan," he said as they concluded, "Ahh don't have the job yet; Ahh hope Ahh can flatter the Board into appointin' me."

"I surely hope so," Evan replied, shaking Hal's hand firmly.

On Monday afternoon, Hal renewed his acquaintance with Tom Steele when he visited the Trudeau Laboratory and the Sanatorium. More familiar with tuberculosis research than inhaled dust diseases, the two fell naturally into scientific chatter about the latest clinical trials and the strains of tubercle bacilli that were turning up resistant to anti-tuberculosis drugs. As the shadows fell longer, Steele, still captivated by Hungerford after all these years, mentioned Springer's visit in July. "Yes, Ahh know Agent Crane," Hungerford replied.

"Is it true you won't sign a loyalty oath?"

Hungerford sighed. "Look, Tom, there is no country I love more than the United States of America. There are things here I don't like, one bein' the way Negroes are treated, another bein' scarin' people about the red menace. Now I don't know what the Russians have in mind, especially now that Stalin is dead, but Ahh have to tell you, Tom, the Communists Ahh've known love this country as much as I do. There may be some who take orders from Moscow, but they're not goin' to win over the vast majority of Americans."

"Then you're not a Communist, Hal?"

"Not now and never have been, Tom. But once you start to intimidate people, asking their political beliefs when those beliefs have nothing to do with their loyalty to this country or to their jobs, you create a bigger menace to democracy than the red one. If the loyalty oath Agent Crane asked me to sign was like the Pledge of Allegiance, you know, where it says, '… with liberty and justice for all,' I'd sign it in a minute. But the oath Crane wants me to sign defines loyalty as not ever being a member of the Communist Party. That oath undermines 'liberty and justice for all.'"

Tom was quiet for a moment. "You know, Hal, Agent Crane tried to intimidate me, asking questions about whether Emily ever talked politics with Norman Bethune."

Hal took Tom's hand. "I hope Crane didn't have anything to do with Emily's death."

"No, I have myself to blame for that," he said, his voice breaking.

Hal changed course. "Ahh don't think either you or I have seen the last of Agent Crane."

Tuesday afternoon, Janet had arranged for a realtor to show Hal various homes for sale in the village and surrounding areas, just in case he should get the appointment.

At the cocktail party, Hal's southern accent and gentlemanly manners flattered the Chandlers and Reillys. Other senior Trudeau staff, including Tom Steele, and a few Trudeau family members were present as well. During a lull in the multiple conservations, Archibald Chandler asked Hal in a benign tone, "What's this nonsense I hear about you refusing to sign a loyalty oath?"

Before Hal could answer, Tom Steele spoke up. "It's not asking Hal's loyalty to the United States. It's asking him to swear he's never been a member of the Communist Party."

"Isn't that the same thing?" Walter Reilly asked.

"No, it's not," Tom replied. Then, with Hal's help, and Janet Warner's, he explained the difference much as Hal had explained it to him on Monday afternoon.

The discussion took another turn when Brandon spoke. "Frankly, I don't see that Hal's refusal to sign the whatever-it-is oath has much to do with the FBI's looking for Communists up here. And now that we have Bethune's own words about what his murals mean, I'm confident the FBI will leave us alone." The conversation tapered off after that as people took their leave.

———◆———

The weather on Wednesday morning was glorious. By nine o'-

clock, their son John off to school, the Warners and their guest were finishing breakfast as the sun rose high enough to stream in through the east-facing windows. Outside, the sky was a deep blue beyond a few stray clouds. The leaves, beginning to turn color, hung motionless in the still air. "What's on the agenda for today?" Hal asked.

Janet looked at Brandon. "Why don't we all go for a hike? I know that's what Hal would like to do."

"No, you two go ahead," Brandon answered. "I've got to prepare for the Board meeting and pick up the Board members arriving later this afternoon." He turned to Hal. "Janet packs a terrific lunch. Enjoy yourselves." He pushed away from the table. "If you'll excuse me, I'm already late for work."

"Where to?" Janet asked after Brandon left. Wearing old cotton slacks, a loose blouse, a Brooklyn Dodgers cap on her head, and a boy scout canteen slung over her shoulder, she showed the contents of a small wicker rucksack to Hal: sandwiches, hard apples, and a small bag of homemade cookies.

"Mah recollection is that it's wise to have some rain gear, a poncho or rain jacket, when you hike in the Adirondacks. And maybe a sweater." She bustled off and returned with the items, including an old sweater of Brandon's for Hal.

"Where to?" she repeated.

"Well, there's a gem of a mountain just the other side of Lake Placid called Mt. Jo. It's not very high, but if you're out of shape and an old man like me, it's a good starter. Great views, too."

"I'm probably in worse shape than you. Let's go," she said enthusiastically. They got into the front seat of the Warners' station wagon, with Janet driving. They headed east toward Lake Placid and a mile out turned right on to the road to

Adirondack Loj. In the clear late-morning air, Algonquin Mountain loomed ahead of them, with the much lower but dramatic steep side of Wallface to its right, above the height of Indian Pass. The road turned to dirt and ended at a parking lot at the trailhead. As they got out, Hal pointed to a trailhead opposite the one they would take. "That's the start of the trails to the high peaks, including Mt. Marcy, the highest in New York. If I get the job of director of the lab, Janet, I hope to climb it while I'm here."

"Can you do it in one day?" she asked.

"Unless I stay here," he pointed left toward Adirondack Loj, "I'd have to start before dawn."

The beginning of the trail to Mt. Jo was almost level before climbing moderately. Hal let Janet set the pace; he had no trouble keeping up, although he was carrying the rucksack and his own canteen. The climb became steeper, often over small boulders, passing two trails a half-mile apart, one coming in on their right, the farther one on their left. They had to scramble over some steep rocks to reach the true bare rock summit, a little over a mile from the start. Janet gasped at the view, so overjoyed that she reached up and flung her arms around Hal's neck. He hadn't been hugged like that for a long time and he waited patiently until she released herself. Facing Algonquin, Janet exclaimed, "I feel like I'm in a bowl surrounded by lush green mountains above me."

From his back pocket, Hal pulled out a battered topographical map and lined it up with his pocket compass on the flat rock surface. They stood and rotated slowly as Hal, his arm extended and finger pointing, traced the arc of peaks from Cascade Mountain to the northeast, to the Great Range to the southeast, to distant Marcy due south, then southwest to looming Algonquin, which seemed higher than Marcy because of its proximity, and then west to Street and Nye. Against the dark green of the evergreens, the hardwoods—birch, maple, beech—dappled the slopes with occasional yellows and reds. Facing Algonquin, they sat on the bare rock, eating lunch in full sunlight.

"Brandon's wrong, you know," Hal said abruptly.

"About what?"

"He thinks that when the FBI sees Bethune's description of the murals, including his verses, they'll conclude he wasn't a Communist when he drew them and leave the Trudeau Foundation alone."

"Brandon does seem to be putting a lot of stock in the murals. But *The Fluoroscope* article is pretty clear." She took a swig from her canteen. "Though I have asked myself, 'Why is the FBI so interested in whether there was a Communist here twenty-six years ago?' The Sanatorium staff has turned over a few times since then, with the exception of Tom Steele and Edgar Wren. Tom's a staunch Republican and Wren is so engrossed in medicine he has never even bothered to marry. The leadership's changed at least three times."

"That's the point, Janet. It doesn't make sense, even if there was a communist cell here in 1927, that it would still be present today. Bethune and the murals are a pretext."

"But if the FBI has to acknowledge that Bethune was not a Communist when he drew the murals, their case would crumble."

Hal chewed his sandwich thoughtfully for a full minute. The air grew perceptibly cooler as a small cloud blocked the sun for a few minutes. "Ahh don't know much about art, Janet, but Ahh think it's something like poetry: The reader can see into it what he or she wants. What the poet or the artist thinks is almost irrelevant when the work becomes public."

"Well, their thoughts carry some weight, but I see what you mean, Hal; the public can be persuaded otherwise." She pulled two apples from the rucksack and offered one to Hal.

The sun reemerged and Hal stretched out against the rock. "Ahh have a feelin' that Arnold Springer is behind the FBI investigation."

Still sitting, Janet turned to look down at him. The sun was in Hal's eyes so he couldn't recognize her features. "How stupid! That never occurred to me," she said, before taking another bite of apple. "If not Springer, maybe one of the Board members."

"Uh huh," Hal grunted uncharacteristically.

"Oh Hal," she cried, "if that's the case, they'll fight your appointment tooth and nail."

"Uh huh," he repeated, melancholy creeping into his voice. He sat up. "And Ahh'd have to give up returnin' to the Adirondacks. All this beauty."

"Brandon thinks the Board is closely divided. They did vote to force Springer to publish the Seventh Symposium. Maybe that same majority will prevail on your appointment."

"It might," he said, as he folded the wrappers of their now-eaten sandwiches and put them in the rucksack. "But Springer hasn't published them and Ahh don't think he plans to. Until they're found, no one will have access to them." He stood up and helped Janet to her feet. "Ahh don't think Ahh have delusions of grandeur, Janet," he said sardonically, "but approvin' mah appointment to replace Springer could bring down the whole edifice." Before he fastened the lid of the rucksack, he peered inside. "Oh look, we forgot to eat your cookies."

"I've had enough. Let's save them for the bottom," Janet replied. Hal hoisted the rucksack on his shoulders and they started down.

———◆———

The Board, meeting in executive session on September 10, started quietly enough with Fred Todd's announcement that the sale of the Trudeau Sanatorium and Laboratory had been set for early 1954, and that preliminary discussions about a gift of land for a new Trudeau Institute on the shores of Lower Saranac Lake were well underway with a wealthy donor. The one remaining agenda item was approval of Harold Hungerford as director of the Saranac Laboratory. Chairman Todd summarized the events leading to Dr. Springer's sudden departure, which coincided with the disappearance of the unpublished papers of the Seventh Symposium. "I don't think it's any secret to say that several of those papers contained research findings on asbestos that could be highly deleterious to their industrial sponsors, laying the basis for product liability suits far costlier than workmen's compensation. Whether Dr. Springer is responsible for their theft and, if so, whether he acted alone, can only be answered by further investigation. According to the contract under which some of the research in these papers was conducted, findings can only be published with the approval of the companies that supported the research. Whether that restriction would stand in a court of law is dubious, particularly as the suppression of the results could harm thousands if not millions of people yet to be exposed to asbestos. Wisely, I believe, this Board voted for publication at its last meeting, knowing full well that it could mean the withdrawal of corporate support, reliance on government funding, and possible law suits against the Foundation."

"Government funding is socialism," one of the corporate Board members shouted.

Patiently, Todd explained that a grant or contract from the federal government did not mean that the government owned the laboratory—the usual meaning of "socialism"— and that scientists outside the government would decide whether an application for federal funds was scientifically worthy. "We are fortunate," Dr. Todd continued, "to have found a replacement for Dr. Springer, Dr. Harold Hungerford, a pioneer in tuberculosis research and management, a Trudeau Medal winner, and, I might add, an old friend of our own Tom Steele. Hungerford is currently a deputy director of one of the institutes that comprise the National Institutes of Health, which, with appropriations from the Congress of the United States, is undertaking a major investment in research at America's universities, medical centers, and other private non-profit organizations. Hungerford's recent experience and his prominence can only redound to the benefit of the Saranac Laboratory and the future Trudeau Institute.

"There is what some of you may consider a blemish on Dr. Hungerford's sterling record, however. He has refused to sign the oath required of federal employees, which makes him swear that he has never been a member of the Communist Party."

"That's more than a blemish," another Board member shouted. "It means he's a disloyal American."

Todd ignored the interruption. "Dr. Hungerford has spent the last few days visiting our facilities. Those of you present at last evening's cocktail party heard him and Tom Steele discuss the meaning of loyalty. Rather than my attempting to defend him, I'd like, with your permission, to ask him to defend himself."

"No," shouted the Board member, "you never should have invited him, Fred, without our permission. You're railroading him through."

"If I had appointed Dr. Hungerford as director without seeking your approval, as I am doing today, you might have an argument. But considering Dr. Hungerford's qualifications, and that no other applicant has sought this position, extending to him the courtesy of explaining—defending himself if you will—is in the best tradition of the Foundation whose trustees we are."

The room had been silent for a minute when a physician scientist Board member raised his hand. "I move we listen to Dr. Hungerford." Two others quickly seconded the motion, which carried with no dissenting votes, though not all hands were raised in support.

After the outcome was clear, Archibald Chandler spoke. "I voted to hear Dr. Hungerford because that is only fair. That does not necessarily mean that I will vote for him as director of the Saranac Laboratory."

The Board recessed for lunch, and when it resumed Dr. Hungerford stood before it. He started by describing his early association with Trudeau as a patient and lauding its extraordinary research "in both tuberculosis, led by my friend Tom Steele, and in inhaled dust diseases." He described his work at Duke and then at the newly founded National Microbiological Institute, concluding by explaining why he would not sign the so-called loyalty oath, adding, "Ahh'd be happy to answer any questions."

The Board questioned him vigorously and he answered calmly, with a touch of humor, regardless of how vitriolic the questions were. When there were no more, Todd thanked

Hungerford, who left the room. The Board debated his appointment for another half hour. In the final vote, Hungerford received a majority of three votes, becoming director of the laboratory as of October 1, 1953. Roger Anderson immediately announced his resignation from the Board and left the meeting.

"Well, looks like Ahh might get to climb Mt. Marcy after all," he told Janet Warner, when he left to close his apartment in Bethesda before moving to the Adirondacks.

Chapter 13

Brandon Warner's hope that the FBI would drop its investigation was dashed on September 22, 1953 when he, Hungerford, Todd, Steele, Springer, and Anderson were served subpoenas to appear before the House Un-American Activities Committee on October 26. Warner's subpoena instructed him to have the Bethune murals with him.

The banner headline in *The Adirondack Daily Eagle* (whose motto boasted, "The Last Eagle in the Adirondacks") the next day declared:

**Trudeau Scientists Called to Testify Before Congress;
House Committee Suspects Subversion**

Drawn from a press release from the House Un-American Activities Committee, the story reported that the Committee had begun an investigation into subversion at the Trudeau Sanatorium and Laboratories. It listed the persons subpoenaed to appear, correctly indicating their relationship to the Trudeau Foundation.

The story continued by quoting the press release: "In announcing the hearing, K. Reginald Palmer, Chair of the Committee, said, 'Communist infiltration of the staff at Trudeau goes back to the 1920s, when an avowed Communist, Dr. Norman Bethune, a patient at the Sanatorium, planted the subversive seed among physicians, nurses, and scientists there. The Committee wants to know whether the seed has sprouted, undermining the strides made in the care and treatment of tuberculosis by the Sanatorium's founder, the late Dr. E. L. Trudeau." At this point in the story, the reporter for *The Eagle* inserted the following sentence: "The Sanatorium has admitted a decreasing number of patients in recent years and is rumored to be on the verge of closing."

The editorial accompanying the lead story, written and signed by Ted Bradley, editor and publisher of *The Eagle*, began: "All the trouble the Trudeau Sanatorium has had recently in attracting patients may stem from a communist plot to undermine one of America's leading institutions in the care and research of tuberculosis. The leaders of the Trudeau Foundation will have their 'day in court' next month when they testify before the House Un-American Activities Committee. Before then, they owe the residents of Saranac Lake and the surrounding area an explanation for why the Sanatorium and its laboratories, the largest employer in southern Franklin County, is on the verge of closing with the resultant loss of many jobs."

————●————

Still shocked from receiving the subpoena, Brandon said to Janet as he finished his coffee, "This is really too much." As was the Warners' custom, Janet had retrieved *The Eagle* from their front step. So stunned by the headline, she had sat at the kitchen table reading the story before making breakfast. Then she laid the paper at Brandon's place. "Did you read the editorial?" Brandon asked as he finished eating. She shook her head no as she refilled their cups. "Bradley says the closing of the Sanatorium, and I quote, 'may stem from a communist plot.' Forget about streptomycin, forget that other sanatoriums are losing patients just as we are." He poured some cream into his freshened cup. "When Fred Todd sees this he's going to explode."

Archibald Chandler called. "Good day, Brandon. I suppose you've seen this morning's paper. What's that old Army expression? Well, 'the shit's hit the fan,' hasn't it? I hope you have good answers for what Ted Bradley has to say."

"Yes, Mr. Chandler, I've seen the paper and there's not a shred of evidence to support a communist plot up here. I was about to call Dr. Todd to apprise him of the situation. I'm going to invite him to come up this weekend so we can discuss it. It will be up to him to call an emergency meeting of the Board, but in any case I'd like the benefit of your wise counsel."

"Thanks, Brandon, I appreciate that. I think it's critical to answer the editorial. Have you thought about a town meeting?"

"No, I hadn't. *The Eagle* is obliged to let us respond to the accusations, to give us more space than a Letter to the Editor. I'll call Bradley this morning and if he is agreeable, I'll start to draft one. Fred, perhaps the others who've been subpoenaed, and you, Archibald, can help with it."

"You're sure none of them—" he stopped abruptly, "or you—are commies?"

The inquisition's begun in earnest, Brandon said to himself. " I can't speak for the others, but I'll tell you personally, Archibald, that I am not, nor have I ever been, a Communist."

"I worry about our new director of the Saranac Lab. I don't suppose he's going to tell the Committee he's clean and be done with it. I'd breathe a lot easier if he did."

"You heard Dr. Hungerford's explanation at the last Board

meeting."

Chandler grunted. "We're getting off the point, Brandon. If Ted doesn't give you enough space, think about the town meeting."

"A town meeting could get unruly, Archibald, but I suppose that's what our democracy was built on. You know, there's nothing for the town to vote on. The Sanatorium grounds will soon be in the hands of the Corporate Managers of America."

After he put the phone down, Brandon told Janet what Archibald had suggested. "Given the red hysteria," she replied, "I shudder to think what the townspeople might do if you met them face to face. You might get stoned to death like Tessie Hutchinson in *The Lottery*."

On Saturday morning, September 28, four of the subpoenaed men sat on the back porch of the Warner home sipping Janet's mulled cider and watching yellow, brown, and a few red leaves float down from the nearby birch and maples to settle on the back lawn. The sun approaching its zenith, but not high in the sky, was bright, casting enough warmth that even with the gentle breeze the men preferred to sit outside, though each wore an outer garment—woolen shirt, sweater, corduroy jacket. None wore ties. Fred Todd had driven up from Manhattan on Friday. Hungerford walked up from the cottage he had rented in the village, and Steele from his home a few blocks away. Archibald Chandler pleaded a competing engagement. "I invited Roger Anderson from West Virginia," Todd informed them, "but he said that since he was no longer on the Board he wouldn't come. Arnold Springer's whereabouts are still a mystery." As they settled in, the four compared notes on being served subpoenas by characters ranging from shabby to elegant. Todd said the one who served him "pretended to be a patient so he could get into my office in Bellevue."

Handsome and very tall, with a distinguished Ivy League accent, Todd began by saying he hadn't expected to return to Saranac Lake so soon. "At least this is a lovely time to be up here, and Brandon and Janet are gracious hosts. I wish our task this morning was as pleasant as our surroundings." He looked at the foolscap pad on his lap. "We all know that the events of the last week threaten the future of the Foundation. I don't think any of us thought our patriotism would ever be questioned, or that we might suffer personally, but what I want to do today is consider how we can best protect the integrity and the future of the Trudeau Foundation in responding to the allegations of K. Reginald Palmer and Ted Bradley. Each of us may be called on by the Committee to answer the 'Are you now or have you ever been…' question, but answering is a personal matter on which our own conscience must guide us. We can discuss it during lunch, which Janet has kindly offered to serve us."

"It might upset mah appetite," Hal Hungerford announced in his southern drawl. Everyone laughed.

"Let me say one other thing to make my position perfectly clear," Todd continued. "I've known all of you since before the war and I'm at least partly responsible for your coming to or remaining at Trudeau. I never once had reason to think that your political beliefs, whatever they might be, influenced your work at Trudeau and I don't intend to start thinking so now. Unlike the Hollywood magnates who fired and blacklisted those who refused to cooperate with the witch hunt, I will stand by you no matter what stance you take before the Committee." He looked at his pad again. "Can someone tell me what triggered the FBI's investigation?"

No one spoke until Hal Hungerford started softly. "Actually, the FBI's investigation began with me." The oldest man present, he was sitting in a Windsor rocking chair and he spoke deliberately in his baritone, southern voice, without stopping the motion of his rocker. "As Ahh told Brandon, when Agent Crane visited me in January to ask why Ahh hadn't signed the loyalty oath, in my innocence, Ahh acquainted him with Norman Bethune, telling him we were both patients at Trudeau in 1927. Now, I'm not bragging about this; in fact, I am deeply sorry to have instigated the investigation." Only the creak of Hal's rocker could be heard for the next few moments until Brandon spoke up.

"Agent Crane drove up here after he had seen Hal. I reported his visit and my response to the Board last February."

"What about the Bethune murals?" Tom Steele asked. "The Committee has subpoenaed them."

"Murals?" Todd asked. "Oh yes, the Board gave you permission, Brandon, to see if they showed Bethune's communist tendencies when he drew them. Did they?"

"We've all looked at them, plus Archibald Chandler and Janet," Brandon replied. "We agree they do not."

"That doesn't sound like enough to warrant subpoenaing the whole lot of us," Fred Todd exclaimed. "Either HUAC is awfully hard up or there's more to it." He thought for a moment. "Did Crane interview Arnold Springer when he was still at Saranac? It's strange that he and Roger Anderson have been subpoenaed."

"Not so far as I know," Brandon replied.

The sun passed behind a cloud, causing a slight chill. Consulting his pad again, Fred asked Brandon for his thoughts on responding to Ted Bradley and *The Daily Eagle*.

"It seems to me," Brandon began, "that the most immediate threat to the integrity of Trudeau comes from Tom Bradley's allegations in his editorial. If ever there was a statement to inflame town-gown relationships, Bradley's editorial was it."

"In this case," Hungerford interrupted, "gown being the hospital variety, not the academic."

"Well, no, Hal." Steele spoke, taking Hungerford's remark seriously, "As scientists, we're looked at as intellectuals, like academics."

"You have a point, Tom," Hungerford replied. "I was just trying to inject a little levity into the discussion."

Warner ignored these interruptions. "Yesterday, I spoke to Bradley and he agreed to give us a full page in *The Eagle*, provided we submit the copy two days in advance and allow his staff and him to question us. He is trying to lay the blame for the imminent closing of the Sanatorium on a communist conspiracy. In my opinion, our reply has to meet this head on in three ways: First, we need to acknowledge that the Sanatorium, like many others across the country, is on the verge of closing and give cogent reasons for this. To deny or ignore this, when in a matter of months it will be a reality, will only shatter our credibility. Second, we have to announce that we have a purchaser for the Foundation's property, and that the purchase will alleviate concerns about job losses when the Sanatorium closes."

"Shouldn't you also say that we want to expand the existing laboratories, probably at another site?" Tom asked.

"Good point," Brandon replied, and made a note of it before continuing. "And finally—and this is probably the most contentious point—we have to explain how this investigation got started."

"Do we have to raise your third point?" Tom asked.

"If our response consists only of the first two points, people will wonder why the Committee picked on the Trudeau Foundation. We must be totally open and candid," Warner argued.

"We can discuss this some more, Brandon," Todd interjected, "but since our aim in responding to Bradley is to placate the village, I see no need to raise your third point. If Bradley or his reporters ask questions about how Trudeau came to be investigated, we'll leave it to Brandon and Hal to respond." No one disagreed.

Janet came out to announce that a buffet lunch would soon be ready. "Would you rather fill your plates and eat around the dining room table or come back out and put your plates on your laps?" Unanimously, they opted to eat inside.

On the way into lunch, Hungerford put his arm around Warner. "Don't worry, Brandon, if Bradley does ask how the investigation got started, nothing you say can put the noose around my neck. I've done that already."

They ate quietly for a few minutes, then Tom Steele spoke. "At the risk of spoiling Hal's appetite, I'd like to bring up our hearing before the Committee." No one objected. "As many of you know, I'm a Republican and a staunch anti-communist, but having observed firsthand how the FBI and the Committee go to extremes in their hunt for Communists, destroying lives and disrupting organizations, I have concluded they do more harm to our way of life than the Communist Party of the United States."

"Janet Warner's food is so good that mah appetite remains

intact despite your intrusion, Tom, but I hope my response will not spoil yours." His look at Tom indicated he was seeking approval to proceed. Tom nodded. "I admit to having discussed these matters with a lawyer versed in the Constitution, something y'all should consider, so I don't claim to be original. Lemme pretend to be K. Reginald Palmer and ask Tom, 'Are you now or have you ever been a member of the Communist Party?' What would your response be?"

"No!" Tom replied emphatically.

"Okay. So now Mr. Palmer asks, 'Have you ever known any Communists?'"

"No again!"

"'Well,' says Mr. Palmer to you in front of the world, 'we have reliable evidence, Mr. Steele, that your wife consorted with an avowed Communist—'"

"I'd tell him it was none of his fucking business," Tom shouted, throwing his napkin on his plate and walking out of the room. The others put their forks down.

"You touched a nerve, Hal," Janet said in a low voice.

"Should I go apologize?" Before anyone could answer, Tom returned, picked up his napkin, and sat back in his seat. "I'm sorry to have lost my temper. Your question cut close to home."

"I understand, Tom, but Ahh wanted to be brutal to show how the Committee has us by the balls. Oh, sorry Janet. No disrespect."

"I've heard worse," she replied.

"You surely don't want to reply the way you just did, Tom. A remark like that would clearly show you held the Committee in contempt, sufficient grounds for sending you to prison if Congress concurred. But even a calm answer could incarcerate you. If you let Mr. Palmer finish his question, asking 'Was your wife a Communist, Dr. Steele?' and you said 'No,' Mr. Palmer or his chief interrogator is likely to reply, 'So-and-so says she was.' Then you could have a costly perjury trial on your hands, like Alger Hiss."

"And if I replied, 'Yes, she might have been before we were married,' then Mr. Palmer could ask who her friends were, and if they were Communists, too."

"Exactly," Hungerford continued, "And if you refused to tell him, you could also be held in contempt. You'd have to worry that someone would contradict you." He stopped to chew a mouthful of food. "The only way you could avoid legal proceedings is to refuse to answer any—underline any—questions about your beliefs. In 1950, the Supreme Court ruled that unwillingness to admit Communist Party membership was adequate grounds for invoking the Fifth Amendment."

"But isn't that tantamount to Tom admitting his guilt?" Fred Todd asked. "The amendment says something like 'you should not be compelled to bear witness against yourself.'"

"Look at the scenario that Tom and I just played out, Fred. No matter what Tom answers, unless he takes the Fifth he can't be sure that the Committee won't dig up another witness who will contradict him. Then it gets back to a perjury trial."

"So taking the Fifth protects you from the Committee citing you, but it doesn't remove the suspicion of guilt. If you were employed in Hollywood, it would probably cost you your job," Janet interjected.

"That's not the case here at Trudeau," Fred reminded them.

"There might be a way to avoid the presumption of guilt, my learned lawyer told me. You could refuse to answer questions about political affiliations, your own or others, because the First Amendment forbids Congress from abridging your free speech. In 1951, the Supreme Court rejected the argument of the leaders of the Communist Party that their advocacy for a socialist type of government did not present a 'clear and present danger' and was protected under the First Amendment. That sent them to jail. Whether mere members of the party, or alleged members, are protected by the First Amendment for refusing to say whether they were or are members has not been adjudicated."

"Thank you, Hal, for that discourse," Fred announced. "Let me remind you that our focus is on protecting the Foundation, not protecting us as individuals. The Foundation will retain counsel to represent its best interests, but you will have to look elsewhere to obtain private counsel." There was general nodding around the table. Fred turned to Janet, "Shall we have dessert on the porch? The sun's out strong and there's hardly any breeze."

Hal Hungerford got up before any of the others and took Janet's hand in his. "If you'll excuse me, Janet, I was going to hike up Ampersand Mountain this afternoon and I'm afraid your dessert will slow me down. So with no disrespect, I'll excuse myself." He said goodbye to the others and headed back to his cottage.

———◆———

The following Monday morning, Warner drove down to the village to hand the Foundation's response in at *The Adirondack Daily Eagle*'s office. Bradley called that afternoon to say that he and some of his staff would like to question Warner about it, as they had agreed. At four o'clock the next day, Warner, Hungerford, and Steele appeared at *The Eagle*'s entrance, an unprepossessing storefront on Broadway in downtown Saranac Lake. The reek of burnt tobacco hit them as soon as they entered through the thin haze that permeated the office. Warner introduced his two colleagues. "I hope you don't mind my bringing along the directors of our two laboratories. They may be able to answer questions I can't."

Bradley nodded pleasantly, introducing the two reporters who accompanied him. Both stubbed out their cigarettes, placing the butts in an enormous ashtray already filled to overflowing. They settled around the ancient oak conference table in Bradley's office; both table and office were about eighty years old. "Well, Brandon, you've pretty well demolished my notion that a communist plot is what's causing the ruin of the Sanatorium, and *The Eagle* is pleased to learn about the impending sale of the property to the Corporate Managers of America. You sure kept that secret."

"Can you tell us a little more about the sale?" one of the reporters asked as he lit up a cigarette.

"Before you do," interjected Bradley, "let me remind you that unless you go off the record, anything you say may be mentioned in our story that accompanies your statement."

"Thank you, Ted, I am speaking here for the record." Brandon turned to the reporter. "Yes. The sale documents will be signed early in 1954. CMA estimates that they will begin renovations in 1955 and should be able to open their offices here in 1956."

"Do you know how many jobs CMA will provide?" the second reporter asked.

"You'll have to ask their executive director, but starting in 1955 there should be construction jobs for the renovation and hiring for longer-term jobs."

"What will you do with the proceeds of the sale?" Bradley asked.

"Although I am not at liberty to give you the price of the sale—"

"I assumed that was the case. That's why I didn't ask." He snipped off the end of a new cigar.

"—I can explain the distribution of the proceeds. First, we will be providing handsome severance pay for every employee of Trudeau, affording them several months in which to find new jobs. Next, we will pay off our creditors, but fortunately we are not heavily in debt due to prudent cutbacks as our census decreased. That still leaves the bulk of the revenue. Our Board, ably chaired by Dr. Fred Todd, has been discussing this ever since the closure of the Sanatorium appeared on the horizon. The Board sees the sale as an opportunity to expand the scientific work of both the Trudeau and Saranac Laboratories. We have begun to look into property along Lower Saranac Lake, which may be available as gift or purchase, to house the new Trudeau Institute. The sale of the Sanatorium will be of enormous help but, frankly, it will not be sufficient to build the new institute, equip it with up-to-date instruments and supplies needed for research, and hire a top-notch staff. We've begun by recruiting Dr. Hungerford," he nodded to Hal, who raised his hand halfway and smiled blandly, "who has been deputy director of the National Microbiological Institute.

"The construction of the new institute will, of course, provide jobs, and many more will be offered once the institute opens. The scientific staff will be significantly increased, and that means more construction to house them. We are planning to replace the traditional curricula for physicians and nurses with courses to train research technicians drawn from the local communities, which Tom will direct. So while I cannot say that we will employ as many people as the Sanatorium, we will continue to employ a large number. Plus, there'll be CMA's recruitment." Both reporters scribbled away as Brandon spoke, unlit cigarettes dangling from their lips.

"Well, that should provide further reassurance to the public that Saranac Lake will not be drained when the Sanatorium closes," Bradley noted. He lit his cigar and then added, "There is still one matter raised by the House Committee that you did not deal with in your article, Brandon. And that is a communist plot on the grounds of the Sanatorium."

Tom turned to Warner. "I guess you were right, Brandon."

Bradley smiled, "Do I hear some dissension in the ranks? We'd like to hear both sides." He puffed on his cigar.

"Some of us thought the points we just made would lay 'the communist plot' to rest, but now that you've raised it, we have to address it. There really is no disagreement." Brandon looked at Tom and Hal, who both nodded.

"Actually," Hal interceded, "it was I who brought the Trudeau Sanatorium to the FBI's attention." He repeated what he told his colleagues that Saturday.

Warner continued when Hal finished. "I wrote the FBI that we could find no evidence that Bethune was a Communist when he was a patient at the Sanatorium, and that careful analysis does not indicate any communist sympathy in the murals he drew when he was a patient here."

Ted Bradley thanked the Trudeau representatives for their candid responses. "I have only one more question, unless my colleagues have others." They shook their heads. "Can you shed any light on why two former members of the Trudeau community were subpoenaed?"

"No, I can't," Warner replied. "In fact, I invited Mr. Anderson to participate in our preparation for this meeting. He declined. I would have extended a similar invitation to Dr. Springer but I could not reach him."

Bradley, followed by his reporters, stood. "Well, that does it. Your statement will appear in Thursday's edition together with our commentary. Good afternoon, gentlemen." The Trudeau contingent was relieved to step into the fresh air.

Warner's statement appeared in Thursday's paper. The accompanying story reported information on the Trudeau Foundation's plans to preserve and enlarge its role in assuring the continued well-being of Saranac Lake and surrounding communities. In a brief editorial, the editor thanked the Foundation for explaining the closure of the Sanatorium to *The Eagle*. "It will be up to the House Un-American Activities Committee to make good its charge, but after speaking with the leaders of the Trudeau Foundation, we see no basis for a communist plot." *The Eagle* did not mention the murals.

Chapter 14

Immediately after subpoenaing the murals, Raymond Conn, the chief investigator of the House Un-American Activities Committee, personally called Brandon. In addition to bringing the murals to the hearing, Conn politely requested that he have full-color photographs of them taken and sent to the Committee as quickly as possible. Warner complied.

Conn asked his staff to hunt around for a prominent art historian with impeccable credentials and an anti-communist bent. They came up with Vladimir Zloyev, professor of art and art history at Cornell University. Raised in Russia, Zloyev's family went into exile soon after the 1917 October Revolution. After studying art in France and England—and speaking French and English fluently, albeit with a Russian accent—he and his wife, also a Russian exile, came to the United States in 1940. Before emigrating, he had written diatribes about the works of the Mexican leftist artists, Diego Rivera and David Siqueiros.

Together with the color photos that Warner supplied, Conn sent Zloyev a copy of the reverential biography of Norman Bethune, *The Scalpel, the Sword*, telling him that the Committee wanted his honest opinion on whether Bethune's murals showed any inclination toward communist values that the artist might have held at the time he drew them.

Hungerford and Steele piled into the Warners' station wagon on Saturday morning, October 24. Driving most of the way down U.S. 9, they did not arrive in Manhattan until early evening. They met Fred Todd for dinner. He had arranged lodgings for them, as well as parking for Brandon's station wagon in New York while they were in Washington. On Sunday, they boarded the Pennsylvania Railroad's *The Senator*. In addition to the one valise that each of them carried, Warner grappled with the long tube containing the murals. They placed their luggage in the rack above their plush seats and tried to relax during the five-hour trip to the nation's capital. While they were waiting their turn for a cab outside the cavernous Union Station, Hal Hungerford asked Brandon what he had done with the murals. Warner looked at the luggage at their feet. The tube was missing. "Oh my god! I left it on the train. Watch my bags, Hal, I've got to retrieve it." He dashed off.

"I don't believe I've ever seen Brandon run so fast," Hal chuckled. "For the shape the murals are in, we might be better off if some cleaning attendant tossed them in the trash. Ahh don't think anybody would profit from stealing them."

A half-hour later, Brandon returned without the tube. "They wouldn't let me on the train, but the conductor recognized me and went to fetch the tube. He couldn't find it but suggested I go to the Lost and Found. I saw the tube there on a shelf. I had to fill out forms, you know, my name, where I lost it, what was in it. It still had the address label with Tom's name on it. I tried to explain that we were traveling together, but that wasn't good enough. Come on Tom, I'll lead you to the Lost and Found and maybe they'll return the tube to you." Hal and Fred minded their luggage.

When they returned with the tube, Hal asked, "Did you check the contents?"

Brandon and Tom looked at each other. "No, we didn't," Brandon replied.

"I think you'd better check it before you hand it over to the Committee. It'd be embarrassing if they opened it up and found nothing in it, or maybe that poster of Jane Russell half-naked in *The Outlaw*."

———◆———

The next morning, the Trudeau contingent arrived at the Old House Office Building off Independence Avenue fifteen minutes before the scheduled time. They were stunned by the enormous Caucus Room, where the hearing was to be held, with its paired Corinthian pilasters spaced along the walls and four elaborate crystal chandeliers suspended from the classically decorated ceiling. A few minutes later, Arnold Springer and Roger Anderson walked in. Fred Todd went over to greet them. Both looked grim and barely shook hands with him. They took seats on the other side of the room from Fred, Brandon, Hal, and Tom. Soon after, the chairman, K. Reginald Palmer, and several Committee members entered the front of the hearing room through a wooden double door with a Greek pediment and took their seats on the long dais. The spacious room was almost full when Chairman Palmer banged his gavel.

Dr. Todd was called first. In a well-tailored gray flannel suit, with a subdued foulard tied in a neat four-in-hand, his lanky six-foot-six frame towering over the clerk as he was sworn in, he cut an imposing figure. For generations, Todd's family had been among the elite of New York society. His uncle had served with distinction in the Republican administration of

Herbert Hoover. Chairman Palmer greeted him effusively, saving his chief investigator the time of asking for his professional credentials. "Dr. Todd," Palmer told the Committee and the audience, "we are honored to have you with us today. In addition to being the chairman of the Board of the Trudeau Foundation and Sanatorium, Dr. Todd is the head of the Pulmonary Diseases Division at Bellevue Hospital and professor of medicine at Cornell Medical College. Dr. Todd, I hope you can assure us that Communists have not infiltrated the staff of Trudeau, one of America's leading clinical and research institutions, or, if they have, that you will root them out."

"Thank you for that gracious and kind introduction, Chairman Palmer." Then Todd read from his prepared statement. "I have been informed by Dr. Warner, the executive director of the Trudeau Foundation and Sanatorium, that the Committee is interested in a piece of art drawn by a patient at the Sanatorium in 1927. I had hoped to procure a large poster of another piece of art, painted at the end of the nineteenth century, but was unable to find a suitable reproduction. You are, I am sure, familiar with it as it was the centerpiece of a campaign a few years ago by the American Medical Association, of which I am a member. The painting, *The Doctor*, by Sir Luke Fildes, shows a pensive doctor sitting by the bedside of a sick child, whose worried father stands in the background. The caption added by the AMA read, 'Keep politics out of this picture.' What the AMA meant was to keep universal health coverage—what the AMA called socialized medicine—out of medicine. Now, I have not been called here today to argue for or against universal health coverage. The message I wish to convey to the Committee is, to paraphrase the AMA's slogan, 'Keep politics out of American medicine.'

"On graduating from medical school, every physician must take an ancient oath that says in part: 'Into whatsoever houses I enter, I will enter to help the sick, and I will abstain from all intentional wrong-doing and harm …' In other words, our loyalty is to our patients.

"Now, there are other occupations in which loyalty to our government is essential to fulfill one's job, but medicine is not one of them. The Hippocratic oath does not call for such loyalty, and the Trudeau Foundation does not demand it of its physicians and scientists.

"I know it is not fashionable today to quote the words of President Truman in his successful campaign for the presidency in 1948, but he invoked the key word in your Committee's name: 'Is it un-American,' President Truman asked, 'Is it un-American to visit the sick, aid the afflicted or comfort the dying? I thought that was simple Christianity.'

"It is my fervent belief that it is un-American for this Committee to interfere with the mission of the Trudeau Foundation—which, to use President Truman's words, is 'to visit the sick, aid the afflicted or comfort the dying,' and to conduct research and provide teaching to improve the prevention and treatment of tuberculosis and other diseases of the lung. Dr. Warner has bent over backwards to satisfy the investigation by the FBI. If you must look for Communists, please do not look among us. Our goals are clear, and if we feel that an employee's conduct overtly interferes with his or her professional work, we will take action. An employee's personal beliefs, by themselves, do not constitute a cause for such action."

Chairman Palmer did not address Dr. Todd as effusively when he finished as when he had started. He simply said, "Thank you."

Next, Brandon Warner was sworn in and his identity established. In his response to questioning by Chief Investigator Conn, Warner summarized his effort to find out if Communists had infiltrated the Trudeau, beginning with Norman Bethune in 1927 and concluding with a history of Bethune's murals and Bethune's article in *The Fluoroscope*, which he submitted as evidence. "I am now willing to state without doubt," he concluded, "that the murals provide no evidence that Bethune was a Communist when he drew them."

"And what about today?" Conn asked. "Are there Communists at Trudeau?"

"Not to my knowledge."

"Dr. Warner, are you now or have you ever been a member of the Communist Party of the United States or any other communist organization?"

"No, I have never been a member of any such organization." Hal Hungerford stirred uneasily in his seat. He had warned Brandon of the consequences of answering the way he did, and he was sure, too, that Janet had advised her husband to take the Fifth Amendment.

"Have you ever known any Communists?"

"I don't know, I may have."

"Do you know Dr. Harold Hungerford?"

"Yes, of course, he is the director of Trudeau's Saranac Laboratory."

"Do you have any reason to believe he is a Communist?"

"I told you I could find no evidence of Communists at Trudeau."

"Are you aware, Dr. Warner, that Dr. Hungerford has refused to swear his loyalty to the United States?"

"I am." He paused before finishing. "That doesn't make

him a Communist."

"That is your opinion, Dr. Warner." Conn paused to drink some water. "What if, Dr. Warner, I confronted you with evidence that you had been a member of the Communist Party?"

Brandon turned pale, his stomach turned over, and he took a few moments to answer. "I would say it was a fabrication."

"Thank you, Dr. Warner, you may step down."

Chairman Palmer called a recess so the murals could be hung in their proper sequence between the pilasters on the side wall opposite the windows. After ten minutes, he reopened the hearings, calling Vladimir Zloyev to testify. A tall, gaunt man with black hair slicked back across his head without a part stepped forward, immaculately dressed in a blue serge suit with a white handkerchief protruding from his suit jacket's breast pocket. As he took a seat at the witness table, Zloyev flicked a tiny bit of lint from the shoulder of his suit jacket. He repeated this several times during his testimony. After stating his name and swearing to tell the truth, his testimony proceeded as follows:

Conn: Please state your occupation.

Zloyev: I am professor of art and art history at Cornell University, Ithaca, N.Y.

Conn: Professor Zloyev, what is your nationality by birth?

Zloyev: I was born in Russia in 1910.

Conn: Are you a United States citizen?

Zloyev: I was naturalized in 1950.

Conn: Are you now or have you ever been a member of the Communist Party of any country?

Zloyev: Why should I be a Communist? For generations, my family—you would call us lesser nobility—owned vast farm acreages outside Moscow, all confiscated in 1917 when we had to flee for our lives. No, I have never been a Communist.

Conn: Do you think that you could evaluate art by a Communist objectively?

Zloyev: Art historians by training must set aside any political or religious bias when they are asked to evaluate works of art.

Conn: Are you acquainted with Norman Bethune?

Zloyev: He's dead, isn't he? [Laughter]

Conn: I meant, are you familiar with his name?

Zloyev: I wasn't until you gave me a book, *The Scalpel, the Sword*, a biography. [He raises the book from the witness table.] He admitted he was a red in 1937.

Conn: A red?

Zloyev: A member of the Communist Party of Canada.

Conn: Professor Zloyev, have you seen the murals painted by Norman Bethune when he was a patient at the Trudeau Sanatorium in 1927?

Zloyev: The Committee provided color photographs of the murals about ten days ago. Not until just now have I seen the actual murals.

Conn: As an expert in the field, what do you think of them?

Zloyev: They are a mess. [Laughter]

Conn: Can you elaborate? You can leave your chair and go to the display.

Zloyev [with pointer in hand, going to the display]: Well, you can see gigantic tears in the first mural. Someone, maybe an angel, is reading from a scroll, only the first word of which, "Norman," is legible. The other murals are in better shape, although an "L" and part of a "Y" are missing from "Hollywood" in the fifth mural. [He points.] The chalk is faded, rubbed off in some places, and the murals show creases from where they have been folded. The face of the angel in the last mural is fuzzy. The verses that Bethune wrote on the bottom of most of them are not entirely legible. In general, the murals have not been well preserved. But having said all that, I have to admit that Norman Bethune could draw. His figures are well proportioned and show real character. What's left of the murals shows a masterful use of color with chalk crayon.

Conn: Do you think Bethune was a Communist when he drew the murals in 1927?

Zloyev [resumes his seat]: Of that, there can be no doubt. He definitely was. [Murmurs throughout the hearing room]

Chairman Palmer: Quiet please. We must have order.

Conn: Please elaborate, Professor.

Zloyev: It's clear from his biography that Norman Bethune was a rebel from childhood, resisting his father's authoritarian mien. And as a young man in World War I, he adopted the same anti-war attitude as the Marxist-Leninists, according to his biographers. In a letter to a friend he wrote, "The slaughter has begun to appall me. I've begun to question whether it was worth it." He came back from the war "wondering whether something lay behind the slaughter and wreckage." Doubting the motives of the Western democracies was clearly subversive. His biographers say that in the mid-1920s, before contracting tuberculosis, he was depressed by "the shabby flats, the unpaid bills, the senseless all-pervading sickness of the boom city of fat America"—he was practicing in Detroit at the time. "This isn't medicine," he would say to his wife, Frances, "It's like putting a mustard plaster on a wooden leg ... A job at twenty dollars a week would have done more for the father of a baby I delivered in an abandoned boxcar than all the wonders that could now be performed for his doomed child." He was angry at his own profession and how it measured success. "When I saved a man's life for nothing I was a failure," Bethune wrote. "Now when I give a simple tonic where a good bracing set of exercises would do just as well, I collect a fantastic fee and am a success." So you see, members of the Committee, Bethune is already challenging the fee-for-service basis of modern medicine. In the 1930s, he openly embraced socialized medicine but he was already preaching it in the 1920s before he drew the murals.

As to the murals themselves, his biographers called them "allegories." Now in my English dictionary, definitions of allegory include "a picture with a hidden meaning." On their face, the murals are about Dr. Bethune's fight against tuberculosis from birth to death. But what is the hidden meaning? [With pointer in hand, he returns to the murals.] Let me show you. Here in the third mural, the adolescent Bethune sets sail in search of fame, wealth, love, and art, the goals of youth in the free world represented by voluptuous, naked maidens pointing the way to the "Castle of Heart's Desire." But as he sails toward the castle he is attacked by swarms of T.B. bats. [He lays the pointer down.]

Now let me pause here to point out, members of the Committee, that these are allegorical T.B. bats. They are, gentlemen, the Communist's perception of the evils of capitalism, wreaking disease and death on exploited workers and peasants. What could be more communistic? [He picks up the pointer.] I quote Bethune's words, "His course is changed, his bark a wreck." Bethune falls in the fourth panel into the "Abyss of Despair" [points to it] and in the fifth [points to it] looks back to see that the "Castle of Heart's Desire" is nothing but a Hollywood set; fame, wealth, love, if not art, are mirages in the capitalist world. He finds momentary respite in the Trudeau Sanatorium, on whose grounds he has drawn the house of Dr. Harold Hungerford [points to it in the sixth panel], a fellow traveler of Dr. Bethune, before returning to the "canyons of the city." Once again capitalism attacks—a gigantic T.B. bat—and the people, the common people, are reduced to ants crowding a large thoroughfare that divides the city.

So, in conclusion, the Bethune murals are an allegory for the evils of capitalism. What could be more communistic?

Chairman Palmer: Thank you for that most illuminating testimony, Professor Zloyev. I see that Congressman Brewster has a comment.

Mr. Brewster (Democrat): Professor Zloyev, wouldn't it be unusual for a Communist to use angels to depict enlightenment?

Zloyev: A Communist will stoop to anything, Congressman, to make his point. In this case, I think Bethune was haunted by his parents, both strict Presbyterians, whom he never renounced. To Norman Bethune, communism was the light of the future in this world or the next. Why not represent it by angels?

———◆———

Harold Hungerford was called next. His slow, deep southern drawl surprised the members of the Committee and many in the audience. They seemed to relax after the tension introduced by the last two witnesses. Conn established that Hungerford had resigned his post as deputy director of the National Institute of Microbiology and had recently returned to Saranac Lake as director of the Saranac Laboratory. Chairman Palmer interrupted Conn to ask a question of his own.

Chairman Palmer: Professor Zloyev just pointed out that in Bethune's mural of the Trudeau Sanatorium, your house is shown just outside the gates of the Sanatorium. I thought you were a cottage mate of Bethune's?

Hungerford: I was. Just as the tombstones in the last panel, and the "free gas" filling station where you could get artificial pneumothorax, were figments of Beth's—uhh, Bethune's—imagination, so too was my house. I was already working in the Trudeau Laboratory in 1927 and Bethune imagined that I would settle down and live in Saranac Lake, outside the Sanatorium.

Chairman Palmer: Where did Professor Zloyev get the idea that you and Bethune were fellow travelers—that is, co-communist conspirators?

Hungerford: You'd have to ask Professor Zloyev. I read the same biography of Bethune as he did and my name didn't appear even once. [He chuckles.] As a matter of fact, Ahh was a little offended that the authors didn't mention me. Bethune and I remained friends after we first met at the Sanatorium. Maybe someone [witness glances at Conn] put words in the professor's mouth.

Conn: So you admit to being a friend of Bethune's?

Hungerford: I never denied it.

Conn: Were you and Bethune Communists in 1927?

Hungerford: I didn't even know what a Communist was in 1927, and I don't think Bethune did either.

Conn: You're not answering the question.

Hungerford: I thought I was. [Laughter]

Conn [showing a sheet of paper to the witness]: Do you recognize this paper?

Hungerford: Yes, it's an oath I refused to sign because it was not germane—

Conn: We are not interested in your reasons, Dr. Hungerford, we just want you to acknowledge that you did not sign the required loyalty oath when you were a deputy director at NIH.

Hungerford: I readily admit that I did not sign it, but with good reason.

Conn: And as I already said, we are not interested in your reasons. Let me ask you one more question. Are you now or have you ever been a member of the Communist Party of the United States or any other country?"

Hungerford: I refuse to answer.

Conn: On what grounds?

Hungerford: On the grounds that my personal beliefs are none of the government's business. That is also why I refused to sign the so-called loyalty oath.

Chairman Palmer [intervening]: Then you are not refusing to answer on the basis of the Fifth Amendment, which the Supreme Court has recognized as your constitutional right.

Hungerford: No, I base my refusal on the First Amendment, which forbids Congress to make any law abridging the freedom of speech. By raising a communist specter, the Committee is telling people it's not safe to express their beliefs; they might lose their livelihood, as has happened in Hollywood. Through this Committee, the Congress is abridging freedom of speech.

Chairman Palmer: You may leave the Committee with no choice but to cite you for contempt of Congress.

Hungerford: I've been warned of that before and, as I just said, Ahh do hold the Congress in contempt if it allows this witch hunt to continue.

Chairman Palmer: The witness may step down. The hearing is adjourned until two o'clock.

———

After lunch, Tom Steele was called to the witness table. Standing next to the tall, obese Conn, Tom looked short and compact as he was sworn in. Of all the Trudeau witnesses that Conn and FBI Agent Crane discussed in preparing for the hearing, Steele was the most problematic, although Warner's refusal to take the Fifth took them by surprise. Crane had thoroughly briefed Conn on Steele, using his recollection of the photographs on Steele's desk to describe his family. He told Conn that he had no doubt that Steele was a loyal American who boasted of being a Republican, but that he might have been shielding his recently deceased wife, whom Bethune could have recruited into the party when she helped care for him in 1927.

Standing in front of the witness chair, Steele took the oath and identified himself. Conn expressed condolences on the recent death of his wife. He then asked Tom to describe his responsibilities at Trudeau. The hearing proceeded as follows:

Conn: For how many years have you been associated with Trudeau, Dr. Steele?

Steele: Since 1927, twenty-six years.

Conn: Do you think Communists have ever disrupted the work at Trudeau?

Steele [not answering immediately]: You mean like organizing the workers to go on strike for higher wages or better working conditions?

Conn: Yes, those are good examples. Would you have condoned strikes for them, Dr. Steele?

Steele: If they disrupted or compromised patient care, definitely not!

Conn: During your many years at Trudeau, did you ever

suspect anyone there to be a Communist, Dr. Steele?

Steele: No.

Conn: Not your wife, Emily?

Steele [taken aback]: No, certainly not.

Conn: I noticed, Tom, that you have not corrected me when I have addressed you as "Doctor Steele."

Steele: I'm sorry, I should have.

Conn: Can you tell the Committee why?

Steele: Because I do not have an advanced degree. [Murmuring in the audience]

Conn: You mean a doctorate. [Steele nods.] Please, can you speak up?

Steele: I don't have either an M.D. or Ph.D. degree.

Conn: Then why are you masquerading as a doctor?

Steele [angrily]: I am not masquerading. Because of my accomplishments, many people call me "doctor." I usually don't bother to correct them. Maybe I should. I don't refer to myself as "doctor."

Conn: You are responsible for diagnosing patients, are you not, Mr. Steele?

Steele: My laboratory establishes the type of tubercle bacillus a patient has and whether it will respond to streptomycin or other drugs. I report that information to the physician who is caring for the patient. He, not I, decides how to manage the patient.

Conn: But if your lab makes a mistake—says the patient will respond when in fact he won't—the doctor has no way of knowing.

Steele: Until the patient doesn't respond, that is correct.

Conn: And we have only your word that you can ensure that your laboratory doesn't make mistakes.

Steele [angrily, his voice rising]: Mr. Conn, I have developed many of the bacterial culture techniques we use at the Trudeau Laboratory, published them, and seen them adopted elsewhere. I daresay I have more hands-on experience than most laboratory directors with Ph.D. or M.D. degrees.

Conn: Very well, Tom. Let me return to your wife. What was your wife's maiden name?

Steele: Jenkins, Emily Jenkins.

Conn: When did you meet her?

Steele: When I applied for a job at the Trudeau Laboratory in the summer of 1927.

Conn: The same year that Dr. Norman Bethune was a patient at the Sanatorium.

Steele: Yes.

Conn: How can you be certain that Bethune was a patient in 1927?

Steele [barely audible]: Because Emily stopped dating me in November of that year. I suspected she was dating Bethune. A few months after he was discharged, we started dating again and remained together until [witness takes handkerchief from pocket, blows his nose, wipes his eyes]—

Conn: Emily died?

Steele [barely audible]: Yes.

Conn: Did Emily ever tell you she had dated Bethune?

Steele [barely audible]: Yes.

Conn: You'll have to speak up, Tom. When did she first tell you?

Steele: Last March.

Conn: In March of 1953, twenty-six years after she dated Bethune?

Steele [softly]: That is correct.

Conn: Why then?

Steele: I explained this to Agent Crane in July. Must I repeat it?

Conn: For the record, please.

Mr. Brewster [member of the Committee]: Mr. Chairman, we seem to be veering into highly personal matters and the witness is plainly uncomfortable. Can we dispense with this line of questioning?

Conn: If the Congressman from Massachusetts will be patient, we will show that Mr. Steele's testimony on these points is highly germane to the purpose of this hearing.

Chairman Palmer: Let's see where this is going, Chuck. Please answer the question, Mr. Steele.

Steele: Emily had learned earlier this year that the murals Bethune drew were being returned to the Trudeau. She feared my jealousy would turn to rage when I saw the mural and recognized her as Bethune's Angel of Death. Hoping to soothe my anger, she told me that she had been his model before I discovered it myself.

Conn: Did you fly into a rage when she told you?

Steele: Yes. We were out walking and I pushed her so she almost fell. [Witness sobs.]

Conn [loudly]: Is that all you did to her? [Witness continues to sob. Growing noise in hearing room.]

Chairman Palmer: We will have a ten-minute recess to allow the witness to collect himself.

Sitting among the observers, Larry Crane was one of the first to stand when Palmer declared the recess. He walked over to Conn and the two conferred for less than a minute. Conn picked up *The Fluoroscope* article from the exhibit table and the two of them walked over to the murals, stopping in front of the Angel of Death.

During the break, Fred Todd put his arm around Tom and offered him a glass of water. When the hearing continued, Tom Steele slumped in the witness chair, emphasizing his short stature. His complexion ashen, his hands tremulous, his tie loosened and his jacket unbuttoned, he appeared older than when he had begun to testify.

Conn: Mr. Steele, I withdraw my last question. I took advantage of Chairman Palmer's recess to compare the photograph of the ninth mural containing the Angel of Death in the reprint submitted by Dr. Warner, which I had not seen before, to the original mural hanging on the wall of this spacious caucus room. [Opening the reprint to the page that showed the last mural, he hands it to the witness.] Tom, would you be good enough to walk to the last mural and tell us how it compares to the photograph taken in 1932?

Steele [steadily]: I don't have to. In the photograph, the face of the Angel of Death is clearly recognizable as that of Emily Jenkins, even to a birthmark on her left cheek. In the actual mural, Emily's—I mean the angel's—face is smeared beyond recognition. [Loud murmurs in hearing room. Chairman bangs gavel. People crane their necks to examine the last mural on the wall.]

Conn: Do you have any idea how the face got smudged?

Steele [after a long pause, the room silent] I did it. [Hearing room erupts, chairman bangs gavel repeatedly]

Conn: Why?

Steele: I didn't want anyone to recognize Emily.

Conn [rapidly]: Why not?

Steele: Because I didn't want the woman I married to be recognized as a half-naked model posing for that Communist,

Bethune. Only God knows what else they did.

Conn: But all that was a quarter of a century before you smudged the mural. And in the interval you and Emily had a happy marriage, raising two handsome boys, and you reached the pinnacle of success as director of the Trudeau Laboratory without an M.D. or Ph.D. [Steele sobs.] May I suggest a more plausible explanation, Tom? The murals were returned to Saranac Lake to see if they provided evidence that Bethune was a Communist when he drew them. When Emily told you that she was the model for the angel in the mural, you realized she would be considered a Communist.

Steele: My wife was not a Communist before we were married, and not after.

Conn [rapidly]: Can you prove it? Did you ever talk politics with her?

Steele: No.

Conn [rapidly]: Why not?

Steele [angrily]: Emily's place was in the home. Raising our boys, cooking, cleaning house.

Conn [rapidly, close to the witness]: She was a registered nurse, was she not? She could think for herself.

Steele: That was before we married.

Conn: Did she ever talk about going back to nursing?

Steele [loudly]: I forbade it.

Conn [pauses]: No, Mr. Steele. Emily Jenkins, if not Mrs. Thomas Steele, was able to think. And when she served as a model for Norman Bethune, the communist thoughts they held in common helped him seduce her.

Steele [calmly, quietly, looking directly at Mr. Conn]: Mr. Conn, your hypothesis is more far-fetched than what I conveyed to you.

Conn: We disagree on that. [He looks at his notes.] I have only a few more questions for you, Tom. How long have you known Dr. Harold Hungerford?"

Steele: Since 1927, when we both worked in the laboratory. We became good friends.

Conn: So good that you recommended that Dr. Hungerford replace Dr. Springer as head of the Saranac Laboratory earlier this year?

Steele: Dr. Hungerford was eminently qualified for the job.

Conn: Even after he refused to sign a loyalty oath when he was in the federal government's employ?

Steele: You and your Committee may think that refusing to sign what you call an oath of loyalty to the United States Government is tantamount to being a Communist, but I don't. I told you before, I had no basis to believe that anyone on the Trudeau staff, then or now, was a Communist.

Conn: Mr. Steele, let me ask you one final question: Are you now or have you ever been a member of the Communist Party of the United States or any other communist or communist front organization?

Steele [sitting erect, hands flat on the table without the least tremor, color in his cheeks, speaking quietly]: "If you had asked me before, I might have answered differently. But now, Mr. Conn, Chairman Palmer, and members of the House Un-American Activities Committee [voice rising], I will simply reply [shouting], It's none of your damn business.

Conn told the chairman he had no further questions. The chairman announced an adjournment until the following morning. He asked all those who had been subpoenaed, whether they had testified or not, to return the next day.

The next morning *The Washington Post* carried a front-page story below the fold with the headline **House Committee Embarrasses Trudeau Scientist**. As a result, more than twice as many people as the Caucus Room could accommodate were in line when the doors opened. People were standing along the side walls and in the back of the room. Chairman Palmer banged his gavel a half-hour late.

The first witness was Dr. Arnold Springer, thirty-eight years of age. His black hair, pomaded and parted down the middle, drew attention from his rather ordinary face. His double-breasted suit made him look bigger than he really was. After the customary swearing in, Springer told Conn that his current employer was West Virginia University School of Medicine, where he was the Clearview Professor of Industrial Hygiene. As soon as Springer said this, Warner and Todd looked knowingly at each other. Clearview was the name of Roger Anderson's company. The proceedings were as follows:

Conn: Can you explain what your position entails?

Springer: In addition to teaching, I conduct research on workplace hazards, particularly inhaled dusts. Our goal is to help industries provide a safer workplace.

Conn: How long have you been at the West Virginia Medical School?

Springer: Two months.

Conn: Before that?

Springer: At the Trudeau Foundation as director of the Saranac Laboratory, doing the same sort of work I do now—except for the teaching. I had been there since I was honorably discharged from the U.S. Navy in 1945.

Conn: Why did you leave Trudeau?

Springer: I was forced to. [Murmurs in the hearing room]

Conn: Please explain.

Springer: Periodically, the Trudeau Foundation holds symposia of interest to physicians and others in the field of pulmonary diseases. The most recent symposium, the seventh, was held at the Saranac Laboratory in September 1952. As head of the laboratory, it was my responsibility to edit the papers and prepare them for publication, as had been done for the previous six symposia. As I read over these papers, I realized that their science did not merit publication.

Conn: On what basis?

Springer: Many of them were based on animal studies without offering a shred of evidence that humans had been harmed by dust inhalation to the extent the experimental animals had.

Conn: Did you share your concerns with Dr. Warner?

Springer: Yes, on several occasions, and he must have shared his concerns with Dr. Todd, the chairman of the Board of Trustees.

Conn: How do you know that?

Springer: Just before the Fourth of July holiday this year, Dr. Warner told me that if I didn't have papers for the Seventh Symposium ready for publication and on his desk on July 6, he would fire me under the authority vested in him by the Board.

Conn: Did you comply?

Springer: No, I did not. Instead of waiting to be fired, I quit. It was not a pleasant way to spend the holiday weekend, but quitting cleared my conscience.

Conn: So you think the entire Board knew what was going on?

Springer: You can ask Roger Anderson, he was a member

of the Board.

Conn [to Chairman Palmer]: Mr. Anderson is scheduled to testify next, Mr. Chairman.

[Turning back to the witness] Why do you think Dr. Warner and the Board were so eager to see the results published if they were without merit?

Springer: Mr. Anderson can answer that better than I, but I do believe that Dr. Warner and some members of the Board felt that the companies that had been contributing to Trudeau could not be trusted to act in the best interests of their workers. The papers that had been presented at the Seventh Symposium, several by scientists at Trudeau, were intent on stirring up the unions and their members by claiming that their workplaces were dangerous.

Conn: Why would they do that?

Springer]: Because there are Communists among them. [Enough murmuring for Chairman Palmer to gavel for order]

Conn: Can you name them?

Springer [pointing to Dr. Warner]: He is, or at least he was.

Conn: How do you know?

Springer: At the beginning of 1940, after Europe had gone to war, I joined the Bethune Society at the University of Buffalo Medical School.

Conn: The Bethune Society, after Norman Bethune?

Springer: Yes. Bethune died in November 1939. After Stalin and Hitler signed their non-aggression pact in August of that year, the Communists reversed course and started a major effort to keep the United States out of the war. At Buffalo in 1940, they set up the Bethune Society to organize the medical students to oppose the war. At the time, I thought World War II was going to be a rerun of World War I and I didn't want to die for no particular cause. So I joined. One of the active organizers was Brandon Warner. [People crane to look at Warner vigorously shaking his head; murmuring in the gallery.]

Conn [after Chairman Palmer restores order]: Are you suggesting Brandon Warner was a member of the Communist Party of the United States?

Springer: If not the party, then its youth arm, the Young Communist League. [Warner draws attention by shouting "No" and shaking his head vigorously.]

Conn: How long did you remain a member of the Bethune Society?

Springer: It disbanded when Germany attacked the Soviet Union in June 1941.

Conn: Are you still a Communist?

Springer [smiling]: When I saw their duplicity—when, after the war, I saw them trying to undermine what we had won in the war, when this Committee exposed how they infiltrated Hollywood—I renounced the party and all it stood for. I am a patriotic American!

Conn: When you and Warner were both at the Trudeau Sanatorium after the war, did you ever talk about these matters?

Springer: Only once. He mentioned to me that he was trying to locate the murals that his hero, Bethune, had painted when he was a patient at Trudeau in 1927. He told me he was in contact with Dr. Hungerford who, he said, was a comrade of Bethune's when they were both patients here and knew the whereabouts of the murals.

Conn: Comrade?

Springer: Yes. Comrade is what Communists call fellow party members.

Warner [from the floor]: Lies, all lies! I insist on the right to reply.

Chairman Palmer: Dr. Warner, this is not a court of law. The hearing is to enlighten Congress on communist infiltration of the Trudeau Sanatorium and Laboratories. Dr. Springer's testimony before this Committee of the Congress, and yours, too, is privileged. If you wish to press charges of libel against Dr. Springer and he repeats his accusation without the protection of the Committee, you are free to do so. [Bangs gavel]

Conn: Were you aware of any other Communists at the Trudeau Sanatorium when you were there?

Springer: Not on the staff, but wives of staff members.

Conn: Will you share their names with us and tell us the basis for your suspicion?

Springer: Gladly. One was Janet Warner, Brandon Warner's wife. She asked my wife to sign a petition asking for clemency for the Rosenbergs after they were sentenced to death in 1951.

Dr. Warner from the witness table [shouting]: That doesn't make her a Communist.

Chairman Palmer [bangs gavel]: Dr. Warner. One more outburst and I will have you ejected from the hearing room.

Conn: And the other?

Springer. When Mrs. Warner asked my wife to sign, she showed her the petition. My wife saw the last person who signed it.

Conn: Who was it?

Springer: Emily Steele.

Conn: I have no further questions.

Chairman Palmer: The witness is dismissed, with kind thanks for his candid testimony. We will have a fifteen-minute recess.

"Ah, now we know who's behind this hearing," Hal

Hungerford commented to Fred Todd sitting to his left. "Springer and Anderson and the companies they represent." Hal turned to Brandon Warner, sitting to his right, and put his hand on Brandon's knee. "You've got yourself in a pretty kettle of fish, Brandon. You should have taken the Fifth."

"How Springer got so many lies packed into a few minutes is quite amazing," Brandon replied. "What can I do?" he asked helplessly.

Trudeau's lawyer, sitting behind Hal, Fred, and Brandon, tapped Todd on the shoulder. "You've got to move quickly, Dr. Todd. If the mining and manufacturing companies are out to slander Trudeau, you should make a statement after the hearing adjourns." He turned to Brandon. "You'd do well to refute Springer's charges as quickly as possible. Your own lawyer can advise you on a libel suit. If you can prove Springer's charges are false, I doubt he'll continue his attack."

———◆———

In questioning Roger Anderson, Raymond Conn asked the question suggested by Dr. Springer: "Was the Trudeau Board informed of Dr. Warner's threat to fire Dr. Springer?"

"At its meeting in February, the Board voted by one vote to have Springer publish the Seventh Symposium papers. I was in the minority. The chairman of the Board, Dr. Todd, took it on himself to authorize Springer's dismissal if he did not publish them."

"In other words," Conn concluded, "his firing was not sanctioned by the Board."

"That is correct," Anderson replied.

"I understand, Mr. Anderson, that you recently resigned from Trudeau's Board. If that is so, can you tell us why?"

Conn asked.

"Once again, at its September meeting, the Board revealed its communist tendencies," Anderson replied. "By a narrow vote, it agreed to replace Dr. Springer as director of the Saranac Laboratory with Dr. Harold Hungerford, whose testimony you heard yesterday. In alliance with his communist friends on the Board, Dr. Hungerford is intent on destroying the very companies that have been at the forefront of improving worker safety. As a representative of one of those companies, and as a loyal American who wants to keep research such as that done at the Saranac Laboratory out of the clutches of the government, I resigned in protest. I will not be associated with Communists."

With that, the hearing ended. Chairman Palmer announced that after a scheduled vote on the House floor, the Committee would convene in executive session to consider contempt of Congress charges against several witnesses. He banged his gavel, ending the public session.

"The press will probably stick around to see if the Committee announces contempt citations," Trudeau's lawyer advised. "That will give you an opportunity to reply to Springer and Anderson."

An hour later, the Committee concluded its executive session and Chairman Palmer announced that the Committee was citing Dr. Harold Hungerford, Dr. Brandon Warner, and Mr. Thomas Steele for contempt of Congress. "The hearings just concluded," the chairman said, "leave open the possibility that the Trudeau Sanatorium and Laboratories are infiltrated by Communists who pose a serious threat to America's leading role in medical research."

Reporters quickly left the Caucus Room and were met by

Todd and Warner, whose reactions they were eager to get. Hungerford and Steele chose not to participate. Standing head and shoulders above the crowd, Fred Todd began in his sonorous voice.

"Ladies and gentlemen of the press, you have just witnessed a shameful attempt to discredit the Trudeau Foundation and members of its staff. I never expected to experience the miscarriage of justice we have just observed in a Committee of the Congress of the United States. As Chairman Palmer reminded us, the House Committee is not a court of law. But indeed it functions as a kangaroo court, jumping over witnesses' right to confront their accusers, prejudicing the public against them.

"Let me respond to Dr. Springer's and Dr. Anderson's allegations. For many years, coal companies—and other companies whose workers have a higher occurrence of lung diseases than workers in other industries—have supported animal research at the Saranac Laboratory.

"The recent animal studies that Dr. Springer spoke about used lower doses of inhaled dusts, particularly asbestos, than earlier studies. Their findings, perhaps to the surprise of the companies involved in their manufacture, have the potential to be much costlier to the companies. They can only be performed in animals. Let me explain. Workers who may have only been exposed for a few years and then changed jobs while they were still healthy are often lost to follow-up. People who have casual exposure, such as children or spouses of asbestos workers, are not even suspected of suffering harm. Animals, on the other hand, can be exposed to varying levels of industrial dusts for varying times and followed until they die. At the Saranac Laboratory, beginning in the 1930s and 1940s under Dr. Leroy

Gardner, animal studies revealed that exposure to asbestos at low doses had harmful effects, including a rare cancer of the lining of the lung, called mesothelioma, after a long delay. These harmful effects have now been confirmed in humans exposed to relatively small amounts of asbestos. Even the general public, ubiquitously exposed to asbestos in insulation and other products, could be at risk of asbestos-related diseases. If so, the companies that mine and manufacture asbestos could be threatened by a host of lawsuits beyond workmen's compensation. Some of the companies that had supported research in the Saranac Laboratory threatened to withdraw support unless the findings of the animal studies were suppressed.

"Ladies and gentlemen, what Dr. Springer did not tell you was that on the same day that he unceremoniously quit his job, without prior notification, all of the papers from the Seventh Symposium and some papers of Dr. Leroy Gardner's, Dr. Springer's predecessor, disappeared without a trace."

"Are you suggesting," a reporter interrupted, "that Dr. Springer absconded with the papers?"

"That will be up to a court of law to decide," Todd replied. "The papers are the property of the Saranac Laboratory. The Board and its attorneys will have to determine how to pursue securing their return."

"Dr. Warner, what about Dr. Springer's allegations that you were, are, a Communist?" a reporter asked.

"And your wife," another shouted.

"As I said in my testimony," Warner began, "I have never been a member of the Communist Party or any communist front organization. I had never heard of Norman Bethune until this past January, when FBI Agent Larry Crane visited me at the Sanatorium. Consequently, I had never heard of Bethune when, as Dr. Springer alleges, I was active in a 'Bethune Society' at the University of Buffalo School of Medicine, from which I graduated in June 1940. If there was such a society at Buffalo, I was never a member. Finally, I did not know Dr. Springer until I met him at Saranac Lake years later. As to my wife, it is true that she circulated a petition asking for clemency for the Rosenbergs. In fact, I signed it, too. The petition did not maintain they were innocent. We both felt the death penalty was inhumane and they should not be executed. That does not make anyone who signed the petition a Communist."

"Springer said you told him that Hungerford was a 'comrade' of Bethune's."

"A complete fabrication," Warner answered.

Fred Todd stepped forward. "I'd like to reply to Mr. Anderson's comment that the Board did not give Dr. Warner the authority to fire Springer. Technically, Mr. Anderson is correct. Recall, however, that in discussing the mission of the Trudeau Foundation in my introductory testimony, I said that 'when we feel that an employee's conduct overtly interferes with his or her professional work, we will take action.' To that I added, 'An employee's personal beliefs do not, *by themselves*, constitute a cause for such action.' In my many years of association with the Trudeau Sanatorium and its laboratories, I have only once known of an employee whose personal beliefs interfered with his professional work. That was Dr. Arnold Springer, when he refused to publish the papers from the Seventh Symposium. As chairman of the Board, I authorized Dr. Warner to discharge Dr. Springer if he did not publish these papers only after the Board, as Mr. Anderson admitted, urged publication of the Seventh Symposium."

Chapter 15

On the train back to New York, Todd told Hungerford and Steele that he'd like to have dinner just with Brandon Warner.

"That's no problem," Hungerford said, throwing his arm around Tom's shoulder. "Tom and I, a widower and an old bachelor, will paint the town red." Tom smiled wanly. "Oops," Hungerford retracted, "Ahh didn't mean red."

At dinner alone with Brandon, Fred came right to the point. "I've got to call a Board meeting in November, Brandon. The business members, Chandler and Reilly among them, will not be happy with the Committee's closing statement that the Trudeau Foundation may be infiltrated by Communists. And only begrudgingly did they give their support to Hungerford as director. You may have earned some favor with them and the other business members by not taking the Fifth, but now you've got to deal with Springer's accusation that you were a Communist in 1939."

Brandon put down his fork and wiped his lips with his napkin. "I had nothing to hide, Fred. I thought answering the big question would boost my stature. I should have listened to Hal Hungerford, and my wife. She thought I should have refused to answer, too."

Seeming as though he had not heard Brandon, Todd continued.

"Without placating Chandler and Reilly, the liberals will lose control of the Board and I may have to resign. That's of little consequence to me personally or financially, but I think it will be the downfall of the Trudeau Foundation. It will have trouble attracting scientists and physicians. A conservative Board could even start its own witch hunt. I know your effort to find Communists in 1927 was well meaning, Brandon, but it set a dangerous precedent."

"How will you placate the Board?"

Fred took a minute before answering, not because he was uncertain of his answer, but because he had explored the options coming back from Washington and was embarrassed to state his decision. "I will have to ask for Hal Hungerford's and your resignation."

Warner laughed nervously. "I knew I'd leave once the sale to the Corporate Managers Association is complete; I guess it will just be a little sooner. Leaving will break Hal's heart. He was so looking forward to reforming the Saranac Lab and living up here. Hal told me that when his boss at NIH was about to fire him, he begged Hal not to be the sacrificial lamb. Hal didn't heed him." Brandon thought for a moment. "I guess that's what Hal and I are now—sacrificial lambs."

———————

News of the hearings reached Saranac Lake before Warner, Steele, and Hungerford returned. *The Adirondack Daily Eagle* sent a correspondent to cover them in Washington and he wired his stories to *The Eagle*, where Ted Bradley and one of his reporters quickly edited them so that the results of the first day appeared before the hearings of the second day had begun.

The morning light flooded into the Chandlers' breakfast room where Caroline Chandler had dutifully folded *The Eagle* to the left of her husband's place setting. She poured his coffee as he sat down and spread his napkin on his lap. He opened the paper, startled by the headline:

HUAC Attacks Trudeau Scientist

By the time he finished the article, his coffee was no longer steaming. Caroline had lingered over her toast and a second cup of coffee while her husband became more agitated as he read. "Disgraceful," he said to her, throwing the paper down in disgust.

"What do you mean, dear?"

"How the Un-American Activities Committee lit into Tom Steele and will likely cite him for contempt." She took the paper from her husband and quickly read the story.

"That dreadful Raymond Conn," Caroline commented, "forcing Tom to break down in public."

The morning after the hearings concluded, Caroline read the story before Archibald came down and knew he would be even angrier. "I told Fred Todd," he almost shouted, "that I suspected Brandon Warner was a Communist and now I think I was right." He continued to read and calmed down a bit.

After breakfast, Chandler called his broker and told him to sell his substantial holdings in asbestos mining and manufacturing companies. "Do it gradually, so we don't start a stampede; they'll lose their value in due time." Next, he called Walter Reilly, his fellow Trudeau Board member. Reilly had read *The Eagle* and had the same reaction. They were surprised that Ted Bradley had not published an editorial retracting his last one and congratulating the Committee for exposing the communist plot. Chandler asked Reilly, "What are we going to do to clean out this nest of commies?"

"You know, Archibald, with Anderson resigning, Fred

Todd and the other doctors have a strong majority. I don't think we can get the Board to do anything."

"I have two ideas, Walter. First, I think we have to appeal to the Trudeau family to intervene. It has a compelling interest in the Sanatorium and Foundation."

"But they have said repeatedly that they have delegated their authority to the Board," Reilly replied.

"But this is an extraordinary situation. Unprecedented."

"What's your other idea, Archibald?"

"That we get an editorial from Ted Bradley calling for the firing of Warner and Hungerford."

"What about Steele?"

"I know Tom and he's not a Communist."

Chandler and Reilly met with Bradley that afternoon. "Sorry, gentlemen," Bradley told them. "I share your concerns, but I'm not going to reverse my last editorial on the subject until I have a chance to talk with Fred Todd."

A few days later, the Trudeau family's attorney told Chandler that although the situation was unusual, "the family will not intervene before the Board responds to the Committee's concerns."

———◆———

As Todd expected, the business members of the Board, including Chandler and Reilly, expressed their anger at the next Board meeting on November 12. "What do you propose we do?" Todd asked the angry members of the Board.

"Get rid of Warner and Hungerford," Chandler said. "Steele is no Communist or fellow traveler. His crime—desecrating the mural—was not politically motivated and he's already paid dearly for it. He can stay. If Congress approves his contempt citation, we can reconsider."

When Chandler and Reilly threatened to resign if the Board did not act, Todd's first thought was to let them. *Then the rump Board can appoint more liberal replacements.* Then he reconsidered. *That might not sit well with the Trudeau family, who had delegated all management decisions to the Board. Not only did they provide their name, but E. L. Trudeau's estate provided considerable financial support.*

Without dissent, the Board authorized Todd to ask for the resignations of Warner and Hungerford. Tom Steele would remain head of the Trudeau Laboratory. Todd asked the Board members not to leak the decisions until he formally announced the resignations.

On November 16, Todd phoned Brandon from his Manhattan office to convey the Board's decisions. He asked Brandon to inform Hal that he would have to leave, too.

After the Board met, Todd called Ted Bradley and told him, off the record, what it had decided. "I can't keep a lid on that, Fred," Bradley replied. "Since you've told me off the record, we will run a news story saying that a usually reliable source has told *The Eagle* about the resignations and the closure of the Sanatorium. I won't write an editorial until the Board officially announces the resignations."

"I don't see that you give us any choice, Ted. The Foundation will have to live with that."

———◆———

On November 19, one week before Thanksgiving, Brandon visited Hal Hungerford at the Saranac Laboratory and relayed the Board's expectation that he would resign. "Ahh need a little while to digest this, Brandon, looking forward as I was to puttin' the laboratory on an honorable footing." Over the weekend before the holiday, he climbed Mt. Mckenzie on Saturday and, on Sunday, Algonquin, second in height to Marcy but half the distance. The weather was crisp and clear with overnight frosts; the hardwoods had lost their leaves. The approache to the summit of Algonquin had patches of ice but Hal managed to skirt them or walk gingerly over them. He had little trouble following the trail up the mountain, but in real life he did not know where to turn next.

As he hiked, Hal began to review his life—childhood in the south; Betty, his one true love; Trudeau and Bethune; Duke; NIH; the last few months at Saranac Lake. A good life that turned on a dime. He played the hearings over in his mind, trying to understand why he deserved censure. *It's not me*, he told himself, over and over. *It's the country gone mad*. As he had never been a Communist, or ever thought of becoming one, he was perplexed when he found himself a pariah, cast out as much as Hester Prynne with her scarlet letter. He was a leader in the field of pulmonary diseases, recognized by numerous awards, including, ironically, the Trudeau Medal of the National Tuberculosis Society. To Hal, being a loyal American did not mean kowtowing to a bunch of witch hunters.

His situation had looked bright, almost too good to be true, when the Trudeau Board appointed him director of the lab. Now all was bleak, the contempt citation hanging over his head and in debt to his lawyers. He thought for a moment that prison might provide a respite, but even at his age it would not be a life sentence. He decided not to submit his resignation until after Thanksgiving.

Chapter 16

Thanksgiving dinner at the Warners' took Hal's mind off his problems. Tom Steele and his two sons were invited, too. By unspoken agreement, the conversation steered clear of the hearings or the future, beyond the next few days, and he had a good time. He announced that he was planning to climb Mt. Marcy, the highest peak in the Adirondacks. "I've never snowshoed, let alone skied, and I'm not going to learn in my old age. Tomorrow's as good a day as any."

"Are you looking for company?" Janet asked. She had not climbed since her walk up Mt. Jo with Hal in September. He smiled warmly at her. Janet had become his best friend after the hearings. She had confided to him that Brandon's willingness to answer the Committee's question infuriated her; they were barely speaking to each other. *I really would like Janet's company*, Hal thought, but he couldn't accept her offer, if that's what her question represented. He was growing too fond of Janet and, despite her recent troubles with her husband, he knew that she was beyond his reach for many reasons, their age difference among them. In addition, he really did want to reach Marcy's summit and she would slow him down. But he didn't want to offend her.

"Ahh'd love your company, Janet, but the only way Ahh'm going to make it to the top and back in one day is to start at four o'clock in the morning—in the dark. That's a mite early for you and Ahh don't think your husband would think it wise, considerin' you haven't been climbing lately." He detected a look of sadness before she smiled and let the matter drop.

"You know, I've lived my adult life here but never climbed the high peaks," Tom Steele commented.

"Well, it helps to start young," Hal replied. "Ahh began as a kid and continued in medical school with the woman who became my wife—"

"I didn't know you were married," Janet interrupted.

"Betty died of tuberculosis in 1924," Hal replied matter-of-factly before continuing. "Ahh hiked when I was up here in the late 1920s, and then at Duke, took excursions to the Smokies, usually hiking by myself, staying out sometimes for two or three nights. That's when Ahh acquired mah sleepin' bag. Still have it, but now Ahh prefer mah bed to a night in the cold." He stopped to take a sip of wine. "At NIH, I occasionally drove out to Shenandoah National Park and hiked in the Blue Ridge mountains. And as Janet knows, I've been hiking pretty regularly since my return to the Adirondacks in September. Ahh'm no longer a speedy hiker; have to stop more often to catch mah breath, wonderin' if mah tuberculosis-scarred lungs are slowin' me, or maybe it's mah weight, or mah age."

Hal stopped briefly at his lab on the way home from the Warners and was in bed by 9 p.m. The next morning, the day after Thanksgiving, he got up at four o'clock, had his usual breakfast of coffee and toast, and packed a bologna sandwich and an apple in his old wicker rucksack, together with a rain poncho, sweater, flashlight, and down sleeping bag—his most expensive possession after his car. He filled his canteen, tucked the slender Adirondack Mountain Club trail book in the breast pocket of his shirt, and in the pitch-black walked to his battered 1947 Chevy, parked alongside his cottage, and stowed his pack in the trunk.

When he turned on to the road to Adirondack Loj, it was still too dark to see Algonquin and Wallface far ahead and he had no clue as to whether dawn would be followed by sunlight. The absence of stars in the pre-dawn mist was not unusual. For what it was worth, the weather forecast on the radio from Plattsburgh had predicted a clear day with a chance of rain on Saturday.

He reached the parking lot adjacent to the Loj around 5:30 a.m., before the day revealed itself. The temperature felt in the thirties, so he took off his heavy wool shirt, put his sweater on, and buttoned his shirt over it. As he walked to the trailhead, he noted a half-dozen cars. *Must belong to backpackers*, he thought, *unless they're earlier risers than I am*. At the register at the trailhead, he took out his flashlight, entered his name, address, and phone number, as well as information about his plans. Destination: Mt. Marcy; Number in Party: 1; Nights Out: 0. He would complete the last column, Time/Date of Return, that afternoon. No one had checked in before him on Friday. Checking the description of the van Hoevenberg trail in the guidebook one more time, he put the book back in his shirt pocket and started out with the aid of his flashlight.

By the time he reached Marcy Dam, Mt. Colden, with its mirror image in the calm water above the dam, was visible. Circling its east side, he noticed that neither of the nearby lean-tos were occupied. The van Hoevenberg trail, with blue markers, swung sharply to the left, up the northeast flank of Marcy. Climbing became a little steep, so by the time he reached the junction of the trail to Phelps Mountain, he was overheated. and paused to take off his sweater, returning it to his rucksack along with his flashlight. He took his first drink of water then emptied his canteen, refilling it from the rapidly flowing Phelps Brook. In his hour and a half on the trail, he had covered about forty percent of the route to Marcy. *At this rate, I'll reach Marcy by ten o'clock*, he thought. He added on two hours for the steeper pitches ahead, concluding: *I'll be pleased to reach the summit by noon. Going faster on the return, I should be back before sunset.* Buoyed by this calculation and the brightening daylight, he began to pay more attention to the forest: to the early morning calls of the sparrows, one of the few birds that did not migrate south; to the skeletal limbs of the deciduous trees; and to the sky, now clear and blue.

In an hour of steady but moderate climbing, slogging through a few muddy spots, he reached Indian Falls, not much more than a trickle in autumn. Turning to his right as he stood on the flat rocks on the top of the falls, he gasped as he took in the McIntyre Range, almost due west. Snowcapped Algonquin, the highest in the range, glowed in the early sunlight. As he stood well below its summit, he couldn't imagine that he'd climbed it. *And Marcy is higher. And if there's snow on top of Algonquin, there must be some on Marcy.* He began to worry whether he had dressed warmly enough, hoping that the noonday sun would melt the snow and keep the temperature above freezing. At the moment, he was perspiring and out of breath, despite having stopped just a minute ago. Sitting on a boulder, he unbuttoned his shirt to let the sweat evaporate and took a *long drink from his canteen. The view and the brook babbling gently— worth living for, worth getting up in the middle of the night for*, he thought as his breathing returned to normal. He felt hunger pangs but decided it was too early for lunch.

The climbing was more difficult now; at the top of every steep pitch he had to rest. It was 9:30 a.m. when he came out on a ridge from which he caught views of Marcy. *Hardly any snow*, he observed. From his guidebook, he calculated that he had walked a little over six miles and ascended about two thousand feet. In the final mile and a half, he would ascend another thousand feet. With difficulty, he set out again, soon coming to the junction with the Hopkins Trail. The forest was behind him now, the trees and shrubs along the trail dwarfed in size. Passing two lean-tos, neither occupied, at 10:30 a.m. he reached the bare rock dome of Marcy, still with a mile to go to the summit and six hundred vertical feet to climb. Cairns and occasional paint blazes replaced the blue trail markers.

He reached the peak almost exactly at noon, just as he had predicted at the junction of the trail to Phelps. Elated with his conquest, he made a slow, clumsy pirouette, admiring the array of peaks beneath him as he rotated. Finishing, he felt a light breeze and noticed clouds obliterating the top of Mt. Whiteface far to the north. "Time for lunch," he said hungrily. While he was eating, two young backpackers joined him, coming up the southwestern flank of Marcy, opposite to Hal's route. They had several days of beard and heavy backpacks, with their sleeping bags stuffed into waterproof sacks and strapped underneath and snowshoes hanging from the sides. "You expecting snow?" Hungerford asked with a derogatory chuckle.

Pointing to the north, one of them replied, "Sure looks like it and it's coming fast." Their original plan, they told Hal, had been to hike to Haystack and then over the Great Range. After some discussion, they concluded, as they told Hal, that the safest thing for them was to backtrack to the lean-tos along the Opalescent Brook trail or at Lake Colden. "The snow will hit the northern side of Marcy first and probably be heaviest there," one of them said. "You're welcome to join us." With several days' worth of provisions, they told Hal that as long as they could get shelter from the storm they weren't worried about getting out. When he politely turned down their offer, they warned him, "You'd better get going." They turned and started back down the trail to the southwest.

They're exaggerating, Hal thought, *probably overeager to try out their snowshoes*. Preoccupied with watching them descend, he was not immediately aware that the sun had disappeared. Only after he shivered momentarily did he realize that the temperature had dropped. He reached into his rucksack and put on his sweater once again. As he buttoned his shirt over it, he decided his poncho would protect him and his pack from the elements and provide an additional layer of warmth. He slipped into the shoulder straps of his rucksack and then pulled on the poncho. Happy and content, he headed toward the first cairn on his way down, the wind in his face, the sun covered by advancing clouds.

At first, the snow fell gently, flakes floating lazily to the rock surface, speckling it as they melted. When he was halfway off the dome the snow came down heavily, starting to stick, making the surface slippery, slowing his descent. He headed toward the next cairn but by the time he reached it, visibility was so poor that he could not locate the succeeding one. Cautiously, he headed downward in more or less a straight line, leaving no trail as his footprints were quickly covered by snow. Visibility was less than ten feet.

He reached timberline at three o'clock; it had taken him longer to come down the rock dome than to go up. There was still no sign of the trail, no gap between the trees, no trail markers. He walked along the timberline for a while, but the dwarfed evergreens provided little shelter from the blizzard.

Hal reasoned that the trees would reduce the snow accumulation below timberline and burrowed into the forest. *One of those lean-tos I passed will give me protection if I can find it. My old sleeping bag will keep me warm; I'm glad I brought it.* The descent was steep and the snow was already up to his knees, making every step an effort.

He had been shivering before he became aware of it. Once he did, the shaking became so violent that he had even more trouble walking. He stumbled and fell into the soft snow, wetting his trousers below the poncho. *Get up, get up*, he warned himself, and with the help of a low tree branch pulled to a stand, uncertain which way to go. His fingers were cold and stiff. The combination of melted snow penetrating his boots and fresh snow coming in over the tops and around the laces wet his feet. He could barely feel his toes.

The light was failing. His watch told Hal it was five o'clock, leading him to conclude, erroneously, that plenty of daylight was left. At about the same time, his shivering stopped. He actually felt warm and fought against taking his poncho and shirt off to remove the sweater. When he came to a spot in which the snow, drifting against the base of a large spruce, had made an inviting white pillow, he decided to lie down to rest. *What more can I do?*

———◆———

The storm did not abate until late Saturday. The road from Route 73 was not plowed until Sunday, and only on Monday did a park ranger discover a lone car in the hikers' parking area. He checked the register at the trailhead, noting that Harold Hungerford, destination Mt. Marcy, was the only person who had not completed the column for time/date of return. No one picked up when they called the phone number he had left. The lone car in the parking area was registered in his name. For the next two days, the weather stayed below freezing. Search parties on skis and snowshoes scoured the area from Mt. Marcy back along the van Hoevenberg trail, as well as the Hopkins trail on to which he might have staggered.

———◆———

On Friday night, Saranac Lake received only a light dusting of snow, which quickly turned to rain. Janet assumed that Hal had gotten back safely, forgetting that the storm could have been much been much worse at higher elevations. She thought Brandon might be annoyed if she called Hal to see if he was all right. *Hal might be annoyed too*, she thought.

Evan Jones called Brandon late Monday morning to say that Hungerford had not yet come to work and that no one was answering Hal's home phone. At home for lunch, Brandon told Janet that Hal had not shown up for work. This time, she immediately went to the phone and called Hal. No answer. She reminded Brandon about Hal's plan to climb Marcy. Sharing her concern, Brandon called the State Police and filed a missing person's report after he returned to his office. A few hours later, the dispatcher called back to report that a ranger had found Hal's car in the hikers' parking lot near Adirondack Loj. Search parties had already been launched on the suspicion that he had lost his way in the blizzard on the mountaintop.

That afternoon, Janet called Hal's home three or four times, never getting an answer. She turned on the five o'clock news on the radio and was horrified when the local newscaster announced, "A search in the snowbound high peaks is on for Harold Hungerford, a scientist at the Trudeau Foundation who is feared missing after he set out to climb Mt Marcy on Friday morning." Later that evening Brandon called the dispatcher, who told him that the search party that skied in from Tahawus on the Calamity Brook trail had encountered two backpackers near Lake Colden who had met a man filling Hal's description on top of Marcy. They had invited him to accompany them down, but he seemed intent on going back the way he had come, directly into the storm.

On Tuesday morning, Brandon told Janet, "I'm going to drive down to the Saranac Lab to see if I can pick up any clues."

"Like a note?" she said with anguish. He shrugged and left.

At the laboratory, Brandon went straight to Hal's office, which was not locked. On the desk he found a manila folder labeled "Personal File." The papers inside were almost entirely handwritten, including the uppermost.

Thanksgiving,
November 26, 1953
To my personal file.

I suppose I have a lot to be thankful for. I am not in prison. At least not yet. And I have upheld a moral standard that would make my daddy proud. Professionally, I've had a rich life that in many ways compensated for a lack of deep, loving personal contacts since Betty died and Beth went his separate way. I was grateful when Brandon Warner offered me the directorship of the Saranac Laboratory, despite my being a pariah, not losing a day's work in the transition from NIH to Trudeau. It was too good to last. At the Board's behest, Brandon has asked me to resign.

In the eyes of the Board, my testimony before the House Un-American Activities Committee changed my presence at Trudeau from an asset to a liability. Being innocent of all charges except refusing to sign the "loyalty" oath, I find this difficult to accept.

Had I not mentioned Norman Bethune's name to Agent Crane when he first visited me, the Trudeau would not have been dragged into these hearings. I count the FBI's investigation directly responsible for the death of Emily Steele, wife of my good friend Tom Steele, who was shamelessly dragged through the mud by the House Committee. In its attempt to slander Trudeau, the Committee was ably abetted by Arnold Springer, who lied about his ac-quaintance with Brandon Warner but is immune to libel charges unless he repeats his lies outside of Congress. More egregiously, he suppressed and then stole scientific pa-pers from the laboratory's files.

My quarrel is not with Brandon Warner, who carried the Board's message of my dis-missal, or with the Board's chairman, Fred Todd, who conducted himself with high moral integrity before the Committee. My hope is that Trudeau will continue to op-erate under standards that match his.

As for me personally, I am not as sanguine as Dickens' Wilkins Micawber that "something will turn up." In any event, on Monday I will submit my resignation. What more can I do?

Midday on Tuesday, December 1, the State Police called to say that a body had been found that carried Harold Hungerford's driver's license. "It was about two hundred feet from the Plateau lean-to off the van Hoevenberg trail," the officer said woefully, "easily visible on a clear winter day. Since we cannot locate a next of kin, Dr. Warner, we would appreciate your coming over to the police barracks at Raybrook to identify the body." Brandon complied. It was Harold Hungerford.

Hungerford's death was the lead story on the front page of *The Daily Eagle* on Wednesday. Buried deep in the story were the following sentences: "Following Hungerford's testimony before the U.S. Congress House Un-American Activities Committee, it was rumored that he was going to resign as director of the Saranac Laboratory. Notified of Dr. Hungerford's death, the House Committee withdrew its citation of contempt."

———

The obituary alongside the story cited Hungerford's professional accomplishments and listed the time of the funeral, with interment at the Pine Ridge cemetery. His grave was not far from Emily Steele's. The funeral was attended by more than one hundred professional colleagues, many of them well-known professors at America's most prestigious medical schools.

In February 1954, Brandon Warner announced that the Trudeau Sanatorium would cease admitting new patients immediately and expected that the last of its current patients would be discharged by the end of the current year. He announced the successful completion of negotiations with the Corporate Managers of America for the purchase of the Sanatorium grounds and the commitment of the Trudeau Foundation to build a research institute elsewhere in the Saranac Lake area.

The U.S. Congress failed to cite Tom Steele and Brandon Warner for contempt. Tom remained the director of the Trudeau Laboratory. Brandon and Janet Warner, and their son John, left Saranac Lake in the spring of 1954 when Brandon resigned to become the director of the United Mine Workers' chain of hospitals. In 1964, the Trudeau Institute, a not-for-profit, biomedical research center, opened at the foot of Algonquin Avenue, near the shores of Lower Saranac Lake.

The Saranac Lake Free Library wanted to display the Bethune murals in 1973 but they could not be found.

Afterword

————◆————

In 2014, a physician friend, knowing of my interest in the Adirondacks, referred me to a recent article in the *Journal of the American Medical Association* about the Bethune murals. The concluding sentence of the article caught my attention: "Although copies exist, the original murals have been unaccounted for and are considered lost at this time." Spending three months of the year near the village of Saranac Lake in the Adirondacks where the murals were last seen, I decided to track down the originals.

Dr. Norman Bethune drew the murals in 1927 while a patient at the Trudeau Sanatorium for tuberculosis at Saranac Lake, New York. After leaving the Sanatorium, he became a leading thoracic surgeon. Bethune declared his membership in the Communist Party of Canada in 1937. The last three years of his life—he died in 1939—brought him international fame.

In 1967, a U.S. Army intelligence officer at Fort Bragg, North Carolina, expressed interest in obtaining the murals from a scientist at Trudeau. It is not clear what stirred his interest; he may have been responding to the scientist's offer to send the murals.

My search of historical documents in the village, as well as personal interviews, failed to provide evidence that the murals were ever sent from Saranac Lake to Fort Bragg. It's remotely possible that they have been hidden, or were intentionally destroyed. More likely, neglect resulted in their disintegration.

The Army's interest in the murals led me to consider them as the basis for a novel that illuminated some aspect of the Cold War. Nothing clicked until I made three discoveries: First, the Seventh Symposium on diseases of inhaled industrial dusts, held in 1952, had never been published, unlike all of the previous Trudeau symposia. Second, the resignation of the director of the Trudeau's Saranac Laboratory, who had organized the Seventh Symposium, was announced by the Trudeau Foundation without explanation in 1953. Third, the Seventh Symposium papers were not found until 1975, a year after the former director's death, when his widow turned them over to the Armed Forces Institute of Pathology.

In investigative journalism that first appeared in *The New Yorker* in 1983, and then in a book, Paul Brodeur implicated manufacturers of asbestos in the suppression of the papers. Some of them were supporting research at the Saranac Laboratory in the 1950s. Brodeur concludes:

> If a significant number of the fifty-odd medical doctors who attended the Seventh Symposium had spoken out or had insisted that its papers and discussion be made public, they might well have blown the lid off the asbestos coverup and saved thousands of lives, untold pain and suffering, and millions of dollars (pp. 179–80).

Only in 1964, twelve years after the Seventh Symposium, did the dangers of low doses of asbestos become public due to the research of Dr. Irving Selikoff. That finally blew "the lid off the asbestos coverup."

It seemed absurd that the Army could glean anything useful

to national security from murals drawn in 1927 by a young
physician preoccupied with the imminence of his own death
from tuberculosis. A more realistic but entirely fictitious scenario is one in which the companies manufacturing asbestos,
threatened by publication of the Seventh Symposium papers,
attempted to intimidate the Trudeau Foundation by claiming
that it had been infiltrated by Communists for decades. And
what better proof could there be than murals on the walls of
the Sanatorium that displayed Bethune's communistic intent?

That Norman Bethune was a Communist in 1927 is open
to dispute. In their definitive biography of Bethune, Roderick
and Sharon Stewart provide little to support the notion that
he had a commitment to political parties or causes before the
Great Depression. Only in the 1930s did he become an advocate for a national health system in Canada and then declare
his membership in the Communist Party of Canada, going to
Spain and China to provide medical assistance to the Spanish
Republic and Mao Zedong respectively. On the other hand,
Allan and Gordon, in their reverential biography, *The Scalpel,
the Sword*, see Bethune as having a strong commitment to social
justice as early as World War I, consistent with declaring himself a Communist in 1937. Bethune, in a detailed description
of the murals in *The Fluoroscope* in 1932, states that they were
drawn "for the amusement of myself and my cottage mates,
the allegorical story of my past life and what I thought the future would be," namely his death and the deaths of his cottage
mates from tuberculosis.

Most of the novel is set in 1953, a year when Senator
Joseph McCarthy had reached the apogee of his red-baiting,
when people were losing their jobs for refusing to state their
political affiliations in "loyalty" oaths or before congressional

committees, and when Ethyl and Julius Rosenberg were executed for conspiracy to commit espionage for the Soviet
Union. It was also the year in which tuberculosis sanatoriums
across the country were losing financial viability due primarily
to the discovery of the antibiotic, streptomycin, which could
cure most patients with tuberculosis. Thus the future of the
Trudeau Foundation was precarious, susceptible to the claim
that it harbored Communists.

The threat to civil liberties, including free speech, made the
early 1950s one of the bleakest periods in our nation's history.
Few people alive today remember the fear that struck artists,
writers, teachers, workers, and others, not without reason as
the black list cost many their jobs. That lack of memory, perhaps, is one reason why Donald Trump's anti-democratic pro-
nouncements and racist policies have gained a foothold. *The
Bethune Murals* serves as a cautionary tale.

———◆———

I have used fictitious names for the principal characters, except
Bethune. Many of them are fashioned after real characters, although I have taken great liberties with their dispositions, tra-
jectories, and actions. I have used real names for a few characters
whose roles in the novel are minor and have given them lines
they could have spoken. These include Frances Penney and
doctors Edward Archibald, Alfred Blalock, Lowrason Brown,
Louis Davidson, and Fred Heise. Those doctors were around
when Bethune asked for and finally received artificial pneumothorax in late 1927, resulting in a remarkable improvement
in his condition. The real scientists, Strasimir Petroff and Selman Waxman, are mentioned in passing.

There is no evidence that Bethune used a female model

when he drew his murals.

The murals were not given to Duke University Hospital. So far as I know, neither the FBI nor the House Un-American Activities Committee of the U.S. Congress ever investigated the Trudeau Foundation.

The quotation attributed to Dr. Louis Davidson on page 80 was taken from the Stewart's *Phoenix*. The quotation attributed to Dr. E. L. Trudeau on page 87 was taken from Hotaling's life of E. L. Trudeau. The quotations from Dr. Bethune on pages 145 and 146 were taken from his "The T.B.'s Progress" in *The Fluoroscope*. Allan and Gordon's *The Scalpel, The Sword* is quoted with slight modification on pages 208 and 209. President Harry Truman's question and answer on page 204 is taken from his public papers. https://www.trumanlibrary.org/ publicpapers/index.php?pid=1991

Tony Holtzman

Bibliography

Allan, T, Gordon S. The Scalpel, The Sword: The Story of
Doctor Norman Bethune, First edition 1952, 320 pages.
Republished 2009 Toronto:Dundurn Press

Bethune, N. The T.B.'s Progress. The Fluoroscope 1932,
1(7). Original could not be located. Reprinted in L.
Hannant, ed. (See below)

Brodeur, P. Outrageous Misconduct: The Asbestos Industry
on Trial. New York: Pantheon, 1985, 374 pages

Halberstam, D. The 1950s. New York:Villard. 1993, 801
pages

Hannant, L. ed. The Politics of Passion: Norman Bethune's
Life and Art. Toronto:University of Toronto. 1998, 396
pages

Holtzman, T. Art of Suffering: The Lost Murals of
Tuberculosis Patient Norman Bethune. Adirondack Life
2016, 47 (1):42-45

Hotaling, M. A Rare Romance in Medicine: The Life And
Legacy of Edward Livingston Trudeau. Saranac
Lake:Historic Saranac Lake, 2016, 336 pages

Link, EP. The T.B.'s Progress: Norman Bethune as Artist.
Plattsburgh, NY: Center for the Study of Canada, SUNY
Plattsburgh; 1991, 27 pages

Malani, PN., Prager, RL. Journey in Thick Wood: Childhood
Henry Norman Bethune. JAMA 2014, 312:1380-82

Medsger, B. The Burglary: The Discovery of J. Edgar
    Hoover's Secret FBI. New York:Vintage, 592 pages

Navasky, VS. Naming Names New York:Viking 1980, 482
    pages

Rhode, M. On Collecting Dr. Arthur Vorwald's Asbestosis
    Records: A Cautionary Tale. 2001, Otis Historical
    Archives, National Library of Health and Medicine.
    https://www.academia.edu/2909506/On_collecting_
    Dr._Arthur_Vorwalds_asbestosis_records_A_
    Cautionary Tale

Riley, H. You Know What? A Selection of Commentaries.
    Saranac Lake:Adirondack Vista, LLC, 2010, 290 pages

Selikoff, IJ, Churg, J, Hammond, EC. Asbestos Exposure
    and Neoplasia. JAMA 1964, 188:22-26

Selikoff, IJ, Churg, J, Hammond, CE. Relation Between
    Exposure to Asbestos and Mesothelioma. N Engl J Med
    1965, 272:560-565

Stephenson, LW. The Blalock-Bethune Connection. Surgery
    2001, 130:882-9

Stewart, R., Stewart S. Phoenix: The Life of Norman
    Bethune. Montreal:McGill-Queen's University, 2011, 479
    pages

Taylor, R. Saranac: America's Magic Mountain. New
    York:Paragon House, 1988, 159-195

Zuidema, GD., Sloan, H. Alfred Blalock, Norman
    Bethune, and the Bethune Murals. Surgery 2001,
    130:866-81

Acknowledgements

If there's one person responsible for my writing this book it is Dr. Avelina Bardwell. Knowing of my interest in the Adirondacks, Avie called my attention to the article about the Bethune murals by Malani and Prager in the *Journal of the American Medical Association* in 2014. That started me on learning all I could about the murals and Bethune's stay at the Trudeau Sanatorium. Amy Catania, the Director of Historic Saranac Lake, was the first person I contacted. Ever since, she has been the muse for this project. Without Amy, I would never have discovered the magnitude of the problem that resulted from the failure to publish the Seventh Saranac Symposium. Amy paved the way for my interviews with knowledgeable people in the Saranac Lake community and conducted one interview for me. Her comments on a late draft of the novel were immensely helpful. Marc Wanner and Chessie Monks-Kelly, colleagues of Amy's, and Michelle Tucker of the Saranac Lake Free Library, were a great help.

Through Dr. Dorothy Federman, who also made excellent suggestions for improving a late draft, I contacted Sue Chapman who introduced me to Kelly Stanyon, Librarian of the Trudeau Institute. Kelly provided me with invaluable correspondence from the archives as well as annual reports and other material. Thanks to interviews with Marjorie Wolinsky (courtesy of Amy), James Meade, and William Steenken Jr., I have a better idea of staff life at Trudeau in the 1950s.

In addition to published work, conversations with Rod Stewart, co-author of Bethune's definitive biography, Jean Mason, and George Zuidema provided information about Norman Bethune and the murals. Jean led me to "Bethune" a documentary produced by the National Film Board of Canada, and to an American movie starring Donald Sutherland as Bethune. Zuidema gave me 8" x 10" full color photographs of the Bethune murals from his collection at the University of Michigan. Photographer par excellence, Nathan Farb, generously advised me on the likely status of old lantern slides of the murals that were in the possession of Historic Saranac Lake. Dennis Costanzo, SUNY Plattsburgh, kindly reproduced Eugene Link's monograph on Bethune for me; it is out of print. Gail Antokal was able to pinpoint the media that Bethune used in drawing the murals.

In addition to Amy and Dorothy, Maryhelen (Mel) Snyder, Susan Bagby, Mina Bancroft Wuchenich, Steven Holtzman, and Deborah Holtzman read and offered constructive criticism of various revisions of *The Bethune Murals*. Mel and Susan who read earlier versions, would probably not recognize the final product. Conversations with my good friends Tom Schneider, Amir Yechielli, and the late Abby Lippman also improved the product. Members of a Menlo Park writers' group. Dante Drummond, Diana Brady, Caroline Chu, Lessa Bouchard, Kathy Boussina, Tom Schneider, and Michelle Shabtai commented on specific chapters.

Editor Lynn Stegner's insightful comments made the book a much better novel.

Finally, Eva Cohen once again did the gorgeous cover design, this time with help from Dr. Norman Bethune.